# LUCIENNE BOYCE

## The Contraband Killings

A DAN FOSTER MYSTERY **FOUR**

# OTHER TITLES BY LUCIENNE BOYCE

*To The Fair Land*

**The Dan Foster Mysteries:-**
*Bloodie Bones*
*The Butcher's Block*
*Death Makes No Distinction*
*The Fatal Coin*

**Non-Fiction**
*The Bristol Suffragettes*
*The Road to Representation: Essays on the Women's Suffrage Campaign*

Copyright © 2022 Lucienne Boyce
Published by Wulfrun Press 2022
Cover Design © 2022 J D Smith Design Ltd

The right of Lucienne Boyce to be identified as the author of this work has been asserted by her in accordance with the Copyright, Designs and Patents Act 1988

All rights reserved. No part of this book may be used or reproduced, stored in a retrieval system, or transmitted in any form, or by any means, electronic, mechanical, photocopying, recording or otherwise without the prior written permission of the copyright holder except in the case of brief quotation embodied in critical articles and reviews.

This is a work of fiction. Names, characters, places and incidents are either products of the author's imagination or are used fictitiously. Any resemblance to actual events or places or persons, living or dead, is entirely coincidental.

ISBN (Paperback) 978-1-9997236-8-2
ISBN (ebook) 978-1-9997236-9-9

# ABOUT THE AUTHOR

Lucienne Boyce writes historical fiction and non-fiction. After gaining an MA in English Literature with the Open University, specialising in eighteenth-century literature, she published her first historical novel, *To The Fair Land*, an eighteenth-century thriller set in London, Bristol and the South Seas.

The Dan Foster Mysteries follow the adventures of a Bow Street Runner at the end of the eighteenth century, and are set against a tumultuous background of war with France and unrest at home.

Her non-fiction books are *The Bristol Suffragettes*, and a collection of short essays, *The Road to Representation: Essays on the Women's Suffrage Campaign*.

She regularly gives talks on both her fiction and non-fiction work, and blogs about suffragettes, suffragists, the eighteenth century and books. She has been a local radio presenter, tutored a course on women's suffrage history, and run workshops on writing historical fiction.

Find out more at www.lucienneboyce.com

# CHAPTER ONE

Dan Foster, Principal Officer of Bow Street, paused in the doorway of the noisy candlelit dining room of the Piazza Coffee House in Covent Garden. Tray-laden waiters weaved elegantly between the tables, depositing steaming dishes, collecting used crockery, nodding acknowledgements to the demands of diners impatient for more meat, more salt, more pudding, more wine, more ale. The dominant smells were beef boiled, beef roasted, beef stewed, and the rich, bitter scent of coffee.

It was the last that tempted Dan, but there was no chance of finding himself a place at one of the tables and ordering an invigorating pot. He located Sir William Addington, Chief Magistrate of Bow Street, at a table in the corner, a generous plateful of food and a half-emptied bottle of wine before him. Dan, his hat under his arm, made his way across the room, scrutinising as he did so the stranger who stood at Sir William's elbow.

He was a slight, dark-haired man with a delicately-boned face, thin lips, and deep-set eyes so dark they seemed black. He wore a fashionably plain dark jacket, well-fitting breeches and expensive boots, but they had the crumpled, tired look of clothes which had been worn all day, and all the previous night too. He was a few years younger than Dan, twenty-five or twenty-six, and like Dan, he was there as a subordinate, standing in spite of the empty chairs next to the magistrate. Not a very eager subordinate either. If he had sighed, yawned and examined his nails, he could not have looked more bored.

"Come along, come along, I haven't got all day," cried Sir William, waving a hurrying hand at Dan. "I have to be back in court in half an hour."

"I came as soon as I got the message to meet you here, sir. If it's about the City Road robbery, I was just on my way to the Lord Rodney's Head in Islington to speak to the landlord. He informed on the two muggins we arrested for it. They say he put them up to it and bought the victim's watch off them afterwards. They're going to hang, but he's going to walk free with a reward into the bargain, unless—"

"Yes, yes, never mind that. Why aren't you wearing your badge?"

Dan looked down at his coat and realised he had forgotten to put it on before he went inside. He wondered if Sir William had sent for him just to check if he was sporting the gilt badge engraved with the words "Bow Street Officer" which the chief magistrate had recently decreed his officers must wear when they were on duty. The patrolmen had a similar badge marked "Bow Street Patrol". An ingenious method, Sir William thought it, of enabling the public to tell the ranks apart, but an inconvenient disclosure if you were negotiating a tavern full of cutthroats and pickpockets. Dan fumbled in his pocket, but Sir William had already forgotten the badge.

"You remember the Barker case?"

Dan's hand fell to his side. "The Customs officer murdered in Kent in spring."

"Aye, and most horribly murdered too. Lowered into a pit and stoned to death."

Barker had worked his way into a gang of smugglers in the guise of a London criminal who had fled the capital after killing a householder in the course of a burglary. He had played the part of daring ruffian to perfection, until one of the gang had followed him to a rendezvous with his commanding officer. It had been a vicious killing and the manhunt afterwards had been thorough. Not a house in the neighbouring villages had been left unsearched, not a cart unloaded, not a man, woman or child unquestioned by the excise men, constables, and militia drafted in to hound down the killers. But whether out of fear or loyalty, no one would impart a scrap of information about the smuggling gang who controlled the district more surely than the King's officers.

"His killers got away," Dan said.

Sir William reached for his glass and took a mouthful of the rich red wine. "Not before Barker was able to pass on some of the intelligence he'd gleaned. Descriptions were circulated to every magistrate in the land months ago. It was beginning to look as if we'd never lay hands on any of 'em. Now one of the gang, Watcyn Jones, has been arrested." He fished a chunk of beef out of his alamode. "The Home Secretary wants him tried at the Old Bailey and hanged at Newgate. We've got to send a clear message to anyone who thinks he can get away with attacking King's men. I'm sending you to fetch him. You'll report to the local JP, Sir Edward Lloyd Pryce." Sir William pushed a bundle of papers across the table. "Your warrants and letter of introduction signed by the Home Secretary. You're to leave at once. Tomorrow if it can be arranged, the day after at the latest. His Grace is anxious to have Jones in London as soon as possible."

Dan gathered up the documents. "Very good, sir." It was not the first time he had been sent on such a mission.

"Constable G – er—" Sir William mumbled over the hard consonant. "Constable Gevans will accompany you."

For the first time, the stranger showed an interest in the conversation. "It's not—"

Dan cut him short. "Constable Gevans, sir? Why not one of the other principal officers?"

"Because you'll need an interpreter and none of the others speak Welsh."

"Welsh?"

"Jones is in Beaumaris Gaol." Sir William caught sight of Dan's expression. "That's north Wales, Foster." He put the beef into his mouth and chewed noisily. "There's one more thing. So far, Jones has refused to answer questions, so anything you can get out of him will be useful. You can suggest there might be a reprieve if he impeaches the rest of the gang, but don't make any promises. Is that clear? Well, what are you waiting for, the pair of you? Didn't I say I have to be back in court shortly?"

Dan bowed and nodded at Gevans to follow him. Sir William snatched up his wine and swallowed another hasty mouthful.

"And put your damned badge on," he called after them.

"Lord!" said the constable when they were outside. "I thought he was going to do himself an injury with his huffing and puffing. And what's all that hullabaloo about a badge?"

Though his accent was not strong, there was no mistaking him for an Englishman. Dan would not have taken him for a parish police officer either. He sounded more like a Westminster scholar than a Westminster constable. They halted in the colonnade overlooking the noisy square where vendors and shoppers tussled with one another for profit and bargains.

"Where is Beaumaris?" asked Dan.

"It's on Anglesey. We take the Holyhead road, as if for the Irish packet boat."

"The mail coach will be quickest, then. The Irish Mail goes from the Golden Cross."

"I know where the coaches go from."

Dan answered this with a crushing look. "If you can't get

us on the Mail tomorrow night, get us on the first stagecoach out."

"Me? Can't you send one of the clerks?"

"I'm sending you."

"But tomorrow? It doesn't leave us much time. Sir William did say the day after would do."

"Time to do what? Just get those places for tomorrow night. Come and see me later to confirm you've done it. I'll be at home." Dan gave his address. "That's all for now, Gevans."

He moved towards the stone steps down to the Piazza.

"It's not Gevans."

Dan looked back. "What?"

"My name. It's not Gevans. It's Evans."

"Why did you say it was Gevans?"

"I didn't. It was Sir William. My name is Goronwy Evans."

He pronounced his name "Gor-ron-oi" with a rolled "r". No wonder Sir William had had problems with it.

"Then I'll see you later, Constable Evans."

Dan strode off across the Piazza in the direction of the Strand. He had a feeling that Evans was watching him, probably muttering something less than complimentary under his breath. Too bad: they were stuck with one another now.

# CHAPTER TWO

A few moments later, Dan was walking along York Street, a spur at the end of Tavistock Street. Most of the terraced houses were four storeys high, sash windowed, the oldest built around seventy years ago. He passed several with shop fronts: a wine merchant, a bookseller, the Bunch of Grapes tavern. Some of them opened on to the street, others had a narrow railed space with steps leading down to a tiny area overlooked by two dusty basement windows. It was one of these buildings that Dan let himself into with his front door key.

They were only a street away from their former home in Russell Street, but this house was a definite step up. The rooms were larger, lighter and airier. The kitchen was in the basement, along with a scullery and pantry, and a housemaid to go with them who slept in an attic room. Aggie was a Foundling Hospital girl, having been deposited there as a baby by her unknown mother fifteen years ago.

The family no longer spent their time sitting in the kitchen. They had a parlour and dining room now, and four bedrooms. One of them would have been his mother-in-law's if she had lived long enough to make the move. Mrs Harper had died that spring after a long decline and a short illness. It had been partly due to the loss that they had made the move. Caroline's grief showed no sign of abating as long as they stayed in the old home. Dan had made a great deal of money on his last murder case, when an open-handed Prince of Wales had paid a generous reward. Added to what he had already saved, he could afford something better.

The thought made him smile. There had been a time when a sheltering doorway felt like a step up. Better than the ash pits of a London brickyard.

A boy darted out of the door from the kitchen stairs. He was aged twelve or thereabouts: like Dan, he did not know when he had been born or who his father was. Also like Dan, he had been a street urchin. Dan had first come across him in Southwark during an investigation. The boy had helped him, something the young Dan would never have done, but then Nick had not known at the time that he was a principal officer. Dan had not liked to abandon the boy after that.

"Mr Foster! Did you get the landlord to talk? Will the footpads hang? Can we go and see it?" He took Dan's hat and coat and hung them on the pegs, smoothing them out as he did so.

"Have to drop that case for now, Nick," Dan said.

He was about to go to the parlour when he heard a wail of distress from upstairs, followed by a child's choking sobs. Caroline must be in the kitchen instructing Aggie about dinner and could not hear it.

"What's the matter with Alex?"

"Dunno."

"You go on in, I'll be along in a minute."

The brightness went out of Nick's face. Dan, who had already forgotten about him, loped up the stairs two at a time. Alex stood in his crib, clutching the rails, his face red and swollen. When he saw his father, he bawled louder than ever. Dan scooped him up.

"Hey, hey, what's all this about?"

He took a clean cloth from a pile on top of the chest of

drawers and mopped up Alex's tears. When he looked a bit less dishevelled and his sobs had faded to occasional hiccups, Dan carried him downstairs, the child's fingers curled tightly around his collar. He had a strong grip on him; a good sign, Dan thought. One day he would be old enough to take to the gym, and in due course, father and son would be sparring like old timers.

Nick, who never went into the parlour when Dan was not there, had gone back to Aggie in the kitchen. Caroline sat by the fire with her Bible open on her lap. A nervous look flickered across her face. It was quickly replaced by defensiveness.

"Didn't you hear him crying?"

"You should have left him. I put him to bed without any supper."

"He's had nothing to eat?"

Dan went to the top of the kitchen stairs and yelled "Aggie!" He went back and sat down opposite Caroline, Alex on his lap.

"What do you mean, you put him to bed without any supper?"

"He's been very wicked."

"Wicked? He's two years old."

"I don't like hearing him cry any more than you do. It's for his own good. Mr Hurst says it's his immortal soul we must think of, not his fleeting worldly comfort."

She was spared Dan's retort by Aggie's entrance. The girl looked at the miserable child on Dan's lap, glanced at Caroline and, seeing trouble brewing, scuttled off to fetch the bread and milk Dan asked for.

"What has your Methodist preacher got to do with my son?" he asked.

"He called on me this afternoon. Alex snatched a slice of cake from the plate when he thought no one was looking. Mr Hurst was most distressed to see such slyness and gluttony in one so young. He says that it is kinder to nip it in the bud now than have him grow up to be a hardened thief and criminal."

"And this is his idea of nipping criminal tendencies in the bud, is it? Sending the boy to bed hungry and frightened?"

"Mr Hurst says that it is better to feel the guidance of a loving parent in this life than roast in the Devil's everlasting fires of hell in the next."

"I'll give Mr Hurst hell fire if anything like this ever happens again."

"But you don't understand. Mr Hurst says Alex's soul is at particular risk because he is a child of sin."

Before Dan could say anything to this, Aggie came in with the bread and milk. He took the bowl from her and started to spoon the food into Alex's mouth.

He waited for the maid to leave before he asked, "What have you told him?"

"No more than the truth. He knew, Dan. He can see into your heart. He knew I wasn't being truthful. He understands sin. He sees how unhappy it makes us and how acknowledging it lifts the burden. He is such a good man. I couldn't bear lying to him, pretending I was Alex's mother."

The spoon paused in mid-air. That meant Hurst had wheedled out of her the story of Alex's parentage. Dan had had an affair with his son's mother, who died shortly after giving birth. He had not known she was pregnant until Alex's half-brother turned up with the baby one day. Caroline had been so furious, Dan left and set up home with his child and Nick. Later she had relented and offered to bring up Alex as her own, and they had made a fresh start.

With the coming of the child, the demons that had haunted Caroline all through their marriage had gone: the rages and jealousies, the drunkenness and tears. Not that Dan denied he had to take some of the blame for her misery. He did not love her the way he had loved her when they first married, and she knew he regretted choosing her over her younger sister. In spite of it, they had found a way of getting along since they had Alex to care for. And Eleanor was safely married now, and he had put her out of his mind. Mostly.

Mrs Harper's death had been a blow, but he had thought the new house had consoled Caroline for her loss. After the excitement of the move and settling in, it seemed that it had not been enough after all. A few weeks ago she had gone to a prayer meeting with one of her friends. The preacher was a celebrity and they went looking for no more than an hour's entertainment. But all that weeping and shaking and hallelujahs: it had been headier than drink, and more comforting.

"Mick!" cried Alex.

Dan resumed his spooning. "But that is what we agreed, Caroline. It's no one's business but our own. And it's better for Alex to leave it at that until he's older. You are the only mother he has ever known…There. All gone now. Good boy."

He put the bowl on the floor, wiped the dribbles from Alex's chin with his thumb and let him settle in his arms. He would wait for him to fall asleep before he took him upstairs. He would not put him to bed on his own again tonight.

"Was today the first time Hurst has called?"

"He's been once or twice before."

"For tea and cake?"

"For readings and prayers."

"Brings the collection box, does he?"

"He needs money for his good works. He doesn't stop at preaching, Dan, though that is labour enough. He wants to set up a soup kitchen to feed and clothe the poor."

"Because he's such a good man. A good man who would condemn a child for a sin he had no part in."

"He wants to save Alex, to pluck him from the flames, pluck us all from the flames."

"How long is this going to go on, Caroline? I've put up with it as long as I thought it was giving you something. Consolation. Comfort. I don't know. But I'm not having this.

I don't want Hurst coming here again. I don't want him anywhere near my son."

"You're forbidding me seeing Mr Hurst?"

"I'm telling you he's not to come here and he's to have nothing more to do with Alex."

"You can't stop me going to his sermons."

Dan acknowledged the truth of this. It would only make things worse if he told her not to go, only lead to anger and resentment. She would not submit to it anyway, and she would not be Caroline if she did. If he was honest, he was glad. It meant Hurst's doctrines had not submerged her nature completely.

Unless she saw through Hurst for herself, the preacher's hold over her would never be loosened. If her eyes were not opened before Dan went to Wales, he would be leaving her and his son unprotected from the preacher's pernicious influence. It did not give him much time to think of something.

For now, though, he had to leave it. Someone was knocking on the front door.

# CHAPTER THREE

"That's for me," Dan said. "Work." He hesitated. "Do you want me to ask Aggie to put Alex to bed, or will you take him?"

"I'll take him."

A truce: their love for Alex could still bring them together.

Caroline glanced at Goronwy Evans as she crossed the hall with Alex in her arms. He whipped off his hat and watched her go up the stairs. Dan had seen the same look in other men's eyes. Evans tore his gaze away from Mrs Foster and looked at Dan with something close to awe.

Dan led him into the parlour. "What progress have you made?"

"I've taken two places on the mail coach for tomorrow evening at seven."

"Very well. Have you a pistol? Or can you only be trusted with a truncheon?"

"I have a pistol."

"Make sure you bring it. We'll meet at the Golden Cross at a quarter to seven. Don't be late."

"Anything else?" Evans's tone suggested he had already put himself out as much as any reasonable man could expect.

"No…Wait! Your lot are mad for preaching, aren't they?"

"My lot? Do you mean the Welsh? Preaching is popular amongst many of my countrymen."

"Have you heard of a preacher called Hurst?"

"I have. My landlady, Mrs Evans – no relation – who is something of a connoisseur, never misses his Fridays."

"Fridays?"

"Monday it's Moody the Congregationalist, Tuesday it's Zinzenden the Moravian, Thursday it's Elliot the Swedenborgian and Fridays it's Hurst the Methodist. Then it's church on Sunday, to make sure she's left no rock of salvation unturned."

"Where does Hurst preach?"

"The lecture room at Beaufort Buildings."

On the Strand, only a few minutes away.

"That's all. Until tomorrow."

Evans, now well and truly dismissed, let himself out of the house. As soon as he had gone, Dan hurried into the hall. He was putting on his hat and coat when Caroline came down the stairs.

"He's worn out, the poor little mite…You're going out again?"

"I've got some business to attend to. I haven't had the chance to tell you yet either. I have to go away tomorrow."

"Why? Where are you going? How long will you be away?"

"A few days. It's nothing to worry about. It's a routine assignment. I'm just bringing a prisoner back for trial."

"Is that what that man was doing here?"

"Constable Evans. Yes. He's coming with me. I need a Welsh speaker."

"You're going to Wales? But why didn't you tell me before?"

"Because I only found out myself a couple of hours ago. And believe me, I'm no happier about it than you are, but I've no choice. The order's come from the Home Secretary himself." He stooped and kissed her on the cheek. "Don't wait up."

"But Dan—"

He had already closed the front door.

He had not gone many steps before it opened again. Dan looked back and saw Nick running after him.

"Mr Foster! You're going away? Can I come with you? I can help you again, like I did in Southwark."

"You heard that, did you?" He had not known the boy was within earshot. "I'm sorry, Nick, it's not possible. You'll be helping me by staying here and keeping an eye on things. And if you do decide to join the Bow Street patrol one day, it's important to keep up with your schooling if you want to get ahead."

Nick thrust his hands in his pockets, circled a toe on the pavement. "But she doesn't want my help."

"If by *she* you mean Mrs Foster, then of course she does. And I don't want her left alone in the house at nights. The best thing you can do for me is go back and have your supper."

"But—"

Dan had heard enough *buts*. "I haven't got time for this now."

Nick trudged back to the house. Dan noticed how tall he had grown in the two years since he had taken him off the streets. He was lanky rather than malnourished, muscular rather than puny. Would he be detective material one day? Dan wondered.

Dan knew the prayer meeting was already underway before he reached the lecture room: he could hear the groaning from the street. A whispering doorkeeper with a cringing manner welcomed him inside and tiptoed him to a seat at the back of the crowded room. Dan put his hat under his chair and looked at the respectable, well-dressed assembly of men and women drawn from the trading or artisan classes. They fixed their reverential eyes on the preacher and burst out with "amens" at frequent intervals. Some enjoyed a good weep; others swayed and keened; many hummed their approval of key points in the sermon.

Hurst, a black-suited pillar of denunciation, stood behind

the lectern at the front of the room. Every now and again he passed a large, bony hand through the dark hair straggling loose about his shoulders, then shook his curled fingers above his head as if to pluck the wrath of God from the heavens. Robbers of widows – damned! Stealers of inheritance – damned! Adulterers – damned! Fornicators – damned! His audience of widow-robbers, inheritance thieves, adulterers and fornicators quivered, shivered and sobbed. This went on for another hour until, with the damning of Papists and unbelievers, their ecstasy of expiation reached a crescendo.

Dan was almost as exhausted as the rest of them as they filed out of the hall, though not so uplifted. The cringing doorman and three cadging cronies rattled black bags which were soon filled with coin. The funds were intended, Hurst had announced at the end of his sermon, for soup kitchens, Magdalene houses, and the sustenance of prisoners languishing in debtors' gaols.

Dan hung back in the passageway until the last of the congregation had departed, then stole back to the lecture room and spied on the men inside. Hurst gathered up his notes, shut his Bible, and sat down, mopping his brow and looking on while his assistants emptied out the bags and counted the cash. This done, Hurst noted the figure in a black book he drew from his pocket, made a calculation, jotted it down, read it out, and shut the book. Cringer took this as his signal to start divvying up the spoils into four unequal piles, the largest going to Hurst.

This was just what Dan needed, and certainly enough to open Caroline's eyes to the preacher's true nature. He was on the verge of strolling inside for what promised to be a most satisfying confrontation when Hurst pocketed his share, stood up and said, "And now for something truly divine."

Cringer sniggered. "Mistress Dolly's tonight, is it?"

Better still, thought Dan. It was unlikely that the preacher was going to Mistress Dolly's to distribute charity to the Magdalenes. Hurst winked at his minions, placed his hat jauntily on his head, said his goodnights and left.

Hurst's flock might be safely penned up by now, but Drury Lane was in full glittering, lusty revel. It was easy to follow the tall man through the crowds of theatre, restaurant and tavern goers, with associated streetwalkers, beggars, thieves and hawkers. Even the narrow court where their walk ended had life in it: a man and woman copulating; a hunched man hurrying furtively away from the lights of Drury Lane; three youths lurching towards one of the cheaper establishments at the end of the court where ancient houses of lath and plaster tottered in the shadows.

Hurst stopped at Mistress Dolly's door and stood in the dim circle of light cast by a lantern overhead. He hammered on the heavy boards and announced himself to the porter who appeared at a small wicket. He unfastened half a dozen locks and bolts, let the preacher inside, banged the door shut, and relocked it. Dan waited a few moments before rapping on the door. The wicket clicked open and a broad face looked out from the grill.

"Fuck off."

The wicket slammed shut. Dan knocked again and kept on knocking until the wicket shot open.

"I won't tell you again."

The face disappeared. The business of the knocking and the wicket was repeated a third time.

"I told you to fuck off."

"If I do," Dan said, "I'll be back with a score of police officers to close this place down."

The man cursed, leaned closer to the bars and peered at Dan. "You're a fucking Runner."

"You're a downy cove. Now let me in."

A moment's hesitation, then, "Wait."

The wicket slammed shut. Heavy footsteps stamped away from the door. Dan moved into the shadows, drew his gun from his pocket and cocked the trigger. Figures silhouetted by the lights of Drury Lane passed across the top of the alley. The copulating couple had finished; the woman adjusted her skirt, the man fastened his breeches. They were all too far away or too wrapped up in their own business to notice if a lone officer should be beaten to death by a gang of bullies. Better to rely on having the weapon at the ready than the public spirit of London's citizens.

One of the bolts scraped back. Dan had not heard anyone approach the door. Instantly, he went on the alert.

# CHAPTER FOUR

The door scraped across flagstones to reveal a corridor lit by a few flickering candles in iron brackets. Apart from the porter, there was no one else there. Dan uncocked his pistol and put it away before stepping into the light.

If the man saw the weapon, he gave no sign. He beckoned Dan inside and secured the door. He led Dan along the passageway and through another door to a cold stone stairwell. The corners were full of dust, mice rustled in the shadows, and cobwebs darkened the upper corners of the dingy walls. The damp, rotten smell of the alley followed them as they climbed.

At the top they stepped through a third door into an above-stairs of carpets, curtains, mirrored sconces, and flower-filled vases. Rooms opened off on either side of a long passage. From them came the sound of rattling dice, clinking glasses, talk and laughter. A bully stood on guard by the curtained window at the end, his arms folded over his chest. He watched Dan with a hostile stare, flexed his muscles and sneered a warning.

The porter took Dan to the last apartment on the right where a woman responded "Come in!" to his knock. He ushered Dan inside and clumped back to his post.

It was a small room with papered walls, china ornaments, demure portraits and classical landscapes. The woman sat at a dainty writing desk. She did not look up and raised a jewelled hand to signal he must wait. He stood by the sofa in front of the fire while she scratched a signature before laying down her pen.

She rose in a rustle of silks. Her figure was slender and she moved with a light, rapid step, as if with the vigour of youth. A strong, sweet perfume preceded her across the room. It made his head swim and tickled the back of his throat. She waved her arm, bracelets jangling, inviting him to sit. He did not move. She shrugged and wafted elegantly onto the sofa. Her face was painted, but beneath the cosmetics the skin was tired and sallow. Her eyes were much older than her dress and manner claimed, and the assumed sweetness in her voice failed to mask the effect of years of gin-drinking.

"This is an unexpected pleasure, Mr Foster."

"How do you know my name?"

"Mangle recognised you. He's not as stupid as he looks."

"That would be difficult. You have the advantage of me. I don't know your name."

"Mistress Dolly, of course."

He smiled. "Then you must be a hundred years old at least. There's been a Mistress Dolly in this court for as long as anyone can remember."

"Mistress Dolly will do. What is it you want, Mr Foster? It must be something special to bring you at last to a place which many of your colleagues have been honouring with their patronage for years. Male, female, neuter? The choice is yours."

"I'm here for one of your guests. Hurst, the preacher. Tell me where he is."

"You know that's impossible. My clients expect discretion. Once word got out that I had done such a thing, I would be ruined."

"I doubt Hurst will talk, and I give you my word I won't."

"The word of a thief-taker? What use is that to me?"

"Keeping your business, if you take me to Hurst. If you

don't, I meant what I said to Mangle. I'll close your card tables, arrest your girls, and throw you in jail for brothel-keeping. That's without taking into account the stolen items we are bound to discover when we start looking about."

Her voice became a deep, ugly rasp. "You know I have only to call out and my men will come running. A dead Bow Street Runner wouldn't be much of a threat to me."

"True. But you don't think I've come here without telling the other officers where I am? If I don't go back to the office tonight, this is the first place they'll look. And I don't think your clients would be too comfortable with a murder investigation taking over their temple of pleasure, do you? Still, if you'd rather protect one client and lose the rest, it's up to you." He gave her a few seconds to think it over. "You'd better be quick. My patience is running out."

She flounced to her feet. "Damn you, Foster, I will repay you for this."

She led him out of the room. The bodyguard unfolded his arms and stepped forward with clenched fists. She shook her head.

"There's no need to trouble yourself, Flitworth."

Dan followed her to the upper floor. Here the furnishings were just as fancy, but the pictures on the walls were of a much less artistic class, having been chosen to inspire and encourage Mistress Dolly's guests.

She stopped. "He's in there. Try not to let the whole house know you're here. Flitworth will wait at the bottom of the stairs and show you out when you're ready."

She left him. Dan looked up and down the corridor. The doors were all closed, but there were signs that all the rooms were occupied: footsteps, water splashing into a basin, furniture creaking, grunts and squeals. No one would be paying any attention to anything beyond their own pleasures. He leaned closer to Hurst's door, heard a woman's voice answered by the preacher's sonorous tones. Dan turned the handle and stepped inside.

Hurst sat on a chair at the foot of the bed, facing the door. He had taken off his jacket and had a large glass of wine in his hand. The bottle stood on a small round table at his elbow. A woman with her back to Dan sat on his lap, her brown hair hanging loose around her shoulders, her legs straddling his so that her nightgown was rucked up to expose thin, bare thighs. She was half the man's size and looked like a child in comparison. She had one arm around his neck, the other hand busy in his breeches.

Dan slammed the door. She gasped and whirled round. A freckled face, startled eyes, a mouth hanging open in alarm. She was not much more than a child, fifteen, perhaps sixteen years old.

"Who the hell are you?" Hurst cried.

"Someone you're going to wish you hadn't met," Dan said. "Let go of the girl."

The preacher struggled to stand up, the wine slopping over the glass. She stumbled off him with an angry "Oi!" She caught her balance and turned to face Dan.

"Mistress never said there'd be two of you. That's extra."

Hurst slammed his glass onto the table. "I think, sir, you have mistaken your room. This girl is mine."

Dan answered the girl. "I'm not here for business. Leave us alone."

"And who are you to give your orders here?" demanded Hurst. He took a step towards Dan, stabbed a pointing finger at the door. "Get out."

Seconds later he crashed back onto the chair. He raised a hand to the red circle around his mouth and brought away blood-smeared fingers.

"Wh…what?"

"'E's a bloody nabber!" the girl screeched.

This cleared Hurst's mind. He lunged out of his chair and made for the door. Dan smacked a backhander across the side of his head that sent him down again.

The girl's eyes widened and she emitted an admiring "Lawk!"

"I said you can go," Dan said.

"Not I," she said, scrambling onto the bed. "Not going to miss this."

"What's your name?"

"Effie."

"Then, Effie, you can make yourself useful. Do you have pen, ink and paper?"

She blinked. He should have known better than to ask.

"Can you find me some?"

"There's a bell for when the cullies want something such as to eat or to drink. Can't say I've ever sent for to write before."

"Try it now."

She padded over to the bell rope by the fireplace. The table had miraculously survived the brawling, and on her way back to the bed she poured herself a glass of wine. Having provided herself with refreshment, she settled down to enjoy the show.

Dan grabbed a chair from the side of the room and set it next to Hurst. He drew his tipstaff, his badge of office, from his pocket and placed it on the table. The preacher focussed on the gilt crown at the top of the handle. He thrust his hand into his pocket and drew out a purse.

"There's no need for this to go any further, Officer. I've got money, lots of money. You can have it. If you let me go, I can get more. How much do you want? You can name your price."

"I don't want your money," Dan said. "Though there is something you can do for me."

"What? Just name it."

"You can write a confession."

The preacher gulped. "A…a confession? But what do you want me to confess?"

Dan glanced around the room. "This will do for a start."

There was a knock on the door. Dan looked at Effie. She rolled her eyes, clambered to the floor, and went and took the tray from the lackey who stood on the threshold, craning his neck in an effort to see what was going on. She kicked the door shut, almost flattening his nose, and carried the writing paraphernalia over to Dan. There was no room for everything on the table so she took the wine bottle back to her perch and balanced it between her thighs while she drank from her glass.

Dan smoothed out the sheets of paper, uncorked the ink bottle, and offered the quill to Hurst. The interruption had given the preacher time to think of a way out of his predicament. He whisked the purse out of sight.

"My dear Officer," he said, "you entirely mistake me. I did not come to indulge in pleasures of the flesh, but to wrestle with the devil for this poor, deluded girl's soul – to save her from eternal damnation and pluck her from the flames."

Effie snorted. "Plucking now, is it?"

"We all know what you're here for," Dan said. "And I know how you're paying for it – with the money you cheated from your congregation at the lecture room tonight. Theft, Mr Hurst, is a hanging matter. Though there's always a chance you'll get off with transportation." Hurst tried to splutter something, but Dan did not give him the opportunity. "I'm offering you a better chance. You write your confession, I publish it, and you make yourself scarce."

"Publish it? I'll be ruined. You have no right to speak to me like this! I am a man of the cloth—"

"You're no more a man of the cloth than I am. Come, Hurst, what's it to be? Newgate and hang, or confess and flee?" Dan held out the pen. "You won't get a better offer from Jack Ketch."

"You've got nothing on me! It's your word against mine. If you don't leave here at once, I shall make a complaint against you. I'll tell the magistrates how you forced your way in here, beat me, robbed me. And I've got the marks to prove it!"

Dan sighed and put the pen on the table. "And I have only to call on the charities you claim have benefitted from your generosity to get all the proof I need. It just means you'll have longer in gaol waiting for your trial to come on. Still, if you prefer to be arrested." He reached in his pocket and took out his handcuffs.

"No, wait! If I give you your confession, you'll let me go?"

"The further you go, the better pleased I'll be."

Hurst snatched up the pen. "What do you want me to write?"

"Well now," said Dan, rattling the cuffs, "let's start with impersonating a minister, gaining money by false pretences, stealing from widows, orphans and the needy, and indulging in low pleasures and lewd pursuits. You aren't writing anything. Here. *I* – what is your first name, by the way? – *Ezekiah Hurst, of* – your address? Put it down. *I, Ezekiah Hurst, of* wherever it is you've put, for I doubt it's the truth, *known to the public as a preacher of the Methodist persuasion, having been discovered on the* – what is the date? – *the evening of the twenty-fifth day of October 1799 at Mistress Dolly's brothel in Wild Court, do hereby confess…*"

"'Ere, you aren't putting me in his confession," Effie squawked.

"There's no need for names," Dan said.

Reassured, she poured herself another glass of wine, snuggled her legs under the bedclothes, and listened contentedly while Dan coaxed the confession out of the wretched trickster.

## CHAPTER FIVE

"It's the back of beyond."

"You'll be back before you know it, son," answered Noah.

Dan held out his hands for Noah to lace up the boxing gloves he wore for training. Though it was early, there were already men sparring on the other side of the curtain that divided the parlour and bedchamber from Noah Foster's gymnasium on Cecil Street, one of the roads off the Strand leading down to the river.

"With a constable! I never saw anyone who looks less suited to the job. The drunks and vagrants of Westminster must think they're being arrested by the nobility. I'd be better off going on my own."

"You never know," Noah said, "if you give him a chance, he might turn out better than you think." The old pugilist winked. "People do sometimes."

Dan smiled ruefully. "You mean like the chance you gave me."

Noah shrugged. "I'll leave it to you to decide, son."

It was not a difficult decision. Noah Foster had first come across Dan as a boy at the Oliver v Johnson fight in Blackheath in 1781, eighteen years ago. Dan had got in a fight over territorial rights with another pickpocket. The lad had been older and bigger than Dan and had given him a good thrashing, but

Noah had spotted Dan's talent in spite of it. He had taken him off the streets, given him a home and a name, trained him to fight and taught him that there was more to life than thieving, cold and hunger.

"At least I was a sharp 'un," Dan said.

Noah laughed. "You were that, all right." He paused. "Talking of sharp 'uns, I wanted to have a word about Nick."

"How's his training coming on?"

"He's not you," Noah said, "but he's eager to do well. A bit too eager sometimes. Takes short cuts. He elbowed his sparring partner in the face yesterday afternoon, all but broke his nose."

"Still too much of the street fighter in him? You got that out of me. You'll do the same with Nick."

"He's been told about it before."

"And how many times did you have to tell me off about biting and kicking?"

"You're an honest fighter by nature."

"I'd have been nothing but a gutter brawler if I hadn't had you for a trainer. But look, Dad, if it's getting too much for you, the gym and everything—"

"Too much? What, you think I'm an old man now? I've been training fighters for two decades or more and I'm not ready for caudles and invalid chairs yet."

"I didn't mean that," said Dan, though perhaps in part he had. "It's just he's a young half-wild thing and bound to be more of a handful than the other novices."

Noah snorted. "And weren't you half-wild? No, Dan, I'm not saying the boy's too much for me. I'm saying that sometimes the wildness never really goes."

"Why should it? It's what kept him alive, what kept me alive. He just has to learn to control it. And let's face it, there must have been times you felt like giving up on me. I'm grateful you didn't, and I know Nick will be too."

"Well," said Noah, his ruffled feelings soothed, "there was that time you tried to run away taking the contents of my cash box with you."

Dan laughed. "Ouch."

Noah patted Dan's hands. "Time to start work."

Dan turned and followed him into the gymnasium. They passed the two sparring rings, the racks of wooden weights, the men shifting around one another and throwing punches with more or less skill. Paul Mattox, Noah's old friend and assistant, was hanging an armful of boxing mufflers on a row of hooks. He looked up and gave Dan a smile made hideous by his scarred mouth and crooked teeth, but it was a cheery, fond smile. The disfigurement was his lot after serving his country in Canada in another long-ago war with the French. It was the result of a blow with a rifle butt and the rough-and-ready army doctoring which was all the treatment the wound had received afterwards.

Noah took up position behind one of the straw punch bags.

Dan paused. "You'll keep an eye on things while I'm gone, and—"

"And I know where your will is. Everything will be fine. Now, watch your footwork."

Dan swung his first punch.

Tom Clifford was working his way through a pile of suspects' descriptions when Dan arrived at Bow Street. The young clerk's face was spattered with the stains that had won him the nickname Inky Tom. Dan had often wondered if it was his way of attracting spills from his work, which was always neat.

"Mr Foster? I hear you're off to Wales."

"This evening. I've some work needs doing in the meantime." Dan took his pocket book out of his coat and extracted Hurst's confession. "I need some copies of this, and then it's to be inserted in the *Hue and Cry*."

"Add it to the pile."

"Can't wait, Inky. I'm on the Home Secretary's business, remember?"

Tom hesitated.

"It isn't very long. And it has to be more interesting than that filing."

The lad grinned. "All right, Mr F."

Dan gave the clerk an affectionate bat with his hat. "It's Mr Foster to you."

He went over to the drawers where the "suspects wanted" material was kept and pulled out the file on the Kent gang. He took it over the road to the Brown Bear to drink coffee while he read it and waited for the copies of Hurst's confession.

The first document was the notice that had circulated in the *Hue and Cry*. The Bow Street news sheet went to all the London police offices, as well as to magistrates around the country who circulated it to parish constables, court officials, local militia and anyone else worth notifying. The descriptions of the wanted men were based on the information Customs Officer Barker had provided.

Tom, efficient as ever, had included a few newspaper clippings. The newspaper articles did little more than remind Dan what a savage death Barker's had been. What was new to him was the announcement that the government had offered a thousand guinea reward for the apprehension of any of the smugglers. Sir William had not mentioned that. Dan wondered what his chances were of some of that coming his way. If he got Jones to give up the rest of the gang, say.

He spent the afternoon delivering copies of the confession to the offices of the *Morning Chronicle*, *Morning Post*, *Lloyd's* and *The Times*. By the end of the day Hurst's misdemeanours were broadcast around London, and within days would be in the hands of every law officer in the country. For completeness, Dan asked Inky Tom to have some handbills printed and distributed in and around Beaufort Buildings.

Then it was time to go home to take leave of his family over tea in the parlour. It was not the first time he had been called away at short notice and by now Caroline was used to the idea, though no happier about it. Dan, mentioning the Home Department reward in the hopes of getting her to see its more positive side, handed half of his cake to Alex.

"Don't give him any more, he won't eat his supper," she said. "I should hope you do earn something more than your usual pay. It's hardly enough for the trouble these jobs put you to."

Dan sneaked his son another piece of cake. Alex went back to pushing a little wooden horse on wheels around the room, steering erratically with one hand and trailing crumbs from the other.

"The horse seems to be a success," Dan said.

It was his latest purchase: Caroline had given him a telling off when he brought it home two days ago. They watched the little boy's bumpy progress. The toy rattled off the carpet, made a head-splitting clatter over the floorboards and passed behind the sofa where Dan and Nick sat.

"Horsey?" she said. "It's his favourite."

"Don't they pay any extra for such jobs, Mr Foster?" asked Nick, moving his feet out of the path of the brightly painted wheels.

"It's not a bad salary, a guinea a day and expenses," Dan answered. "Though they'll argue about those if you don't have proof down to the last penny."

"What Mr Foster earns is no one's business but his own," Caroline snapped. "It's hardly enough for all the disruption these trips cause. Goodness knows how long I'm to be left to manage on my own."

Dan could have reminded her that she had Noah Foster and Paul Mattox to call on if she needed help, and that her sister Eleanor and her husband, Sam Ellis, were only a few minutes' walk away on Long Acre. And she would not be all on her own. Nick would be there: the boy was tough and well able to take care of himself and the family. But he thought it wiser to say none of these things.

The horse's wheels rattled on the wooden floor. Caroline pursed her lips at the noise but refrained from criticism. She was trying hard not to send Dan off with scolding and tantrums ringing in his ears.

The clock on the mantelpiece chimed softly. Dan put down his unfinished tea and checked his watch.

"Time to go."

He and Caroline stood up, their attention momentarily drawn away from the child who was passing in front of Nick. There was a bang, a crash, and Alex burst into tears. The horse lay on its side, three wheels spinning, the fourth knocked out of alignment.

Dan picked up his son and tried to hush his heartbroken sobs of "Horsey's broken!"

"Never mind, son, Dad'll mend it."

"I said that wasn't a toy for in the house," Caroline said. "And you haven't got time to mend it now."

Dan kissed his son. "Grandad will do it. Nick can take it to the gym next time he goes." He looked at the damaged toy. "It must have caught on the chair leg."

"Yes, I think it did," said Nick.

Caroline flashed a suspicious look at the boy, but there was no time to develop whatever thought had flickered into her mind. Dan handed Alex to her, and she and Nick followed him into the hall. Alex, still crying, buried his head in Caroline's neck and could not be persuaded to turn up his face for a goodbye kiss or wave to his father.

Dan put on his coat and snatched up his travelling bag, hastily packed with clean linen, his razor in its battered case, spare Bow Street issue shot and powder flask, and his tipstaff. It would have no jurisdiction in Wales, but he carried it all the same. Money, valuables and pistol he kept about him. He stuffed the packet of food Caroline had prepared for him in his coat pocket and did not see the piece of paper fall out of it, or notice Nick pick it up, glance at it, and put it in his own pocket. It was out of sight by the time they shook hands, and then Dan was off, leaving in a whirl of scolding and tantrums after all.

When Dan arrived at the Golden Cross, a crowd had gathered as usual for the nightly spectacle of the departing coaches. The vehicles with their high-mettled horses were drawn up in a line in front of the inn, the drivers, guards and post boys resplendent in their various liveries. In the crowded yard passengers clung grimly to their luggage, or watched it safely deposited in the boots of their conveyances. The lights of the inn and the lamps on the coaches reflected in the gaudy paintwork of the gleaming carriages. Horses stamped; people chattered, laughed, and shouted; harnesses jingled.

Dan pushed through the press of people. He found Evans flirting with one of the maids who circled the yard selling food and drinks. Brandy and hot water, in Evans's case. The Welshman held up his glass.

"Can I get you one?"

"No. Is our coach ready?"

Evans gulped down the last of his brandy, winked at the girl and returned the glass to her tray. "Over there."

Every now and again cheers went up as the most celebrated drivers in their great caped coats swaggered into their seats. The thrilled spectators swapped tall stories: one driver could knock the pipe out of a man's mouth with a crack of his whip. Another was famed for his entry into the Lion at Shrewsbury, a passage that was not for the faint-hearted, involving as it did a gallop up and over a steep and narrow bridge past the tavern, wheeling back and trotting briskly through the archway into the yard to shouts of "Mind your heads!" to the outside passengers. Another had never been out-galloped on the flat; although it was illegal to race the coaches, the winners were no less lauded for all that.

To shouts of "Let them go!" coach after coach sprang away: the quarter to seven fast coach to Ely, the Cambridge post coach, the North Wales New Coach, the *Sociables*, the *Dukes of York*, the *Royal Charlottes*, the *Marquises of here-and-there*, the *Mercurys*, the *Wonders*, the *Expeditions*. The seven o'clock departures were already waiting: the mail coaches to Cirencester, Oxford, Ipswich, Newmarket and more.

Not for the Royal Mail the brash purples, blues and yellows of the commercial vehicles, but the dignified black, maroon and Post Office red with the royal coat of arms on the door. The guard stood beside the Irish mail coach in his scarlet coat and gold braid, a horn slung over his shoulder, pistols at his belt and his blunderbuss in his hand. He was a bow-legged man in his forties, wiry and short enough to have ridden as a post boy in his youth.

He raised his fingers to his forehead as Dan and Evans approached. "Name's Garing, Principal Officer Foster." He puffed out his scarlet chest. "We are all on the King's business. You can rely on us to get you to Anglesey in good time, sir."

Dan nodded politely, then drew Evans to one side and muttered, "First rule: don't talk about our business." He pulled his watch out of his waistcoat and said aloud, "The driver will have to get a move on then. It's nearly seven."

The ostler at the horses' heads guffawed. Garing smiled and drew out his own watch.

"It wants three minutes yet. Suggest you climb in, gen'men."

Dan opened the coach door and threw in his bag. There was no need to leave it in the boot as they were the only passengers. He stepped in after it. The constable followed and placed his bag carefully on the floor between his feet.

"Look sharp!" Garing called.

The ostler leapt to attention. The horses tossed their heads. The crowd fell back. The maids stopped calling their wares and fixed their eyes on the open door. A tall, broad red-faced man in a caped coat and great boots emerged from the taproom. He carried a whip in one hand and adjusted his hat with the other. With barely a pause in his step he swung himself up into the driver's seat. No word of greeting passed his lips, no acknowledgement of the existence of other mortals at all. Garing disappeared and the rocking of the coach signalled that he had taken his place on his seat near the mailbox. One of the stable boys darted forward, checked that the passenger door was closed, and skipped nimbly back.

"All right inside and out!" roared the driver.

There was a piercing blast from Garing's horn. The coach leapt forward. Lights, faces, barking dogs, cursing porters, whining children, scurrying servants, waving friends and weeping wives were left behind in a blur. Dan tilted his hat over his eyes and went to sleep.

## CHAPTER SIX

At one o'clock on Monday afternoon Dan stood on the landing stage at the George Inn at Bangor, watching two ferrymen piling luggage into their boat. On the Anglesey shore, across the cold grey water lying under a cold grey sky, he saw a long two-storey inn set amongst outhouses and stables. In front of it stood a couple of coaches with their teams harnessed. One was the replacement mail coach that would complete the journey to Holyhead, so there was no need to risk the vehicle they had arrived in on the Strait. Beyond the inn there may have been an island, there may not. The drizzle blotted out all except near objects.

Ferries seemed to attract bad weather. The rain had started as soon as they stepped onto the boat across the estuary at Conwy this morning, had been squalling off and on ever since. The boat had rocked crazily all the way over, and the rowers had warned the passengers to sit quietly in their places. There were a dozen altogether, some of them pale and trembling, others with their eyes firmly shut. There had been relief all round when they reached the shore safely.

Now there was another stretch of heaving water to cross. It did, though, look preferable to the alternative Evans had pointed out to Dan from the top of a steep mountain road after they left Conwy. Dan had looked out of the coach window over a low wall at the edge of the precipice. In some places it was only three or four feet high, in others it disappeared altogether to be replaced by a slight bank which gave all too clear views of the sea lashing the rocks two hundred feet below. Beyond that a bleak extent of sands drifted into the strait.

"If you got a ferry from there, you'd be in Beaumaris directly," Evans said.

"From where?"

"From the sands. You walked across until you came to the boat, about four miles."

Dan could not see any roads. "How do we get down there?"

"No one goes that way anymore. It's too dangerous. Get the timings wrong and you'll be caught in the incoming tide and drowned. This, the Penmaenmawr road, is the travelling road now. It's been much improved over the last few years."

If this was an improvement, Dan supposed that only Welsh mountain goats had used the old road. And someone ought to tell the Conwy to Bangor turnpike trustees to lay out a bit of money on raising the wall.

The luggage on the landing stage belonged to the family huddled nearby, a couple in their fifties and a girl who was no more than eighteen. They had arrived at the George Inn, an impressive building overlooking the Menai Strait from the top of a sloping garden, in a private post chaise. The father had a country squire's plump and port-coloured complexion. His pendulous lip over an ample double chin and slightly protuberant eyes gave him a perpetually affronted air. This was no false impression, for his conversation was one long complaint.

"If they aren't careful, they'll have those portmanteaux in the water. Do these boats never leave when they say they will? Can't you speak up?" The last to his wife, who had attempted a soothing murmur. She fell into a flustered silence. "And you, miss, what do you find to ogle at?"

His daughter pouted and turned her attention back to her family. "I'm sure I don't know, Father."

She had, in fact, been looking at the tall booted figure whose eyes glinted mysteriously from beneath the brim of his hat. Dan had not noticed her interest in him.

The Royal Mail driver approached him and tipped his hat. "I leave you here, sir."

Dan responded to the well-used phrase as every traveller must. He retrieved a half crown from his purse. With drivers changing every fifty miles or so, he thought, you paid so many tips on top of your fare you could almost buy yourself a coach of your own. But he knew the men relied on the money, their wages not being the most generous. Odd how the men who did the hardest work got the least for it.

The coachman showed his approval by accepting the tip and trudged towards the George.

The guard, Garing, knelt on the roof of the coach and threw down mail bags to the clerk from Bangor Post Office. He jumped down and the two traded paperwork. Garing shouldered the bags which were destined for the Dublin Packet and headed for the slipway. Evans appeared at Dan's side, having fortified himself against the chill water with a glass of something, and the passengers took their places in the boat.

As soon as they were on the Strait the clouds darkened. The drizzle sank to meet the swell, soaking their coats, the sails, the boat rails, the horses, the halo of the girl's hair beneath her hood. By the time they stepped out onto the slippery rocks on the other side, the rain was falling in wind-driven sheets and the waves had begun to make the boat a decidedly unpleasant place to be.

A sign on the inn proclaimed it to be the Three Tuns. Aside from its cluster of buildings, Porthaethwy seemed to consist of nothing. There were very few houses, chiefly inhabited by the ferrymen.

Garing loaded the mail bags onto the waiting coach, and

minutes later the Royal Irish Mail clattered off into the murk. The ferrymen deposited the family's luggage by the other vehicle and went away.

"Where's that blasted coachman?" demanded the squire. His wife and daughter were unable to answer and, grumbling, he drove them inside.

Dan and Evans went in after them. In the parlour, candles had already been lit although it was only the middle of the afternoon. A fire burned in a great stone hearth, throwing up shards of red from polished glasses, tables and tankards. The woman behind the bar added to the attraction of the scene. It all looked very promising – except she regretted to inform Evans that they did not have a hire coach available to take them the last few miles to Beaumaris. The conversation left Dan with the impression that it took a very long time to say anything in Welsh.

"How far is it?" he asked.

"Five miles," Evans translated, while the woman looked on with friendly concern.

"Then we'll walk."

Evans looked at the rain pelting against the window, the wind-whipped branches of the solitary tree outside the building, and the blazing fire logs. Dan had already moved to the door, and the constable had no choice but to pick up his bag and set off after him. The barmaid looked at him enquiringly; miserably he explained their intention. She shook her head, tutted, and voiced her concern.

"What's the problem?" asked Dan.

"She says it's not a good idea with this storm blowing. The road will be dark and it's none too safe in places. She says we should wait here until it blows over."

"Which will be when?"

"In the morning."

Dan hesitated. It had turned into a filthy day and they were travel-stained as it was. Besides, after two nights sitting up in a coach, the prospect of a bed was attractive. Added to that, by the time they got to Beaumaris – assuming they did not lose their way – there would not be much of the day left to transact any business.

While they waited downstairs for the fire to be lit in their room, they took off their coats, shook off the drops and draped them over the back of their chairs by the hearth. Evans asked for beer, a coffee for Dan, and ordered supper.

The rain pelted against the windows, the fire crackled, women's voices drifted from somewhere in the building, high and volubly Welsh. A smelly old dog padded in, took one look at them and padded out again. Evans gulped his drink, tapped his foot, glanced restlessly about him.

After a while, a girl came and told them their room was ready. The constable jumped up.

"I'll take the bags up," he said. "You stay here and warm yourself."

"Take my coat too," Dan said.

Evans followed the girl out of the room and up the stairs. The front door opened, admitting a gust of wind, men's voices, heavy footsteps. A wet, weather-beaten group tramped past the parlour to a snug further along the corridor. Businessmen from the look of them, on their way to or from the mainland: solicitors perhaps, cattle merchants, or land agents. The front door opened again, but this time it was someone leaving. He scurried past the windows, his hat pulled down, shoulders hunched against the rain.

Dan finished his drink and decided to follow Evans to the room. He went into the passage, rang the bell, and asked the girl to show him up. She led the way with a candle in her hand, for the storm had brought night into the house early. She lit a candle in the room and left him.

The room, which overlooked the darkness that was the

view across the Strait, was empty. The massive four-poster bed had clean sheets and feather mattresses, and there was a wash stand with a pitcher of water, clean towels and a fresh ball of soap. Dan's coat hung on the door.

Dan suspected they had been put into one of the best chambers, but decided not to protest about the expense. There was no telling whether they would get anything half so comfortable in Beaumaris. He caught sight of himself in the mirror over the fireplace, unshaven, bordering on unkempt. He had missed his morning sessions in the steam bath next door to Noah's gym, where he went after swinging clubs, punching a straw bag, and sparring. He would send for a barber in the morning, have a good shave and trim before he introduced himself to Justice Lloyd Pryce in Beaumaris.

For now, he took off his jacket, necktie and shirt. The water was cold, but clean. He washed his face, arms and torso. Evans had left their bags on the bed. They both carried cylindrical travelling bags with shoulder straps and strap-and-buckle fastenings, except Dan's was newer, but in the shade cast by the bed curtains it was difficult to tell them apart.

The first one he picked up emitted a faint clinking. Was the constable carrying bottles of spirits? There was surely no need; there were ample opportunities to buy drinks at the coaching inns along the way. Yet on the journey Dan had not seen the constable consume anything other than the occasional glass of rum punch to wash down the lukewarm food and watery coffee served to travellers in a series of indistinguishable dining rooms.

Should he open the bag? He had no reason to do so. The man was entitled to carry bottles about the country if he wanted to. Even while he thought this, Dan's fingers reached for the strap, as if searching came too naturally to a Bow Street officer to resist.

Footsteps approached the door. Dan dropped the constable's

bag back onto the bed, opened his own and pulled out a shirt. Evans came in, bringing rain and chill air with him. He took off his hat, poured the water from the brim, and wiped his face.

"You've been out in this?"

"I fancied a look around."

"You can't have seen much of the little there is to see in this weather."

"I saw enough."

Dan put on his jacket. "Supper should be ready soon."

"I'll be down in a minute."

Evans stood in his wet coat, one hand in the right pocket, while Dan crossed the room. Dan pulled the door to behind him but held it open a fraction so he could look back inside. The constable brought out a package wrapped in sacking and tied with string. The package was not big enough to be a bottle of gin or brandy. Evans opened his bag and tucked it carefully inside. Only then did he remove his coat. Dan closed the door and crept down the stairs.

The family from the landing stage was already seated around a table in the parlour, the father consulting a bill of fare while a waiter looked on.

"No need for fish or soup. We'll have beef chops. Are the vegetables and bread included? No. Then two servings between us will be enough. A bottle of claret, and make sure to draw the wine fresh off the barrel. I'll have a beefsteak. And tell my driver to put the luggage in the coach and be ready to leave in half an hour."

"Yes, Mr Roberts," said the waiter, with just enough deference to avoid accusations of insolence. Either he did not mind whether or not he got a tip, or he knew his customer well enough not to expect one.

The waiter left. Roberts leaned back in his chair with a satisfied air. "As I always say, there's no need to pay the prices they charge at the George."

"You do always say it," said his daughter, adding "Papa" as a softener.

Evans arrived, and the London men ordered their own meal. Dan drank soda water and his companion sent for a bottle of wine. The fire crackled; the grumbling tones of the waiter interspersed with sympathetic female clucks came from the passageway. Dan guessed the man was voicing what he thought of Roberts.

The food was good, and Dan let himself enjoy it. Idly he watched Mrs and Miss Roberts pick at their chops and sip from their half-filled glasses while Mr Roberts feasted on his steak and the lion's share of the wine, bread and side dishes. He pushed away his empty plate, told the women they did not want tart or pudding and coffee could wait until they got home, and rang for the bill.

"How old's your son?"

Dan looked at the constable. "What did you say?"

Evans sucked in his lower lip. "I only asked how old is your son?"

Dan hesitated. "He's two."

"What's his name?"

Dan watched the waiter bring the bill to the other table. "Alex."

"You must be missing them."

"What's this?" Roberts cried. "I didn't order this ale."

"That's what your coachman had," the waiter answered.

"He was told he could have bread and cheese. I'll not pay for his toping as well. Take it off."

The waiter rolled his eyes, pocketed the bill and took it away to make the alteration.

Dan nodded at Evans's wine bottle. "Don't sit up too long over that. We're making an early start in the morning."

He left the room with Roberts's voice following him. "They'd eat you out of house and home if you let them. Come along, don't dawdle. I want to be back at Plas Gwyn before suppertime."

## CHAPTER SEVEN

By morning, the rain and mist had cleared and Dan got his first look at the island on the walk to Beaumaris. It was not much of a road, narrow and rutted in places, with long stretches of mud through gloomy tunnels formed by the overarching trees. It wound around wooded slopes from which threads of rainwater splashed down, gushed across the road, and poured off the island, taking much of the surface with it.

Overgrown banks edged the waterline, tangled and steep in places. Gulls shrieked over the glittering water. Along the water's edge oyster catchers stabbed at the wet sand with long curved beaks. A cormorant stood on a rock thick with dark green weed, its wings spread out to dry. Dan spotted houses built on tiny islands that could only be accessed by boat or narrow causeways. Otherwise there were few buildings. On the opposite side of the Strait, the houses, inns, warehouses and offices of Bangor straggled along the shore under drifting plumes of smoke. Behind them the land rose away, with the mountain range of Snowdonia looming in the distance.

There was no traffic and the running water, the wind in the trees, the chatter and rustle of birds were the only sounds. Even so, whenever the vista across the water opened out, it put Dan in mind of the Thames. Rowboats, wherries, fishing boats, pilot boats and sailing ships jostled one another along the waterway in an apparently chaotic coming and going, a chaos that represented trade, work, wealth, regulation.

He saw that there were landing places all along the Anglesey coast. Some were dignified by stone ramps and mooring stations, usually close to places where a spur of the road ran to the water's edge, or at the mouth of a river, and presumably used by local ferry operators. Others were merely little crescents of mud and stone, or flat rocks that could be traversed on foot. No wonder smuggling was so easy.

Evans swung along beside him, occasionally breaking into a tuneful whistle which Dan quelled with a look. The constable sang or hummed to himself instead, so softly that Dan could not complain. Besides, it was a fine day, and fine to be out walking in it after the cramping journey. If Dan had not had the constable at his side, he might have broken into song himself.

The road climbed down gently until it ran alongside the Strait, turned a corner and came to a spit of land. On this was a shipyard with a hull on the stocks. Workmen swarmed over and around the half-built vessel, filling the air with the sound of their hammering, drilling and sawing. Thick smoke rose from braziers, and at the forge a smith shaped iron in a din of bellows, beating, and hissing water. A crane dangled a load of planks, men shouted, and there were snatches of song.

"That must be Gallows Point," Evans said. "No gallows now though."

Half a mile beyond the Point lay Beaumaris, a cluster of irregularly shaped slate roofs spiked with the masts of ships lying at anchor. Here and there portions of city wall still remained. The tallest structures were a church tower and, at the far end of the town, the ruined towers of a castle.

The quayside was crowded with seamen and customs and port officials. Everyone seemed to have business there. Women bought fish, farmers brought in butter and cheese, clerks and merchants checked cargoes. Those who did not have business went there anyway. A schoolmaster herded a group of truanting boys, lured by the whiff of adventure that clung to the seagoing vessels, back to their lessons. Idlers who enjoyed watching other people labour lounged about the wharves. Servants with laden baskets stopped to flirt and gossip.

There were shops and offices in the town too. People could consult a solicitor, shipping agent or corn factor, take their horses to be shod or tools to be made or repaired, order a saddle or a pair of boots. In spite of this variety of enterprises, it was the maritime smells of fish and brine, tar and timber, that dominated.

The two officers halted outside the Bull. Dan was surprised to see that Beaumaris had such a substantial coaching inn since it was miles off the route of the Royal Mail. Then he remembered Evans had mentioned an older and more perilous crossing which had been abandoned in favour of the ferry from Bangor. With no Royal Mail to serve, the Bull's heyday might be over, but it looked as well-appointed as any London inn, and better than Dan had expected.

On the other side of the road stood the courthouse, a small, cramped-looking building. The castle ruins lay a short distance away, surrounded by a sluggish moat. Untidy nests straggled over the ramparts, and the grass around the walls was dotted with heaps of masonry. A wagon had drawn up beside one of these, and three men were loading stones onto it. The sea clawed at the edge of the marshy land, and the ever-present Snowdonia range dominated the opposite shoreline.

Dan consulted his papers. "We need directions to Henlease."

"Henllys," Evans said. "They won't know where you mean if you say Henlease."

Dan put the papers back in his pocket. "You ask."

Evans moved towards the inn door.

"Not in there."

"We could get a bit of lunch."

Dan pointed at a high stone wall beyond the courthouse. "That's the gaol, isn't it? We'll ask while we're there."

"We're going there now? I thought you had to see Justice Pryce first. And shouldn't we sort out some rooms?"

"That can wait."

With a wistful glance at the Bull, the constable followed Dan. The prison doors, heavy oak studded with iron, stood open on to a short stone passage blocked at the far end by an iron gate. A tall, brawny man with a stick and a bunch of keys hanging from his belt walked across the yard, kicking aside the indignant hens scratching at the ground. He ignored the men at the gate until Evans called to him in Welsh.

He thrust a warty face arranged around a large flat nose at the bars and asked what they wanted. At least Dan assumed that was what he asked, and in no very helpful tone. Evans peppered his reply with his own, Dan and Justice Pryce's names and titles. The turnkey's manners improved by stages with the mention of each one and culminated in a tip of the hat. He unlocked the gate and admitted them into the yard.

"He's taking us to Mr Braillard, the governor," Evans said.

The gate clanged behind them. The turnkey relocked it and led them across the stones. Their footsteps echoed from the walls. Several small grated windows overlooked the yard, but no faces appeared at them. Their guide unlocked another door and led them into the building. They passed a bare room with a slimy wooden bathtub on a stone floor. At the end of the corridor, a door stood open on to a steamy kitchen with greasy rivulets running down the walls. A plump, grimy woman presided over a pair of frowsy female prisoners who had just taken delivery of a basket of small loaves. This was the prisoners' daily allowance unless they could afford to buy better provisions from the turnkey, a transaction he would encourage as he would make a good profit from it.

A barred window looked out on to a small inner yard. It was a dark, dank place to take exercise, and was empty. The turnkey knocked on an office door and led them inside.

Governor Braillard detached himself from his desk, hand outstretched, and said in English, "Principal Officer Foster! It is an honour, sir, an honour! We have been expecting you. Everything is in good order, the prisoner all present and correct. He is ready for you to examine now. You have only to say the word and I will take you to him myself. If there is any way in which I can render assistance, you have only to say the word. If you wish to inspect the gaol, you have only—"

"To say the word," Dan said, returning the handshake. "Thank you, Mr Braillard. I don't doubt that all is in order. I will look in on the prisoner for a moment."

Dan and Evans left their bags and the party went back along the corridor and up a flight of stone stairs. They walked along a stone passage with cells on either side. Each had a small ventilation grate over the door, but rather than letting in fresh air, it only let out foul: a fug of damp straw, stale bedding, unwashed men, and full chamber pots. The turnkey loosened the stick in his belt, rapped a warning on one of the doors, and opened it.

The only light in the room came from a tiny aperture high in the wall. Watcyn Jones lay on an iron bed. He rose reluctantly to his feet. He had come in with enough money to buy a few comforts, including freedom from fetters, as well as the unlit candle on the table and the remains of a loaf and a jug of beer.

He flicked back a strand of greasy black hair and stared at Dan and Evans. Dan returned the look with a careful scrutiny of the man for whose safe delivery to London he would soon be responsible. The prisoner was in his early twenties, short and stocky. He had large hands with thick, swollen knuckles. A brawler's hands, Dan thought, with a fighter's shoulders and arms, and the sly eyes of a dirty fighter at that. He wore heavy woollen breeches of indeterminate colour, a coarse shirt and a dirty red scarf. His blue flannel jacket was fastened with large brass buttons and spattered with food stains. He could never have been dapper, and the weeks in prison had not improved the look or smell of him.

A silver chain in his waistcoat struck an incongruous note. He could not have much use for the seal hanging from it. Men like Jones did not write the kind of letters that needed sealing. If they could write at all.

"This is Watcyn Jones?" Dan said.

"The same," answered Braillard.

"Is he in good health? No gaol fever about him?"

Jones had understood, and before Braillard could answer, he said, "Aw, ain't that nice? He's come to ask after me. And him a perfect stranger and all."

The turnkey snarled something in Welsh, presumably along the lines of only speaking when he was spoken to or he'd soon know about it. Jones grinned, releasing a gust of foul breath from between brown teeth.

Dan said, "Dan Foster, Principal Officer of Bow Street, is asking."

Jones raised his eyebrows. "They've sent a Runner?" He jerked his head at Evans. "Who's your monkey?"

The turnkey's stick cracked cross his arm. Jones staggered, cursed in Welsh, and straightened up, still grinning.

Dan frowned at the turnkey. To the governor, he said, "His health?"

"All the men in my care are in good health," Braillard answered. "He's well enough to stand a whipping."

"There'll be no whipping. I'll be back for him tomorrow. Give him a bath and clean linen. And no visitors."

Jones blinked away imaginary tears. "What, can't a son say goodbye to his dear parents?"

"I doubt we'd tear them away from the alehouse long enough," Braillard said.

They left Jones standing in the middle of the cell, his parting words ringing after them: "Till we meet again, Bow Street."

"He's a nasty one," Braillard said as they walked away. "You had better be careful, Officer Foster."

"Mmm," said Dan. He had met men like Jones before. Under their bravado there usually lurked a cowardly bully.

They went back to the governor's office to collect their luggage.

"I will make sure your instructions are carried out," Braillard said. "And if there is anything else, you have only to say the word."

"Thank you, there is nothing else save directions to—" Dan hesitated.

"Henllys," said Evans.

"I will take you there myself," Braillard offered.

"That won't be necessary, thank you. If you could just set us on our way. Good day, Mr Braillard."

The men shook hands, then Braillard and the turnkey escorted them across the yard and out of the prison. The iron gate clanged shut behind them. Dan took in a deep breath of sea air. It was always a relief to leave a prison behind.

"Do you really mean to start back to London tomorrow?" Evans asked, as he and Dan walked out of Beaumaris and followed a road along the shore through grazing land dotted with stands of ancient trees.

"I do."

"It's very quick. I mean, we've only just finished one journey. I thought we'd at least have a day to rest before we had to set off again."

"We're not here on a grand tour, Constable."

Evans fell silent. A cart toiled along in front of them, two men leading the horses. When they came up to it, Dan recognised the men who had been collecting their load of stones from the castle. They tipped their hats as the two officers strode by. Before long, Dan and Evans reached the turning in the road that led to Henllys and started up a long, gradual slope.

## CHAPTER EIGHT

Dan and Evans reached the summit of the lane and passed under the shade of an ancient oak tree. They turned right through open ornate gates, followed the drive along the foot of a small wooded hill, and rounded a corner to see Henllys mansion in front of them. Beyond the entrance the drive continued left, and then swung behind the house to the stable and coach houses.

Dan rang the doorbell. After a few moments, a butler opened the heavy oak door. He tutted at them and pointed in the direction of the hammering and sawing coming from the side of the house.

"He thinks we're tradesmen," Evans said, and explained who they were.

"Principal Officer Foster to see Sir Edward?" said the butler, changing to English. "I will take you to Sir Edward at once."

They followed him around the corner of the mansion, where a row of bay windows overlooked the Strait. The middle bay and its tall sash windows had been removed and the wall covered with scaffolding. Half a dozen men laboured in and around it. The trampled lawn was covered with workmen's carts and piles of bricks, sand and timber.

The workmen looked up, but did not stop working. The reason for their diligence was not hard to guess. Two gentlemen stood with their backs to Dan and Evans, consulting an architectural plan. From the shorter man's deferential manner, Dan guessed that the other was Sir Edward Lloyd Pryce. The magistrate cut a tall, fine figure with his straight back, wide shoulders and narrow hips shown to advantage by a well-tailored jacket, breeches and boots. The profile he turned towards the architect was equally well proportioned, with an intelligent blue eye, a shapely mouth, straight nose, and locks of fair hair tumbling from beneath the brim of his hat.

"The Bow Street officers are here, Sir Edward," said the butler.

The men turned round. Evans gasped, but quickly stifled his revulsion at a furious glance from Dan. Not quickly enough for Sir Edward, who had already taken offence.

Dan resolved to let the constable know what he thought of him at the first opportunity. Irritating a man whose co-operation they needed was hardly a good start. More than that, it always angered him when Paul's scarred mouth elicited a similar reaction from newcomers to the gym seeing Noah's old friend and assistant for the first time.

True, Sir Edward's face was a shock. The right half was as handsome as his profile had promised, but the left was covered in shrivelled red skin which puckered around a black silk eyepatch. Half his outer ear was gone, and the tight skin tugged at the side of his mouth so that his lips were permanently set as if in a faint smile. That he was very far from smiling at his visitors was clear from his icy tone.

"You are the men who will escort Watcyn Jones to London?"

At the name, the hammering and sawing stopped in mid-stroke and all heads turned towards them. The foreman shouted a warning and the men made a show of busying themselves while straining to listen in on the conversation. Since most were Welsh speakers, it would have done them little good if they had been able to hear it. Only one of the bricklayers seemed to follow the talk. He was a young man seen to advantage in his shirtsleeves, his muscles rippling, his soft curly hair blowing in the breeze. A man who knew he drew the eyes of the girls, and sometimes of the ladies too, and was not likely to miss an opportunity to do so.

"We are, sir," Dan replied. "I am Principal Officer Dan Foster of Bow Street Magistrates' Office, and this is Constable Evans. This is our warrant."

"It's an honour to meet you, sir," Evans said.

The magistrate, who had clearly been expecting something more boorish, gave the constable a second look as he took the document from Dan.

"Which part of Wales are you from, Constable? Would I know your family?"

"Ruthin, Sir Edward. My father, Reverend Gerallt Evans, is a master at Ruthin School."

"Is he? Didn't he write a monograph on the etymology of *Ordovices* and the location of the lost town of Mediolanum?"

"He did." Evans recited: "*A discourse on the true origin of the name of Ordovices given to that tribe of Ancient North Walians also known as Ordevices, Orodvicae, and Ordolucae; together with an exact delineation of the boundaries of their territory; and shewing the certain location of the town and fort of Mediolanum.* I served as his amanuensis before I went to Cambridge," he added.

"Did you? I've got a copy somewhere. I'll see if I can find it for you."

Dan, who had never heard of Mediolanum, let alone that it had been mislaid, coughed.

Sir Edward, reminded of the business in hand, said, "You must be in need of refreshment after your journey. We'll finish this discussion later, Mr White."

"Very good, sir," the architect answered. He beckoned to the foreman and began to brief him on his client's revisions.

"Well, let's go and look at this." Sir Edward pocketed the warrant. Behind them, the workmen bombarded the young bricklayer with questions.

On their way back to the entrance, Dan looked through the sash windows. The rooms had been stripped bare, and the floors were littered with building debris and battered and scuffed by the builders' boots. Wallpaper hung off in strips, the plasterwork was dirty and the wainscoting chipped. That so little care had been taken to protect the decor suggested that the plan was to replace everything.

"I'm having a new entrance put in," Sir Edward explained. "With Tuscan columns and a balustrade. The rooms on the ground floor at this side of the house will be refashioned to make dining and drawing rooms that overlook this." He waved his hand. "It's a fine prospect, is it not? The island you can see is Puffin Island. The birds that nest there in the spring are quite a delicacy here. Yonder is Lord Penrhyn's estate, and that is Penmon Point, and there's the Great Orme. And over there is Penmaenmawr."

"Yes. We travelled over it in the mail coach," Dan said. He did not add that he had been glad to leave it behind.

"This entrance will be blocked up," Sir Edward said, as the butler held the door open for them. "Thank you, Davies."

They entered a hall panelled in aged oak and furnished with a heavy table and a coat stand with a frame beneath for sticks. It seemed a grand enough entrance to Dan, though perhaps dark and old-fashioned. Davies disappeared through a door leading to the kitchens and Sir Edward led them past the empty rooms. The rugs in the corridor had been taken up and there were pale rectangles on the wall where paintings had hung. Dust sheets draped over the closed doors.

The magistrate took them into a book-lined room at the rear of the house and gestured to them to take a seat in front of his desk. He sat behind it and opened the Home Department document. Through the window behind him, Dan saw that the library overlooked wooded countryside which opened out into wide tracts dotted with the occasional house or church. Two riders approached the house at an easy pace.

"When do you plan to take him?" Sir Edward asked as he scanned the pages.

"Tomorrow."

Sir Edward looked up. "You don't waste any time, Mr Foster. But Mr Braillard, the prison governor, will have to be consulted."

"Not intending any discourtesy, I've already spoken to him, sir. The Home Secretary's orders are definite on the need for haste."

"And you intend to carry out your orders. You'd make a good sailor in His Majesty's Navy."

A maidservant brought in tea and handed it around. Dan took a drink, but refused the fruit cake. Evans helped himself to the biggest slice. The riders, Dan noticed, had swerved to their right and were making for the Henllys stables.

"These are all in order," Sir Edward said, "and of course you don't need my endorsement for a Home Department warrant. Naturally, I will give you all the assistance you require."

"Thank you. With your leave, we'll get back to Beaumaris."

Evans hastily took a big bite out of his cake.

"Where are you staying?"

"We haven't taken any rooms yet."

"Then you must stay here. That is if you don't mind a bit of dust and noise and being crammed into cramped quarters. I'll have the housekeeper prepare your rooms."

Dan glanced around the room. The wealthy obviously attached a different meaning to "cramped quarters" from the rest of the world.

"That's very kind of you, sir."

Sir Edward smiled. "It is more convenient for me, if I'm

truthful. I intend to accompany you to the gaol. Jones's fate is as inevitable as it is well-deserved, and I would be failing in my duty if I was not on hand to make sure he meets it."

"You know the man?" asked Dan. The riders had drawn close enough for him to see that one of them was a woman, her dark blue habit spreading across her horse's flank.

"There can't be a magistrate on Anglesey who doesn't know him, or his family. His father's a miner on Parys Mountain, and his mother and sister are cobbers; their job is to break up the ore. A drunken, wastrel lot who've all been arrested for thieving, poaching and smuggling at one time or another. But in that, they are like all the Amlwch miners."

"Then I'm surprised they've not been transported before this."

"There is never anyone to stand witness against them. On the contrary, if an alibi is needed, there's never less than half a dozen willing to swear it. That's the way these people are. They are a lawless lot, Mr Foster.

"The worst of it is that Wat Jones is regarded as a hero on Anglesey. Smugglers have always been popular amongst the lower orders, who regard the excise laws as impositions by the English and the flouting of them as the resistance of tyranny. Yet if we don't raise the taxes to prosecute the war, they will soon discover what tyranny is when the French invade. But Captain Williams can tell you more about Jones than I can. I believe that is him now."

Rapid footsteps approached the room. The door opened and a man in riding boots and breeches strode in, his face flushed from fresh air and exercise. He removed his hat and beamed at the company.

"Good afternoon, Ned. I gather these are the Bow Street men."

"They are." Sir Edward made the introductions.

Williams took up a stance at the side of the fireplace in front of a sofa and cluster of chairs.

"Is Lady Charlotte not joining us?" asked Sir Edward.

"She's gone to change her apparel. So, Foster, you've come to take our prisoner off our hands. And good riddance too. We've been trying to bring the villain to justice these three years or more."

"Captain Williams and the Loyal Anglesea Volunteers assist the excise," the magistrate said. "He was instrumental in Jones's arrest."

"And glad to be so," the captain said. "Rightly, though, the credit belongs to Commander Bevan. If it hadn't been for the watch he and his riding officers keep, we'd never have known Jones was back on the island. He'd rejoined his old gang. We'd put them out of action once already, or thought we had. That was in '96, during a landing at Moelfre. Most got away, Jones amongst them, but two were captured and transported. Jones turned up in Kent, as we now know, and the rest lay low. But it wasn't long before they were up to their old tricks. Bevan discovered that an Irish vessel was due to rendezvous with them at a cove near Amlwch. We were waiting for them. The first we knew that Jones was back with them was when one of Bevan's men brought him down."

"What happened to the rest of the gang?" asked Dan.

"Escaped, unfortunately. Still, if the transportation of two of their number wasn't enough to warn them off three years ago, let's hope a hanging does the trick."

"I doubt that these punishments have any such effect, even when they are witnessed by those who might benefit the most from them," Sir Edward said. "The awful impression they first make soon fades. These people have short memories and little capacity to retain ideas."

"Because they're not used to full effect," said Williams. "Too many of your brother magistrates regard the laws as over-strict and the duties as over-burdensome. They're as willing to buy their tea and brandy from a smuggler as they are loath to send him to Botany Bay." Sir Edward was about to protest, but Williams prevented him. "Come now, Ned, you know it as well as I do. Eh, Mr Foster? We catch 'em, and they should hang 'em, isn't that the way of it?"

Dan, who had seen more hangings than he cared to remember, some deserved, some not so much, preferred to leave the debating to drawing room politicians. "I've no experience of dealing with smugglers."

"Evans, you agree with me, surely?"

"I believe that in some cases hanging is the only possible punishment," Evans said, "but it is an awful thing, not to be handed down lightly."

He spoke like a man used to debating over teacups. What with that and the way he'd paraded his learning and polite background to impress their host, Dan found it harder than ever to imagine how he'd come to end up as a Westminster constable.

It was not a bad answer, though. Sir Edward thought the same for he smiled, though Dan noticed that the smile ended in a spasm of pain.

"Come, Williams, you are allowing your enthusiasm for the law to carry you away," he said. "The administration of justice must surely be free of passion."

Williams laughed. "And I am a passionate man? Well, you've always said so, Ned. And maybe you're right."

Was Williams conceding his passionate nature or Sir Edward's argument about justice? Perhaps both, thought Dan.

"I'm certain that Jones's is a case where hanging is the only possible punishment," Williams resumed. "The way that excise officer Baker died—"

"Barker," said Dan.

"Barker, of course. When do you expect to take Jones off our hands?"

"Tomorrow."

"Quick work! Good. What's the plan?"

"I'll hire a carriage from the Bull to transport the prisoner to the ferry, and take a post chaise in Bangor."

"There's no need to hire a carriage," said Sir Edward. "Since you are staying here, you can use mine, and as I said, I shall accompany you to the goal." He massaged his forehead above the eyepatch.

"And I'll arrange a few volunteers to provide an escort," said Williams. "I'll send the order immediately."

"Do you think we need it?" asked Dan.

"Well, there's bound to be some resentment when it gets around that Jones is leaving," Williams said. "Which it will, trust me. It can't do any harm to keep the rabble at a distance."

By now the colour had gone from the right side of Sir Edward's face, though the skin on the left was the same painful red.

Williams moved towards the bell pull. "Perhaps the officers would like to go to their rooms now?"

Dan took the hint and stood up. "If you would excuse us, Sir Edward."

What seemed a long silence while they waited for someone to answer the bell was broken by a brisk rap on the door and the housekeeper, a stout matron in a neat grey gown, came in. She took one look at her master and glowered at the captain, as though she held him responsible for Sir Edward's condition.

"Mrs Jenkins, be so kind as to show our guests to their rooms," said Williams.

She led the officers out of the room, muttering to herself in Welsh.

# CHAPTER NINE

In the evening, the party gathered in a drawing room opposite the dust-sheeted doors. All was quiet now the workmen had gone home, leaving the site tidy and the unfinished doorway boarded up. The curtains had not been drawn, and Dan looked out at the lights of scattered houses shining coldly in the darkness. The night blotted out the fields and woodland. Inside, the room was warm and welcoming, decorated in light greens and rose pinks, and scattered with elegant chairs and sofas.

There were two additional guests to dinner. Captain Williams introduced Dan and Evans to Commander Thomas Bevan, the excise officer whose efforts to guard the Anglesey coast he had praised. Bevan was a short, slight man with a sharp face, thin sandy hair, and small pale eyes, the skin around them wrinkled, Dan supposed, from gazing out to sea on the lookout for smugglers.

As soon as the captain had drifted off to get himself another drink, Bevan said, "Sir Edward and I are cousins. I belong to the Shrewsbury branch of the family. It was Sir Edward who set me in my present career. It is one to which I have devoted myself, in spite of all difficulties. People wonder why we catch so few smugglers. I say it's a wonder we catch as many as we do. It's easy for you city folk to talk, but you can have no idea of what's involved."

"I think I've some experience of chasing villains," Dan said.

"Anglesey has a hundred and twenty-five miles of coastline," Bevan continued, taking no notice. "If we had ten times the number of customs officers, it would be impossible to patrol it all. I've six men in Beaumaris and one cruiser with a nine-man crew, and she's laid up for repairs, which means I've only horse patrols to send out at the moment. The locals are no help. Ask them a question and they just stare back at you, bleating '*Dim Saesneg*' – No English. I'm sure the beggars are only pretending. But what can you expect of such people? They've no principles. The farmers lend the smugglers their horses, the fishermen let them use their boats, the young men help to land the goods, the women carry packets of tea into town hidden under their skirts, and even the children keep lookout for them."

Dan let him drone on. He sipped his soda water and glanced across the room. He had not expected to see Sir Edward again that day, but he seemed to have made a full recovery from his attack. He stood by the fireplace with a man who could only be his brother, Stephen Lloyd Pryce. Where Sir Edward's face was marred by his injuries, Stephen's was twisted by discontent and peevishness. His black suit and white cravat proclaimed his clerical profession, a common resort of the gentry's younger sons. The eldest gets the big house, the estate, and the money. Even so, Sir Edward's life had not been all roses.

"He got it at Camperdown," said a voice in Dan's ear. He turned to see Williams holding a replenished glass.

Dan remembered the battle. Two years ago, Admiral Duncan had smashed the Dutch fleet near the Texel, ending fears of an immediate invasion by the French and their allies. The war was far from over, though, and the threat was still there in the background. The British and their Russian allies were fighting in Holland now and trying to persuade the people to rise up against the Republic that had been foisted on them by the French.

"Ned was a lieutenant on the *Ardent*, one of the vessels which engaged the *Vrijheid*, the Dutch flagship. His ship took a pounding and her casualties were the heaviest of the day. Captain Burgess died before the battle was ten minutes old, and forty men were killed. Over ninety wounded were carried down to the cockpit with appalling injuries. Ned and several others were caught in the blast when some cartridges near a hatchway exploded." Williams paused. "None of which he will tell you himself. He never talks of it."

"The wound still pains him?"

"It does."

The door opened and Bevan broke off in mid-sentence. Evans's eyes widened and he took a sharp breath. Stephen Lloyd Pryce's plaintive voice cut across the sudden silence.

"—and the expense of extra coaching for his arithmetic, for he is sadly behind—"

The reason for the stir stood on the threshold dressed in a dark blue silk gown. Simple in design and modest in cut, it set off Lady Charlotte's figure and complemented her dark eyes and golden hair. The sleeves were long, ending in white lace, and she wore no bracelets. Her only jewellery was a pair of small sapphire earrings set in delicate golden filigree.

Sir Edward held out his arm and she glided to his side. Stephen Lloyd Pryce took a sulky draught of his wine.

"My dear," Sir Edward said, steering her towards Dan and Evans, "here are the Bow Street men I told you about."

Dan gave an awkward bow. She smiled graciously.

"You are very welcome, Mr Foster. Your presence here has lifted a burden from Sir Edward's mind."

"I am glad if that is so," he said gruffly.

He was spared having to make polite conversation by Davies's announcement that their meal was ready. Lady Charlotte held out her hand, inviting Dan to move towards the dining room. Her sleeve slipped back, revealing four dark circles in a close line along her wrist. Hastily she pulled down the lace, and he pretended he had not seen the bruises. Smiling up at her husband, she placed a hand on his arm and the couple led their guests into dinner.

They gathered around a massive dining table on old high-backed chairs in a room panelled in oak. A fire burned in a stone-canopied hearth, and they ate under the gaze of Sir Edward's stiff-collared ancestors. Stephen Lloyd Pryce said grace, then, between loading his plate and filling his glass, resumed his conversation with his brother, pressing on him in a low voice the many and varied costs of putting a son through school. Sir Edward attempted to join other discussions, but Stephen always brought him back to his own pecuniary needs. Dan had no doubt that the cash box would be opened before the evening ended, nor that Stephen already knew it. Yet he continued to urge his case with the air of a man with an unanswered grievance.

Dan only needed to kick Evans under the table once to stop his lovesick staring at Lady Charlotte. At the end of the meal, she retired to the drawing room. There was no long sitting to drink toasts. Sir Edward proposed the health of the King and confusion to his enemies, then they rejoined their hostess in the drawing room for tea. The guests all left before nine, Bevan to his lodgings in Beaumaris, Stephen Lloyd Pryce to his rectory and wife at the tiny village below Henllys, and Captain Williams to his house, Ty Coed, which was near the coast by Mariandyrys, four miles north of here. He could have stayed the night, and it was clear from Sir Edward's references to "your room" that he often did, but he said he had one or two things to see to, and he and his horse knew the way well enough to have no qualms about travelling in the dark.

Dan and Evans took candles from the hall table and went up to their rooms, which were next door to one another. Evans was slightly flushed from the wine he had taken, though he was not drunk. It had not been that kind of evening. Sir Edward kept a generous table, but not a debauched one.

The fire in Dan's room had been lit, the bed turned down, and his nightshirt left folded on the coverlet. He took off his jacket and cravat and sat on an armchair to remove his boots. But he did not get into bed straight away.

All in all, Henllys seemed a well-regulated household, and a happy one. The servants were sober and polite; they did not cringe, fumble, drop plates, spill wine, or dart grudge-filled glances at their master or mistress. As for Sir Edward and Lady Charlotte, they gave every impression of being an affectionate and attentive couple. And yet there were those bruises…an accident, most likely. And after all, it was no business of his.

He finished undressing, got into bed and blew out the candle.

# CHAPTER TEN

Dan and Evans stepped out of Sir Edward's carriage at the edge of the crowd milling around the prison gate. Sir Edward and Williams were on horseback, the captain in his volunteer's uniform of red coat with blue trimmings. He had summoned half a dozen cavalrymen, sons of the squirearchy and clergy, who vied with one another for the splendour of their turnout. The horsemen held the jostling people back as the magistrate and officer dismounted and followed the Bow Street men into the prison.

The pockmarked turnkey took them to Braillard's office where they found Jones and a prison guard standing in front of the governor's desk. Jones was not as rank as he had been the day before, having been washed, shaved and provided with clean linen as Dan had requested. Not that any of them would be too fresh after two days cooped up in a coach.

"Why are they here?" demanded Jones, brandishing his manacled hands at Sir Edward and Williams. "I ain't got nothing to say to them."

"Remember who you're speaking to," Braillard said.

"What, the gentry, is it? Gentry my arse. You think you'll hang me, but I'll see you all dead first, you and all the squires and justices and officers. You're all as guilty as me."

"That's enough, Jones," Braillard said.

"It ain't half enough. You think I don't know who runs the trade on this island, who's behind it all, sitting in their big house on the wealth the poor man has made for him – the poor man who takes all the risks!" He jabbed a finger at Dan. "I tell you what, Bow Street, it ain't me who's going to swing. Not when I tell 'em what I know. I'll tell all their names, and I'll tell who rules the roost here. They're all in on it, but there's one will fall further than all."

Chains rattling, he lunged at Sir Edward. Williams darted in front of his friend to block off his attack. Before the captain could draw his sword, Dan, Evans and the guard had hold of Jones. He struggled in their grip, kicking and spitting.

"I'll see you all dead before I hang, and then I'll see you in hell!"

He almost broke free to make another dive at Sir Edward, but Dan stopped him with a punch to the midriff. He doubled over and staggered against the wall, his hair falling over his eyes, his scarf and jacket awry, his big fists clenched. Dan signalled to the others to step back and give him some air.

Jones shook his rats' tails off his face and wheezed, "You can take me, Bow Street. There's nothing and nobody to keep me here. I can't get off this shithole island quick enough."

From the safety of his desk, Braillard said, "If you have information about criminal activities on Anglesey, Jones, you need to tell us. It will go in your favour if you do."

"Not I! Not till I'm in front of the London magistrates. And then we'll see whose neck stretches the longest."

"It will go against you if you withhold evidence," the governor warned.

"I wouldn't waste your breath, Braillard," said Sir Edward. "I doubt very much that the fellow knows anything."

"You'll just have to wait and see, won't you?" retorted Jones. He straightened up. "I'm ready to go, Bow Street."

Dan took his handcuffs out of his pocket and asked the

guard to take off the manacles. Jones held out his wrists and stood quietly while the switch was made. Braillard led them out of the building. They crossed the yard, Dan and Evans flanking Jones.

The prisoners, who had been confined to their cells, were waiting with their faces pressed to the gratings. They cheered when Jones came into view and shouted good luck and defiance. Jones raised his cuffed hands, took off his hat and waved it at them. Dan had seen men go to the gallows like this, playing up to the crowds. By that time, there was not much left to them but a brief popularity, which they ensured by facing their fates with displays of bravado.

The turnkey unlocked the gate and they stepped into the street. The crowd had grown, and included many women and children. There was more cheering, more encouraging cries, and again Jones strutted and waved.

Dan could imagine the stories that would be told afterwards: of the bold Welshman who defied the English laws, and how they dragged him away to be tried in an English court, and hung on an English tree; of daring night-time escapades on the beaches, dramatic chases on the waves, and romantic interludes on the shore; of hidden tunnels and caves and secret signals; of a smuggler so notorious that one of the legendary Bow Street Runners was sent to fetch him. Dan knew that truth and legend had never mixed, especially when it came to idolising thieves and murderers. Tales for children and fools, and certainly not enough to inspire courage in anyone's breast. The sword at Williams's side, the pistols which Dan and Evans carried, the volunteers' muskets, the prison guards, the stern presence of the magistrate, all kept the people at a cautious distance.

"Could we send one of the men ahead to ensure that the ferry is waiting?" Dan asked Williams.

"You'll do, Pallister." Williams singled out one of the riders, a handsome young man on a well-bred horse, who proudly accepted the order and with much flourish and drama cantered away.

Dan and Evans got the prisoner into the carriage and climbed in after him. Surrounded by the horsemen, they moved off. The crowd surged after them. Shop- and innkeepers stood in their doorways and watched the cavalcade pass. Maids and housewives hung out of windows, blowing kisses and fluttering handkerchiefs. The pavements were lined with onlookers, all wishing Jones well. Several times, Sir Edward turned and ordered them to disperse.

Most of them drifted away at Gallows Point, where the shipyard workers downed tools to watch Jones go by. A few tagged along a little further, but by this time they had seen all there was to see, which did not include any glimpses of the prisoner as Dan had drawn down the blinds in the carriage. Before long the road was empty. Sir Edward waved farewell and fell back.

Dan was glad to pull the blinds up and relieve the stuffy gloom. He had not considered the hangers-on to be any great danger, but it was better to be rid of them for it was always possible for a crowd to turn into a mob. Jones slumped in the corner in glum silence, his eagerness to be carried to London leeching out of him. Perhaps it had occurred to him that revealing a master criminal's identity was one thing, getting anyone to believe him another. Evans sat beside him, his arms folded across his chest, gazing out of the window.

The horses' hooves beat a steady rhythm. Occasionally the carriage lurched into a hole or rut, and Sir Edward's coachman shouted and cracked his whip. Williams and his men disappeared and reappeared at the windows as the road narrowed and widened.

They reached one of the landing places Dan remembered seeing on the way into Beaumaris. It lay at the end of a short track, close to a small river estuary. The river ran down a steep wooded ravine and under a low bridge to the Strait. Later, he learned this was Cadnant.

"Whoa! Whoa!" The coachman's panicked cries unnerved the horses, who whinnied, skittered, and came to lurching halt.

There was shouting outside, then Captain Williams's voice rose up in haughty command. "Step aside!"

"Why have we stopped?" asked Evans.

"I don't know," Dan said.

He drew his pistol, signalled to Evans to do the same and reached for the door handle. In the same instant, a pair of masked faces appeared at Evans's window. One of the men wrenched the door open and snarled an order in Welsh.

"Damn you!" Evans said, and fired.

The shot went wide, succeeding only in enraging the attackers. They hauled the constable out of the carriage and flung him on the ground. Before Dan could defend Evans, the door on his side opened and a stocky figure wielding a pistol leaned into the carriage. Dan braced himself against his seat, drew back his foot and planted a kick in the man's chest which sent him flying. His pistol went off, the ball cracking through the roof. Almost as loud was the sound of his head hitting the ground, knocking him unconscious.

Jones whimpered and cowered in his corner, his arms over his head. Dan shoved him between the seats.

"Stay down!"

He jumped out, leapt over the man sprawled at the roadside and, crouching, ran along the side of the carriage. The coachman had jumped from his seat and struggled to control the plunging horses. In the road ahead, Williams and his men, guns drawn, faced a line of five men armed with pistols and cutlasses. Sailors' weapons, and though there was no uniformity in their dress, their short jackets, wide trousers or breeches left undone at the knees, round-brimmed hats and knitted caps distinguished them as mariners. They had all tied their neckcloths over their faces.

"I said get back or I'll fire!" Williams cried.

From the sound of it, Evans was putting up a fight. If he was overpowered, there would be two men free to fire at the cavalrymen's backs. Dan turned back the way he had come to circle the coach and help the constable see off the threat.

A shot rang out behind him. He skidded to a halt. One of Williams's men slumped over his horse's neck and slid slowly to the ground.

"Hudson!" yelled the rider next to him. He bounded from his saddle and dragged the fallen man to the side of the road. The coachman, meanwhile, dived for cover behind the horses.

Where had the shot come from? Dan peered up at the wooded hillside. A second shot cracked the air. The man holding Hudson yelped, let go of his friend and clutched his arm. One of Williams's men fired into the trees. Two more shots answered. There was more than one gunman hidden up there.

"Williams, dismount and get your men off the road!" Dan shouted, but in the confusion of gunfire and startled horses, the captain did not hear.

A bloodied Evans scrambled to Dan's side, his pistol reloaded and the two guns he had taken from his attackers thrust in his belt.

"What's the plan?"

"To keep the men in the roadway busy while the others take cover under the bridge," Dan said.

Evans cocked his pistol. "I'm ready."

Dan shouted again. "Williams, get your men off the road!"

This time the captain heard him, but before he could act, a commanding voice rang out.

"Stand aside, boys." The words were slightly muffled, but the Irish accent was unmistakeable.

The line of sailors parted and their leader stepped forward.

The lower part of his face was covered by a scarf, his eyes shaded by a cocked hat. He wore a dark jacket, green breeches and high boots, all faded and weather-beaten. He pushed a figure in a scarlet coat in front of him. It was Pallister, the young man Williams had sent ahead to the ferry, his arms tied behind his back, his hat gone, his face bruised, and a gun held to his temple.

"Drop your weapons or this lieutenant's mammy will be weeping tonight," the Irishman said.

"To hell with you!" Williams raised his pistol.

"Lower your weapon, General," the other retorted, "or you'll be the next to die after this lad."

To emphasise the point, another shot from the hillside embedded itself in a tree trunk behind Williams.

Evans aimed his pistol in the direction of the sound. A bullet scuffed the ground at his feet.

Dan stood up. "Do as he says."

"You don't mean it?"

"We're surrounded, they've got a hostage, and we're already two men down."

"Surrender without a fight?"

"Do it, Constable."

Dan stepped into the open and threw down his gun.

"Good," the Irishman said. "Now the rest of you."

"It's no good, Williams," Dan said.

"Blast it!" Williams cursed, but Dan was right. His pistol and sword clattered to the ground. "Put down your weapons, men, and dismount."

Evans stood up, shaking his head in disbelief, and hurled his weapon onto the growing pile.

The man kneeling by Hudson tottered to his feet. He clutched his arm and blood seeped through his fingers. "He's dead," he said, through chattering teeth.

The Irishman rapped an order. Two of his men collected

the weapons, others seized the horses' bridles and led them away. The man Dan had knocked out and the pair Evans had fought emerged unsteadily from behind the carriage. Three gunmen dropped down from the scarp onto the road. As far as Dan could tell from the few words that passed between them, most of the crew were Irish.

Their captain, his grip still tight on young Pallister, bawled, "Wat Jones!"

The only answer from the coach was a sob.

"I said, Wat Jones, are you there? Come out where I can see you."

The coach trembled and a timid head peeked out of the door.

The Irishman laughed. "Well, Wat, are you going to come with us or would you rather stay with them?"

Jones perked up. "I'm with you, friend." He got out of the carriage and scuttled over to his rescuer.

The Irish captain sent one of his men to keep watch on the slipway. The rest herded Dan, Pallister and the others into the middle of the road. Williams took his scarf from his neck and tried to staunch the bleeding from the wounded man's arm.

"Leave him be," the sea captain snapped.

"I'll not have the lad bleed out on us." Williams knotted the scarf tight above the wound. "You'll do, Vaughan."

The seaman shrugged and left him to it. "Who's got the key to the cuffs?"

"I have," said Dan.

"Hand it over. Slowly. Don't try anything or I'll blow your brains out."

Dan reached into his pocket and brought out a key attached to a large metal ring.

"Throw it over here."

Dan threw the key just short of the sea captain who told one of his men to pick it up and release Jones.

Jones rubbed his wrists. "Told you it wouldn't be me that hanged, didn't I, Bow Street?"

The ambushers rolled the dead man to the roadside, made the rest sit back to back in a circle and passed a rope around them, looping it around their wrists as they went. Evans was on Dan's right, one of the volunteers on his left, and his back was pressed against Williams.

Jones picked up the discarded handcuffs. "Let me help." He knelt down and snapped them around Dan's wrists. "How'd you like that, Bow Street?" He dangled the key in Dan's face, and with a sudden flick, hurled it towards the Strait.

"I'm going to like watching you hang," Dan said.

"Looks like it, don't it?" said Jones. "With you sitting there like that, and me standing here, a free man."

Dan met his gaze. "There's only one way to stop me coming for you."

Jones's smirk faltered. He turned to the nearest crewman.

"Give me your gun, mate."

The man glanced at the Irish captain, who hesitated, then handed over one of the guns from his own belt.

"Be quick."

Williams struggled against his bonds, drumming his feet in helpless rage. "If you kill him, Jones, I'll hunt you down, by God, I swear it!"

Jones pointed the gun at Dan's chest and cocked the trigger.

"The boat's here!" shouted the lookout on the slipway.

"Time to go," the Irishman said. "Leave him."

Jones cursed, uncocked and lowered the pistol and put it in his belt. He clenched his fist and smashed it into the side of Dan's head.

"That's the one I owe you."

Dan let himself go with the punch and fell against the man next to him. He could just hear Williams's frantic cries through the ringing in his ear. Dust and pebbles stirred up by the gang's retreat swirled in front of his eyes. He blinked, shook his head, and swung himself back into an upright position.

The sailors scrambled into the boat. The last two pushed it off and jumped in as it moved into the current, the rowers pulling at the oars. As they settled into their places, they unwound their scarves, but were already too far away for Dan to see any of their faces clearly. The captain held out his hand and demanded the return of his pistol. Reluctantly, Jones drew it out. The captain snatched it off him, aimed at a gull bobbing on the water, and pulled the trigger. There was no flash of powder, no ball, and the gull bobbed safely on.

Jones's mouth fell open. The men roared with laughter, as if there had never been such a good trick played before. By now they were passing around a bottle. The scene was getting smaller and smaller, and Dan's last sight of the escaped prisoner was him sitting in the boat, the bottle to his lips, his head flung back.

# CHAPTER ELEVEN

The captives were still struggling against their bonds half an hour later when Evans said, "There's someone coming."

A horse plodded towards them from the direction of Porthaethwy. A woman's voice drifted through the trees, alternating between indignant high notes and contemptuous lows. Occasionally, a man briefly interrupted her in a wheedling tone.

A middle-aged couple leading an unkempt pony with a pannier on its back rounded the corner. The man's red face and unsteady steps explained the woman's rage: he was drunk. Nonetheless, he was first to catch sight of the carriage slewed across the road with its doors swinging open, and the saddle horses cropping the roadside grass nearby. He shuffled to a halt, bringing the old pony to a tired standstill. He took off his hat and scratched his head. Then he saw the circle of officers trussed up in the dust. His mouth fell open, first with astonishment and then with glee. He hee-hawed with laughter, doubled over and slapped his thigh. His wife snatched the hat off him and hit him across the shoulders with it, her voice rising to a pitch almost beyond human hearing.

"We've a wounded man here, you blockhead!" Captain Williams cried. "If you don't cut us loose at once, you'll have the magistrate to answer to. Damn you, you clown," the last prompted by frustration because neither of them understood him. "Evans, tell him if he stands there gawking much longer, I'll kick him into the middle of next week."

Evans translated the useful parts of Williams's demand. Either the surprise of hearing his own language or the reference to the wounded man silenced the drunken peddler. He peered at the fainting soldier propped up by his companions, a blood-drenched scarf wrapped around his arm. As if this was not unnerving enough, only a few feet away lay a corpse, his arms flung wide, his eyes open, and the hole in his chest glistening with gore.

Evans told him to hurry up. Hastily, he drew out a knife and cut the ropes. He boggled at the handcuffs, but the look on Dan's face silenced his exclamations and after severing the cords around Dan's arms he quickly moved on.

The released men stretched their limbs, rubbed their wrists, and looked so grim and vengeful the peddler stepped back in alarm. His wife scuttled behind him, hung on to his arm and blinked nervously at the soldiers. Williams told Evans to send the couple away. They were happy to go, though the pony did not share their sense of urgency and, in spite of all their pulling and pushing, moved off at his former placid pace.

The coachman checked Sir Edward's horses and, satisfied that they were unharmed, walked them forward to straighten up the carriage. Williams knelt beside Vaughan and tightened the tourniquet on his arm.

"How is he?" asked Dan.

"I've done all I can for him," the captain answered. "We need to get him to Doctor Hughes in Beaumaris. He's the coroner as well as the physician. He can look at Hudson at the same time."

"Better lift them into the carriage…What are you doing down there, Constable?"

Evans's head bobbed up from the waterside. "Looking for the key to the cuffs."

"Don't waste your time on that. It'd take you a month of Sundays. Make yourself useful and give the men a hand."

Evans, muttering about ingratitude, scrambled back up the bank and joined the volunteers. The pain of being lifted woke Vaughan for an instant, but he was soon unconscious again. They made him as comfortable as they could on Sir Edward's plush seats, and then went to fetch the horses.

"Jones and his gang have made fools of us," Williams said bitterly.

Dan hardly needed reminding of it. "It wasn't your fault. Jones was my responsibility." He looked out over the Strait. There was no sign of the rowboat, no clue as to where it had gone. "And now there are two murderers to catch."

"They'll be long gone. They'll have a ship waiting for them somewhere."

"They might not have made it to the ship yet. They could still be on Anglesey, or at anchor off shore."

"If they are, it won't be for long. Jones made the mistake of staying on the island once. He won't do it again."

"All the same, we should look. We could send the Revenue cutter."

"We could, but I doubt they will be in these waters by the time we do. They will be well on their way to Ireland or France. But if you think it is worth it, I will send for Bevan as soon as we reach Beaumaris. There's a blacksmith's at the shipyard. You can get the cuffs taken off there. I can take Vaughan to the doctor. We'll rendezvous at the Bull."

The volunteers returned with the horses, and offered the chance to go on horseback, Evans took it. Dan, who only rode when driven to it by necessity, and now hampered by his fetters, went in the coach with Vaughan. The cavalcade travelled towards Porthaethwy a short distance until the coachman could turn the carriage, then doubled back to Beaumaris.

The news of Jones's escape got there before them, broadcast

by the peddler and his wife. When Dan and Evans arrived at the Bull, a crowd had reassembled outside. It was not a sympathetic crowd, jeering and catcalling as the two pushed their way through. One wag asked in English, "Lost something, Officers?", but most of the heckling was in Welsh. It was easy for Dan to ignore, but something one youth said made Evans lose his temper and he went for him. Dan dragged the constable inside.

They found Captain Williams in a private parlour with Commander Thomas Bevan and prison governor Braillard. Evans poured a glass of brandy from the bottle on the table and offered it to Dan, who shook his head impatiently. It was high time the constable noticed he never touched spirits. In fact, high time he attended more and grumbled less in general.

"I'll have coffee."

Williams rang for a servant and gave the order.

"This is a pretty plight!" Braillard said, when they were all settled. "Two men shot, and Jones escaped only hours after he left my custody."

Bevan flashed a foxy smile. "Of course, no blame can attach to you, Mr Foster. You London men can hardly be expected to know Anglesey ways. It was hardly fair of your superiors to send you when the Beaumaris gaolers have always managed to transport prisoners to London in the past."

Dan took a sip of his drink. "How soon can you launch the cutter?"

"Unfortunately, I am unable to do so," Bevan answered. "If you remember, I mentioned last night that she is in the shipyard, having sustained some damage in heavy weather last week."

"You can get them to hurry the work along, can't you?" asked Williams.

"I can certainly try, but how co-operative the shipwrights are likely to be is another matter." Bevan shrugged. "Anglesey."

"Are there no other boats on the island?" Dan asked. "There must be some at Holyhead."

"I can send to Holyhead and see if the customs men there can spare a vessel. But they have their work cut out too. Nevertheless, we are used to working with limited resources, and I do still have the horse patrol. We'll follow the coastline north around Penmon. The boat that carried Jones away was heading that way when last seen. There are plenty of places along the way where a ship may ride in safety. We may not have the expertise of you city police, Mr Foster, but we know our own little patch. Though I agree with Captain Williams that she is unlikely to be in these waters now, we may be lucky. Someone may have seen something."

"When can you start?" asked Dan.

"I have already summoned my men. They should be here soon and we'll be off within the hour." There was time to top up his glass in the meantime, and he did so.

"Since Jones was no longer my responsibility," Braillard said, "I don't know what I can do, but if there is any help I can give, you have only to say the word."

"You can tell me if Jones had any visitors," Dan said.

"Only his sister. She used to bring him food. He told her not to bother, said her cooking tasted like turds. He usually threw it away."

"Where does she live?"

"She lives in Amlwch with her parents, close to the port," Bevan said.

"About fifteen miles away," Williams put in.

"Then I'll go to Amlwch tomorrow."

# CHAPTER TWELVE

"I fear Captain Williams and Commander Bevan are right," said Sir Edward. "Of course, we will do what we can, but there is very little chance of finding Jones now."

It had been dusk by the time they left Beaumaris, shortly after Bevan rode off with his men. Sir Edward sat at his desk in the library at Henllys, writing by lamplight a list of the tasks to be done: descriptions of Jones and his rescuers to be sent to all island magistrates and circulated to justices throughout the kingdom. Customs and excise officers on both sides of the Strait to be notified. Notices prepared to be read out in churches and placed in newspapers, advertising the reward of a hundred pounds offered by Sir Edward for information leading to an arrest.

Dan and Evans sat in front of the magistrate, and Captain Williams sprawled in an armchair by the fire. Darkness had fallen, and Dan could hear but not see the wind whipping the trees. It had carried cloud over the island with it, further obscuring the night.

"I am not going back to London without him," he said.

"Then we must hope the commander's efforts bear fruit," Sir Edward replied. "In the meantime, there is nothing we can do but wait."

"I don't intend to sit around waiting."

"But what can you do?"

"I can try and discover the identity of his accomplices. That might give us some idea of where they've gone. Captain Williams, did you recognise any of the men who attacked us?"

"Unfortunately, no."

"You don't know if any of them were with Jones the night you arrested him?"

"It was dark, they had covered their faces, and there was a great deal of shooting and confusion."

"But you must have your suspicions of who was involved. People Jones is known to associate with."

"There's no shortage of suspects," Sir Edward said. "Any man on this island. Whole families, whole villages, whole trades: they're all involved in smuggling."

"What about the Irish captain?"

"There are lots of Irishmen in the business," Williams answered. "The Irish don't have to pay the duties we do, so they buy in goods from France, store them in Dublin, and bring them over from Port Rush. They're usually well-armed, too."

"You said that it was an Irish vessel Jones and his gang were due to meet the night of his arrest. Do you recall the name of the vessel?"

"I don't, though Bevan might."

"Then we'll ask him. As for Jones, if smuggling is so widespread, it stands to reason that someone will know something. We'll start with his family, especially the sister, find out who his friends are, visit his usual haunts."

Williams raised an eyebrow. "I had no idea there was so much method to your work." Neither, it seemed, had the constable, who was looking at Dan as if he had suggested they should go out looking for Welsh dragons.

"There might be another line of enquiry," Dan said.

"Which is?" asked Sir Edward.

"How they knew where to ambush us."

"I wouldn't read too much into that," said Williams. "It's long been known that Jones was going to be transported to London. They've probably been ready to move for weeks. All they had to do was keep a lookout for the officers from London, and their ears open in the local taverns, and maybe their purses too. Add to that there aren't many ways to get off the island, and it would be a fair guess that you'd be taking the Holyhead road. It is the main route. Then there's only one road between here and Porthaethwy. And as you saw for yourselves, Cadnant was an ideal spot."

"It would still be worth questioning the turnkeys. One of them might have talked."

"They'll be unlikely to admit it," said the captain, as Lady Charlotte came in.

The men stood up and Sir Edward stepped forward to meet his wife. His desk was to the side of the room. Perhaps that was why she did not notice him as she entered, and hurried instead towards the man standing by the hearth.

"Jack – Captain Williams – you are safe!"

The captain bowed. "I am quite unharmed, Lady Charlotte, as are Mr Foster and Mr Evans."

She looked at the officers. The bruise on Dan's face had started to come out. "Mr Foster, you are hurt. I will ask Mrs Jenkins to find you some salve."

"There's no need to trouble yourself, ma'am," Dan said.

"My dear," said Sir Edward, "you must not upset yourself. As you see, they are all safe and well."

She blinked away a tear. "Forgive me, Edward. They said there was a man killed. I thought that you had gone with them, and I was afraid—" She raised a handkerchief to her face.

"There was another man injured," Williams said, "but he will recover."

"And you are sure you have taken no hurt?"

"None at all."

"Yes, Providence is indeed to be thanked for your safe deliverance," said Sir Edward. He guided Lady Charlotte to the sofa. "Let me fetch you a glass of wine."

"Thank you," she said in a weak voice.

He brought her the wine and sat down beside her. She smiled bravely at him. "Please, don't let me interrupt you. What were you talking about?"

"Officer Foster was just impressing us with the working methods of a Bow Street officer," said Williams.

"What are you going to do, Mr Foster?"

"Only what routine dictates, ma'am."

"He intends to start his enquiries at Amlwch tomorrow," Sir Edward said. "On that point, Officer Foster, do you wish to ride or order the carriage? Either is at your disposal."

Evans brightened up at the mention of riding. His face fell when Dan answered, "I would prefer the carriage, if it is convenient to you."

"And you can't think of going there without an armed escort. It is a dangerous, lawless place. Williams, we must take some of your men with us."

"Must you go?" Lady Charlotte cried. "Surely you've risked enough today."

"But, my dear, I was not involved in the ambuscade," Sir Edward said.

She gave a dainty sob. "Of course, I know that, but you were almost killed by that wicked brute at the gaol."

Sir Edward patted her hand. "I was never in any danger, and I shall be perfectly safe tomorrow with Williams and these officers."

"I appreciate the offer," Dan said, "but this sort of work is best left to a law officer. There is no need to accompany us, or trouble the volunteers. However, if you could provide us with pistols, I would be obliged."

"Of course," the magistrate said, "but pistols on their own will not be enough. I must insist on an armed escort."

"It's too heavy-handed, and likely to cause more trouble than it might save. It would really be more of a hindrance than a help."

"It seems to me, Ned," said Williams, "that when you've got a Bow Street officer giving you advice, you'd be foolish not to take it. After all, Officer Foster has more experience in such matters than we do. Better let him get on with it, I say."

"It really would be best, sir," Dan said.

"Very well," said Sir Edward. "No volunteers. But at least let myself and Captain Williams accompany you."

Williams laughed. "I think what Mr Foster is trying not to say is that you would be the biggest hindrance of all. The good people of Amlwch do not love a magistrate. Mr Foster would be obliged to put all his resources into protecting you."

"Captain Williams is right," said Lady Charlotte. "The officers must go on their own."

Evans nodded vigorously. Dan wondered if he would have agreed with the lady if she had suggested they all fly to the moon.

Sir Edward hesitated. "In that case, then of course, I will not go."

"Now I, on the other hand," said the captain, "know Amlwch and its citizens very well, having accompanied Commander Bevan there on many occasions. And, since it was one of my men who was killed, I have as much desire to catch the villain as do you, Foster. I will be coming with you."

"But—" cried Lady Charlotte.

Her husband had already started to speak and did not notice her stifled exclamation. "There!" he cried. "You must agree to this, Foster. And, while the investigation might be yours, you are in my jurisdiction, and on this I do insist."

Dan considered the offer. The captain knew the island, he

knew Amlwch, and he had been involved in run-ins with the smugglers. If they should catch up with Jones or any of his mates, another gun would not come amiss.

"Agreed," he said.

# CHAPTER THIRTEEN

Dan did not have an opportunity to write a report to Sir William Addington until the captain had gone home and the family had retired for the night. As soon as he got to his room, he lit the wax candles in the twin-socket candlestick on the desk. The fire gave out a little extra light, but the corners of the chamber lay in shadow.

He found pens and paper in the desk drawers and settled down to his task. It was not an easy one. The chief magistrate would be furious when he learned that a straightforward prisoner escort had gone so badly wrong. With the Home Secretary, the Duke of Portland, breathing down his neck, Sir William might well carry out his favourite threat of demoting Dan to the foot patrol. He might also summon Dan back to London immediately in order to do it.

Allowing two and a half days for his letter to reach London on the mail coach, and granting Sir William a few hours' deliberation before he penned his wrathful response, and two and a half days for that response to wing its way back, Dan reckoned he had at least six clear days to find Watcyn Jones before he knew whether his orders were to stay and continue the search, or go home in disgrace. It might be longer if he took into account common delays caused by the late arrival of the packet boat with the Dublin mail, accident, or bad weather.

Perhaps he would be lucky. Perhaps he would even have Jones back in custody in good time. If not – that was something to think about later.

He jotted down the heads of his report. The house was quiet; the only sounds were his pen scratching, mice scuffling along the wainscoting, the coals settling. When he looked through the window, which he did frequently, he saw pale clouds scudding across the sky.

The night seemed to drag on, but when he consulted his watch, he had only been working for an hour. The fire burned low. An owl hooted in the woods close by. Listening to the eerie, mournful note dying into the darkness, he did not find the prospect of being summoned back to the noise and glare of London so unattractive. He pictured Covent Garden with its street lights, link boys' torches and carriage lamps; the ceaseless racket of footsteps, hooves and wheels; people tumbling in and out of eating house, brothel and tavern; the street criers and ballad singers; the incoherent shouts of brawling drunks…and realised that the raised voices and scuffles were real and came from Sir Edward's room, which was next to his.

The noises stopped and for a moment he thought he had imagined them. Then he heard a cupboard door open and the clatter of objects hitting the floor. Another minute of silence was followed by booted feet stamping across the room. The door crashed open and someone came out to the landing.

Dan took the candlestick off the desk and opened his own door. Darkness lay to left and right, broken by a rectangle of light from the adjacent room. Sir Edward was descending into the dark stairwell, holding a shuttered lantern to see his way. He had no coat or hat, and his shirt was open at the neck, hanging loose over his breeches and boots. The faint light cast his face in hollow shadows, one deeper than the rest. He had not put on his eyepatch, and without it, his eye socket looked like a fathomless hole, empty as a skull's.

Dan glanced into his room. Boots and shoes were strewn across the floor. The bedding had been dragged off the mattress. A small bedside table lay on its side in a tangle of blankets, surrounded by a scattering of bottles, tumblers and books. It looked as if the argument had degenerated into a fight. Except there was no one else there.

Sir Edward was in the hall struggling with the bolts on the oaken door when Dan caught up with him.

"Sir Edward, is it intruders?"

Sir Edward did not answer. He wrenched open the door and ran out of the house, leaving it wide open. As far as Dan could see, he was unarmed. If he was not after a burglar, what was he doing? Was he going to meet someone? But who could it be, and why in such clandestine fashion? And if it was a prearranged appointment, why was he only half-dressed?

Dan had neither weapon nor lantern. He put the first right by arming himself with a stick from the coat stand. For the second, the candles were no use to him out of doors, so he blew them out and left them on the table; his eyes would get used to the darkness. He pulled the door to behind him, but did not shut it.

He could not see Sir Edward, but a glimmer of the dim lantern light bobbing downhill set him on the trail. He was moving quickly, and Dan had to break into a run to catch up. At the bottom of the grassy incline, Dan saw the glint of water flowing around scattered stones half-buried in mud. It was not enough to make a stream and petered out long before it could reach the shore, disappearing into a line of trees and undergrowth.

Sir Edward had disappeared too. Dan stopped and looked around. Before him was the Strait, edged by a border of rock, mud and sand. He wondered if Sir Edward was going to rendezvous with someone at the water's edge. But what kind of meeting took place on the seashore in the dead of night?

In the prison, Jones had blurted out: *you think I don't know who runs the trade on this island, who's behind it all, sitting in their big house on the wealth the poor man has made for him.* Men facing the noose were apt to make wild accusations, and Dan had not set much store by it. But it had been Sir Edward Jones had gone for.

Could it be that there was something in it after all? That Sir Edward was connected with the smuggling trade? The magistrate had been quick to discredit Jones – *I doubt very much that the fellow knows anything.* But Sir Edward, the hero of Camperdown? Besides, Dan could not see any vessel, neither sailing ship nor rowing boat.

Behind him, the house loomed atop the rise, its chimneys jutting into the sky, its windows blank, and the tracery of scaffolding criss-crossing the frontage. To the right, darkness, sea, woodland. To the left, the same. All was still and quiet, and he began to think Sir Edward had started back when he heard a choking sound.

He circled towards the noise, which was a little above him. Sir Edward stood on the slope, gazing out across the water, his hair ruffled by the wind blowing off the land, the lantern at his feet. He was signalling to someone!

Dan halted in the shadows under the spreading branches of a tree. For a man who had been in the Navy, Sir Edward was surprisingly inept at signals. The beam from the open shutter lay in a line across the ground and would not be visible to anyone unless they were floating in the air above it.

Sir Edward made no effort to adjust the lantern. He stood there, his hands hanging limp at his sides, mumbling and shaking his head. His voice rose to a piercing wail, gurgled into moans, and broke out in unrestrained weeping. Dan had never heard a man make so desolate a sound.

After a few moments, Sir Edward's sobs came less frequently and his breathing grew calmer. His shirt fluttered about him. He shivered, yet remained motionless in the chill night air. Dan's mind raced: should he risk embarrassing his host and intervene, or should he tiptoe away, forgetting what he had seen? But Sir Edward was trembling so violently Dan could hear his teeth chattering. That decided him. The man could not be left here in this state.

Dan coughed and stepped noisily from his hiding place. In spite of this announcement of his presence, Sir Edward did not seem aware of it.

"Come along, sir, it is time to go indoors."

Sir Edward turned towards Dan, his eye unfocussed and unrecognising. He muttered something that sounded like "jump in the sea".

"You come in now, sir," Dan said.

He picked up the lantern, shifted it and the stick into one hand, took the magistrate by the arm and led him back up to the house. Sir Edward made no resistance. Once or twice he stumbled, but Dan saved him from falling. It was slow going, but they reached the door eventually. It was still open, but someone had relit the candles Dan had left in the hall. He guided Sir Edward inside.

Lady Charlotte, a shawl drawn about her shoulders, stood anxiously by the table.

"There you are!" She rushed to her husband's side. He gave her an imbecilic smile.

"He walks in his sleep," she explained in a low voice. "He will be better once he's back in his bed. Would you lock the door? I'll take the key."

Dan did as she asked while she fussed around Sir Edward. "You're chilled to the bone! Come along, my love, back to bed."

Dan picked up the candles and took hold of Sir Edward's right arm. He shuffled quietly between them, climbed the stairs like a child, as if he had not quite learned the knack yet. Lady Charlotte had set a night light on his hearth and removed the traces of his rampage: straightened the bed, restored the table, put his shoes and boots back in the cupboard.

"I can manage now," she said.

"I'll help." Dan closed the door and put the candlestick on the mantlepiece.

They manoeuvred Sir Edward across the room and sat him on the side of the bed. His eye was closed and he lolled like a loose-limbed doll. She pulled off one of his boots, Dan the other. She unbuttoned his breeches, unlaced his drawers, and pulled the shirt over his head. When they had got him into a nightshirt, Dan lifted his ice-cold feet into the bed and lowered him onto the mattress. Lady Charlotte pulled the blankets over him. His face on the pillow might have looked serene if it had not been for the twisted mouth, drawn skin and empty eye socket. She gazed down at him, her face half-shadowed by the flickering candles.

"Does this often happen?" asked Dan.

She straightened the covers below the sleeping man's chin. "He can go for weeks without an attack, but when he's tired or troubled, he's liable to succumb. I've been expecting it since you and Constable Evans came. The business with the prisoner has worried him. I came to check on him and saw that he had gone. Your door was open too, so I guessed you had gone after him."

"And you tend him on your own?"

"When I can. Sometimes I have to send for Mrs Jenkins."

"Because he's too agitated to manage?"

"Yes."

"And he's sometimes violent, isn't he? He gave you those bruises on your wrist."

"No!" She raised her eyes to Dan's face. "It isn't him. He can't help himself. He never remembers what he's done, and if he did, it would break his heart. He couldn't live with the shame. You must not tell him, Mr Foster, you must never tell him."

"But doesn't he wonder how you come by the bruises?"

"I hide them from him, or I tell him I got them when I was out riding, or that I tripped. Anything."

"Wouldn't it be better if he had medical attention?"

"He's seen doctors. None of them have helped, and I will not send him away. I would never do that." She turned from the bed. "He will sleep now. I don't know how to thank you, Mr Foster. You've already done so much, but I must implore one more favour from you."

He spared her the trouble of asking. "I shan't speak of it to anyone."

They left the night light burning and said their goodnights. The report lay on the desk where he had left it, waiting for his final flourish. It would have to wait.

*"I trust you are being a good boy for your mother. Your loving Father."*

Dan put down his pen, folded the paper and placed it inside the letter for Caroline. It would be a new thing for her to get a letter from him. He had not written before when he had been away from home, either because he had been working undercover, or because he had been too busy. Or because he had not wanted to. Not that he had covered more than a side now, hoping he found her well and telling her he did not know how long he would be delayed.

He wondered if Noah had mended the wooden horse, broken the day he left London. He thought of adding a sentence to her letter, telling her to make sure Nick took the toy to Noah when he went to the gym. But he had already sealed it and time was moving on. He told himself she would not forget and placed the letter next to the much thicker packet addressed to Sir William Addington at Bow Street.

He had ended his report on a positive note, reassuring the chief magistrate that he had a plan, that it had every hope of success, that he expected soon to have Jones back in custody. He doubted Sir William would put much faith in the plan – Dan did not have much faith in it himself – but by the time the report reached London, it would already be well underway.

It was still early. The workmen had not arrived, and the servants were the only people moving about the house. He rose, stretched, put on his hat and coat and went downstairs.

The front door was still locked and Lady Charlotte had the key, so he made his way to the back stairs. He followed the sounds of clattering pans and chattering women to the kitchen. The cook and a pair of kitchen maids stared at him, hands poised over mixing bowl, chopping board and saucepan. He spotted a door at the end of a flagged passageway that opened on to a courtyard and headed towards it, managing to explain, by pointing and gesturing, that he was only passing through to get to it.

Cellars and pantries lined the passage. In the scullery, a girl stood at the double sink beneath a high window. She had lifted a pot from a bowl of greasily steaming water, dipped it in the cold rinse water, and was putting it on the wooden draining board. She started at the sound of his footsteps and glanced over her shoulder. But he had already gone by, taking with him an impression of black hair, dark skin, fluster and untidiness.

The clouds of last night had cleared. A cold breeze stirred the clear air. Birds sang from high and low; every tree and bush seemed to harbour trilling, cooing or piping. The sounds of men's voices drifted from the stables, the occasional whinny and tap of hooves, a boy's whistle. They would be getting the chaise ready soon; he had arranged for them to make an early start.

He walked round to the side of the house. The half-built doorway was still boarded up, the window shutters closed, the scaffolding empty. Dan took off his jacket, scarf and shirt and draped them over one of the scaffold props. The air felt good on his skin and he stood there for a moment, breathing in deep draughts invigorated by their passage over the Strait. Though the sky over Henllys was clear, on the opposite shore the range of Snowdonia was obscured by swathes of white mist lit here and there by slanting rays of the morning sun.

He ran on the spot to warm up. When he had tested the weight-bearing capacity of the scaffolding, he used it to raise himself up and down. He had no clubs, but he found a couple of bricks and swung these around. Then he did a bit of sparring, dancing from side to side and forward and back, throwing punches, expelling air on each outward movement.

He was sweating by the time he had finished. He grabbed his clothes, went back to the courtyard and into the house through the door by which he had left. The scullery door was still open, but the girl was not there. Dan found a bucket, put it in the deep stone sink and filled it with water. He helped himself to one of the towels from a wooden airer next to the hot water copper in the small whitewashed annex, put it on the draining board and sluiced himself down.

He finished by ducking his head, his eyes screwed up, his fingers groping for the towel. They met only damp wood. He stretched further. Still no towel. It must have fallen on the floor. As he raised his head and blinked water out of his eyes, someone pressed the soft cotton into his hand. He jerked upright, droplets spraying from his hair.

The scullery maid stood beside him, holding out the towel.

He snatched up his shirt. "What are you doing there?"

She did not understand his words, but she realised that she had in some way displeased him. With a dismayed cry, she thrust the towel at him and ran out of the room.

"No, wait, I didn't mean—"

She had gone, her light steps replaced by the crunch of boots. Evans appeared on the threshold. He grinned.

"You want to watch that dusky maiden. The other servants think she's a witch. I heard them talking."

Dan dried his hair. "Did you want something, Evans?"

Still smirking, the constable said, "The cook said she'd seen you come this way. I only came to say the captain has arrived. Breakfast," he added, "is served in the dining room." As if, having caught Dan washing in the scullery like one of the lowest of the servants, Evans thought he would naturally head to the kitchen for his meal.

"I'll be up in a minute."

With a final leer, Evans strolled away.

Dan threw out the water, cast the cloth into the bucket and finished dressing. He would have liked by some means to explain to the scullery maid that there was no need to be frightened of him, but there was no sign of her.

In the dining room, Williams was clearing a plate of eggs and bacon. Sir Edward sat next to him drinking coffee, a half-eaten roll on his plate.

"Good morning, Mr Foster," said Sir Edward. "I hope you slept well?"

"I…yes," said Dan, too surprised to manage anything smoother.

Sir Edward did not notice the brief awkwardness, but Evans raised his eyebrows at Dan as if he was the quiz of the season. Dan scowled at the constable, who hastily put his face straight.

Lady Charlotte, who breakfasted in her room, had not exaggerated when she said her husband never had any recollection of his night-time fits. Apart from the shadows under Sir Edward's eye, Dan would not have recognised him as the stricken man he had helped to put to bed last night.

"No word from Bevan yet," Sir Edward said. "I expect we will hear from him before long. In the meantime, I'll send one of the servants to take the letter to the customs officers in Caernarfon this morning, and I'll have the notice about the reward drafted by the end of the day."

Dan poured himself some coffee. For a moment he considered slurping it from his saucer just to see how Evans reacted, but managed to restrain himself. When they had eaten, Williams went to the stables to chivvy the coachman. Sir Edward took Dan and Evans to the gun room to choose some pistols. They pocketed powder and shot, left the magistrate to his business, and set off.

# CHAPTER FOURTEEN

They drove down to Beaumaris and out again on a long, steady climb past Baron Hill, the home of Viscount Bulkeley, the Major Commandant of the Loyal Anglesea Volunteers. They could not see the mansion from the road, though Williams assured them it was there, looking down on the town from its eminence.

The road led them through woodland and farms, the terrain scattered with standing stones, its rugged surface occasionally relieved by regularly shaped mounds or barrows. The slopes of some of the larger of these were ridged with rings of stone, others topped with ruins. On the bare top of one of the mounds, Dan saw a group of men and women piling up branches and old timber.

"What's going on there?" he asked.

"They're building an All Hallows Eve bonfire," Williams said. "You don't see the fires very often now, though they used to be lit from hill to hill. Stamping out pagan practices is one thing church and chapel agree on. Not to mention that these occasions usually involve drinking, dancing and games liable to end in romping and kissing." His grin suggested that he was speaking from memory. "They've put their pyre on a Druidical tomb to entice the dead to join them."

"It's not a tomb, it's a hut circle," Evans said.

Williams laughed. "I couldn't tell a cairn from a cromlech. But you don't look like the typical antiquarian, Constable. In my experience, they tend to be antique reverend gentlemen."

"I'm not, but I was brought up by a father – who is an antique reverend gentleman, by the way – who is."

"Pardon me, I meant no offence."

Evans smiled. "None taken, I assure you. And your description is apt. Digging around in old bones and parchment is a pursuit for old men with too much time on their hands."

Evans had not been so slighting of his father's pursuits when he told Sir Edward about them, Dan observed. But then, they were hardly likely to impress the captain in the same way as they had his more studious friend. Which conversation more truly reflected Evans's attitude? Dan had no doubt it was this one. Perhaps his distaste for his father's interests went some way to explaining how a clergyman's son ended up as a constable.

As they travelled north, the road followed the coastline, and a flat, monotonous way it was. They passed miles of mud, marsh and sand bordered by miles of water and sky, and inhabited by enormous flocks of birds dibbling along the shoreline. There were not many houses, and settlements were few and far between. A shipyard enlivened a wide bay and a port where several small vessels lay before a cluster of low houses and taverns. This, Williams informed them, was Red Wharf Bay, its creeks and coves popular with smugglers.

From here there was little to interest Dan, and it was not until Williams said, "There's Parys Mountain," that he sat up and took notice. He leaned across the constable to get a better look out of the window.

It did not look like much of a mountain, and Dan thought it would hardly have qualified if it had not been for the levels it dominated. Square buildings, tall chimneys and round towers broke the stark outline of its bare sides. Billows of dark smoke hid the summit and drifted towards the town of Amlwch half a mile below. From the road, the mountain sides appeared as streaks of grey, pink, orange and yellow, with gullies and craters marked by shadow. Carts crawled up and down the tracks on their way to and from Amlwch port.

A sulphurous smell caught at Dan's throat. Closing the window did not keep it out and it grew stronger as they approached the town. Since there was no avoiding it, they could only do what the Amlwchians did and go about their business as if it did not exist.

They left the carriage at a large, decent-looking inn near the market. A well-mannered landlord, delighted to have such a fine equipage in his yard, came out to greet them, and summoned a pair of smart grooms to see to the horses.

Apart from the smell, Amlwch was an unremarkable place and, with its churches and chapels, less devilish than Dan had been led to expect from Sir Edward's warning. However, he was no stranger to life around wharves and quaysides. The changed character of the area around the harbour made it a microcosm of Billingsgate, Wapping or Southwark. The streets were stinking, narrow and muddy, gloomy even in daylight, and well provided with dung heaps, rivulets of foul liquids, and rubbish tips.

The harbour lay beneath them, a deep pool with a narrow entrance on the seaward side, and a long, thin creek running into it from the land. Here, a line of ships was moored side by side in pairs. Though Dan was no mariner, he could see that getting in and out could not be easy, and ships would have to wait days or even weeks to load and unload. It was the same on the busy Thames, except that here, none of the ships were very large. Some were small pilot boats waiting to guide ocean-going vessels heading for Liverpool.

Carts rumbled along the road above the port, where relays of labourers with wheelbarrows unloaded the copper ore and tipped it into three large open bins on the quayside. A smelting works belched smoke and smuts from its high chimneys, and a candle manufactory vomited the offal odour of animal fat, but it was still the sulphur from the mine that dominated.

They turned into a row of one-storey cottages with thatched roofs patched with mould and holes. Their way was blocked by a muck-coated pig. It gazed up at them with hatred in its eyes, its glistening nostrils flaring. Then it tossed its head, turned its back on them, trotted along the street, and paused to sniff at a dark bundle at the side of the road.

When they came up to the bundle, they saw it was a man slumped against the wall with his knees drawn up, his head thrown back, his eyes closed and his mouth open. His sunken face and wrinkles could have been those of a sickly youth or an aged man. A badge on his ragged jacket displayed the letter "P" for "pauper", signalling that he was in receipt of parish relief. It did not need a London detective to work out how he had spent his money. His loud snoring proved that he was alive, if not well, so they left him and the pig to get better acquainted and knocked at one of the houses.

Footsteps slapped towards the door and it juddered open. A woman, who looked much as the pig might have done if it had been dressed in a dirty patched skirt, tattered shawl and stained bodice, stood on the threshold. She tried to close the door, but the captain pushed past her and ducked into the rancid gloom. Dan and Evans followed him inside.

As miserable hovels went, the Jones family home was a prime example of its kind. A wispy fire burned in an ash-strewn hearth beneath a blackened chimney. A pot of something scummy simmered over it. There was a wooden bedstead in the corner with a crumpled heap of odoriferous bedding on it, and a chamber pot in need of emptying underneath it. The loaf of bread on the rickety table looked as if it had been stored in the coal scuttle, and the wooden platters and mugs next to it had never known water or cloth.

A man sat by the fire in a broken-down chair, a glass of brandy on the hearth beside him. He looked up at them with bloodshot eyes, but took no other notice of them. He resumed his mournful contemplation of a pair of metal cockspurs that lay in his lap on top of a cloth bag of the sort used by owners to carry birds to the cockpit. An open wicker basket stood at his feet, but there was no bantam in it. The bird had probably been slaughtered in last night's battles. By its death, Jones had lost the investment he had made in feeding and training it, and his stakes in the betting too.

Dan saw all this in the scant light let in by a pair of small windows. Williams, meanwhile, opened the warped door to the cottage's only other room, revealing a bed, chest of drawers and another chamber pot.

"No one there," he said, "and there's no other way out."

The woman padded back to the fireside on filthy bare feet, picked up a wooden spoon from the table and lowered herself on to the stool by the cooking pot. She stirred the mess, her head twisted over her shoulder, her eyes fixed on the strangers.

"Owen Jones," said Captain Williams, "you know why we're here." Jones had nothing to say to this and Williams continued, "We're looking for Watcyn. Do you know where he is?"

Still meditating over his dead favourite's weapons, Jones muttered, "*Dim Saesneg.*"

The captain glanced at Evans, who repeated the question. Jones looked at him as if he had spoken Greek. Evans pressed for an answer, which was brief and delivered in a sepulchral tone.

"He says he doesn't know," Evans reported.

"Has he been here?" asked the captain.

"He says his son's stupid, but not that stupid."

"When did he last see him?" asked Williams.

"He says he hasn't seen him."

Evans put the questions to Wat's mother with the same results. Williams shrugged at Dan as if to say, *you see what they're like*. Owen Jones sniggered and said something which made his wife cackle.

"What did he say?" Dan asked Evans.

"Nothing."

"I asked you a question, Constable."

"He says, you're the – er – officer Wat put the cuffs on."

"Is that what he said?"

Evans shifted his feet. "The daft bugger."

Dan turned to Owen with a friendly smile. Owen's grin broadened. Still smiling, Dan said to Evans, "Ask him where the brandy came from."

Evans did so. Owen's face fell. He stuttered a dismayed protest, gave up, and clamped his mouth shut.

"Perhaps we should search the place," Dan suggested.

When this was conveyed to Owen, he paled and started to bluster. His wife dropped the spoon. Her hands flew up to her face and she rocked back and forth, moaning and mumbling.

"Though," Dan said, "a keg or so of smuggled brandy doesn't interest me that much. Still, if you won't talk to me, I've got to do something to make the trip worthwhile." He waited for Evans to translate this. "Have a look round, Constable. Start in the other room."

"*Sefwch!*" Owen cried. Stop!

Evans looked at Dan, who nodded. The constable relayed Dan's questions and Owen's answers.

"It's true. I haven't seen him. Didn't even know he was back on the island until you arrested him."

"And you've no idea who helped him escape?"

"No."

"You didn't go to see him in prison, either of you?"

"No. Elin did, though. His sister."
"Where will we find Elin?"
"She's at the works."

"There was nothing here before this," bellowed Samuel Brooks, the manager of the Parys Mine.

He waved his hand, encompassing the kilns and precipitation pools, sheds and warehouses, flues and engine houses scattered across the site, beyond the cluster of offices. The gesture captured the chasm beneath them, riddled with caves and tunnels. It took in the clouds of dust rising from the chasm floor, the brimstone fumes given off by the ore baking in the kilns, and the acrid clouds of gunpowder smoke.

"Nothing but gorse," Brooks shouted above another explosion and the accompanying rumble of falling rock.

Now the gorse had gone, along with any grass, trees and shrubs. There were no birds, no animal tracks or burrows, and nothing grew or grazed in the surrounding fields. The only water was the copper-rich liquid that seeped out of the mines. Looking down into the opencast at the miners balanced on wooden platforms built against the cliff face, Dan thought he would take his job with its dangers and frustrations over theirs any day. The men hung in mid-air, gouging the ore out of the mountainside and sending it crashing to the floor. Below, scores more of them collected it up, hammered it into pieces with heavy mallets and threw it into buckets. These were hauled up to the surface by the two-man operated winches set on unrailed platforms protruding over the void. One had just sent an empty bucket bobbing back down with a miner standing on it, holding on to the rope.

"And it's brought much prosperity to the island, along with gainful employment for men who would otherwise only idle their time away in drinking and thieving," said the captain.

"Eh?"

When Williams had repeated his remark, Brooks shouted back, "They're idle enough as it is. You have to keep the Welshman on a tight rein or else he's liable to forget why he's here."

It was no wonder the man was hard of hearing, thought Dan. He raised his voice above the noise.

"We are here to speak to Elin Jones, if you wouldn't mind taking us to her now, Mr Brooks."

"Eh? Oh, yes, of course. She's in the sheds." The manager tore himself away from what was to him one of the most sublime views the principality had to offer and led them along a track between heaps of mud and stone. Some of the men broke the rhythm of their work to watch them go by, others paid no attention but dully laboured on.

"We're at full stretch at the moment, owing to a big Navy order for copper for ships' bottoms," Brooks enthused. "Got to do our bit to beat Frenchie."

"It is every man's proud duty," Williams said.

"Eh? Here we are."

Brooks led them in at the front of a long, low building. Another entrance at the back faced the winching platforms so that the men could wheel in barrows of ore as they came up. Inside, the air was thick with dust and filled with the sound of hammering. Over fifty women worked here, each seated between a heap of ore and an iron slab, some accompanied by children who worked alongside them.

The overseer came towards them out of the murk.

"This is Mr Foster, a Bow Street Runner from London," yelled Brooks, pulling out a gold watch. "He and his colleagues wish to speak to Elin Jones." He snapped the watch shut and replaced it in his waistcoat. "I must attend another appointment. Captain, Officers."

The overseer touched his hat, and when Brooks had gone, he consulted the woman nearest to him. She had the look of an aging prize fighter. On her left hand she wore a thick glove, its fingers encircled by iron rings. Dan soon saw, though, that it had no pugilistic purpose. She used it to pick chunks of ore from the pile beside her, which she placed on the knock stone and broke up with a hammer.

The man spoke to her in Welsh. She removed the scarf she had tied around her mouth to keep out the dust and replied in the same language, one of her eyes fixed on Dan, possibly because she could fix it nowhere else owing to her squint. She waved her hammer at the back of the shed.

They weaved between the women to the back of the shed. Behind them the pugilistic crone called to her neighbour, who called to her neighbour, who called to hers, until from all over the shed came a babble of Welsh interspersed with "Bow Street Runner". The women and children gaped at the strangers from London, giggling and nudging one another, but the hammering continued unabated.

They reached Elin Jones, who ignored them and continued with her work until the overseer said a few sharp words. After a second or two, she put her hammer and glove on the knock stone and stood up. She was a scrawny woman in a heavy skirt several inches short of her shabby boots. Like the other women, she wore a filthy apron. Her hair hung in lank rats' tails so like those sported by Watcyn Jones, there was no doubting she was his sister, older by four or five years.

"Is there somewhere quiet we could go?" Dan asked the overseer.

He scratched his head. "Outside?"

What with the winches, carts, barrows and hammers, it was not much of an improvement behind the shed. At least they could not be overheard. Elin Jones unwound her scarf from her head and neck and gazed sullenly at the ground, only glancing at the captain and Dan when the overseer, speaking in Welsh, mentioned their names. Dan thanked him and said they could manage. The man went back into the shed to quell the women's gossip.

"Tell her why we're here," Dan said to Evans.

"I know why you're here," she said in English. She smirked. "You're the trap he put the cuffs on. It was the talk of the taverns last night."

"Was volunteer Hudson the talk of the taverns too? And Barker the customs officer in Kent, lowered into a pit and stoned to death?"

"Wat didn't kill them. He hasn't killed anyone, and you can't prove he did."

Williams laughed. "Gentle as a lamb and innocent as a newborn."

She rounded on the captain. "He never killed no one!"

Dan cast an impatient glance at the captain. "He's an accessory to the murder of Hudson, and unless we find out who pulled the trigger, he's the one who will pay for it. Same goes with Barker. We can't prove your brother didn't kill him unless he tells us who did. So it's in his best interest if we find him. And then, if he helps us, maybe we can help him."

"What do you care about his best interest? You want to hang him for something he didn't do."

"Not if he didn't do it, but running away like this only makes me think he's guilty."

"And why should he stay to have you pin it on him? He'll be miles away by now. I hope he is."

"Or maybe you know he is. You visited him in prison, didn't you? When was the last time you went?"

"I took him some food last Sunday. No law against that."

"And did you help him plan his escape?"

"I know nothing about it."

"Do you know who did help him?"

"How would I know?"

"You know who his friends are."

"He's got lots of friends."

"Because he's such charming company," said Williams.

She glared at the captain.

"And he didn't ask you to carry messages to those friends?"

"No."

"What, didn't he trust you?"

"He did! He was only thinking of me…that it would be safer…"

"Safer for him." Dan laughed. "So he didn't trust his own sister."

"He did. He did trust me."

"He's gone off without you, and you didn't even know he was going."

"I did! He told me everything. He—" She broke off.

"In that case, you'd better tell me. If you don't, I'll arrest you for aiding an escape."

She looked at Evans, who explained the threat in her own language. She responded with a furious stream of Welsh.

"She says she won't tell you," Evans said.

"Very well, give me your cuffs. If you could make sure she doesn't make a run for it, Captain."

Elin, seeing herself hemmed in, embarked on another tirade which Evans left untranslated. Dan took the cuffs from the constable and snapped them open. She cried out, a single word. The same he had heard Owen Jones use: *sefwch*.

Head bent, plucking at her skirt, she mumbled, "He never said a word, not so much as a hint. I don't know where he's gone, or who with. And if I did, you're the last person I'd tell. I'm losing money standing here. If you've nothing more to say, I'm going back to work."

Dan nodded at Williams, who stood aside to let her go. She turned on her heels and stalked back into the shed.

Williams laughed. "Touched on the raw there, Foster. But if she doesn't know anything, we're at a dead end."

"Not yet," Dan answered. "I'm going to speak to that overseer again."

# CHAPTER FIFTEEN

"Who were his workmates?" the overseer in the copper ladies' shed repeated. "Not sure I can remember. It's two year or more since he worked the mine."

"But he must have had friends," Dan said.

"Friends?" the other said doubtfully. "Well, of course, the men work in teams, and each team arranges with the manager to work a bargain – a part of the mine, see – and sells the ore they find there to the owners for an agreed price. But the teams and bargains change all the time. Areas get worked out. The men make new partnerships."

"So which team did Jones work in?"

The man drummed his fingers on his jawbone. When this failed to refresh his memory, he said, "You could ask Hugh the Store. He knows them all."

He directed them along the track to a brick building with a tiled roof. Inside a couple of men lounged against a counter in front of shelves of mining gear stretching to the back of the warehouse. Hugh the Store had spread out a line of chisels of varying sizes for the men to examine. From the care they were taking over their choices, it was obvious that the purchase price had to come from their own pockets.

The three men ignored Dan and his companions and continued their discussion. Hugh cracked a joke; the miners looked at Dan and laughed. It was not hard to guess why: the fame of the handcuffs had preceded him. They had a great deal more to say about the chisels and would have carried on saying it, but Dan was not in a waiting mood.

"Since you've obviously got all day, you won't mind if I interrupt, gentlemen."

The storekeeper, like other supervisors and managers they had met, spoke English. After a moment's hesitation, he gathered up the tools and sent the miners away.

When they had stomped out and banged the door after them, he said, "What can I do for you, Officer?"

But in answer to Dan's questions, he knew nothing and could remember nothing.

"Not much help there either," said Williams when they went outside. "Looks like we've had a wasted journey, Foster."

"If the teams negotiated with the management, there might be records," Dan said. "Let's go back to the office."

Brooks was about to lead a group of tourists around the mine. The party consisted of two clergymen, an artist with a sketchbook, and a young man Dan would hardly have noticed if he had not shuffled behind the others and pulled his collar up and his hat down. As it was, Dan marked the heavy face and full mouth with its slight overbite, the intense dark eyes, and short black hair. He further noted that his appearance was a blend of gentleman, student and vagabond.

The gentleman was suggested by good linen and black silk scarf; the student by his assiduous note-taking; and the vagabond by his greatcoat, pantaloons buttoned close above his ankles, leather satchel slung across his body, and stout boots. It was practical wear for someone who spent a lot of time on the road who, while he had sufficient money and leisure to make a tour, was not rich enough to afford a carriage and so travelled as a pedestrian. Why the sight of two London police officers should alarm him was not so easy to explain.

Dan's observations were quickly made and as quickly filed away for no particular reason but habit. He asked Brooks about the records, and the manager called over one of the clerks. He then summoned his little band of sightseers and led them out to the works, with the pedestrian taking care to be the first outside. The door closed behind them, muffling the noise of the works and Brooks's booming, "There was nothing here before this…"

The clerk, whose English was excellent, produced a ledger. He moistened his finger and thumb before turning over each page and dawdled his way through it until he found what Dan wanted. Jones had teamed up with Robert Griffith and his two brothers. Where could they be found? They were here, working. Can we talk to them? If you wish. Can you send for them? I can send one of the boys with a message, but there's no guarantee they'll come. Then can you show us where they are?

The clerk led them outside and up the track. He stopped near one of the winch platforms and pointed.

"They're down there."

Dan gazed into the chasm. "And how do we get down there?"

"There's the slow way," the clerk said, swinging round and pointing at a track which followed a roundabout path to the floor of the mine. "Or there's the quick way."

"What's the quick way?"

The clerk, still pointing, swung back. Dan followed the line of his outstretched arm to the edge of the platform, where one of the men leaned out and grabbed a bucket that had just come up from the floor of the mine.

"You can go down in one of those."

"Shit," said Evans.

Dan pretended he had not heard this, but the winch operator was not so tactful. As he helped his colleague haul the ore towards the pile where it would wait to be broken into still smaller chunks before going to the women in the sheds, he told him about the clerk's sport with the English. Of course, no one expected them to descend by the miners' method. His companion joined in his laughter with a wheezing haw-haw, which he ended by lobbing a ball of spit into the abyss.

"Seriously, Foster," Williams said, "you aren't considering it?"

"These people are not what you'd call helpful," Dan said in a low voice. "If we take the slow way, I wouldn't put it past one of them to drop down and warn the Griffith brothers. They'll make themselves scarce, and on a big site like this, we could be looking for them for hours. If you prefer, you can stay here, Captain."

"And miss the fun?"

Dan said to the clerk, "Your men can lower us down. I'll go first."

The clerk's eyes popped, but he gave the order. The winchman stared at Dan in disbelief. His mate wiped the sneer off his face and muttered something that might have been "I'll be damned".

The men emptied the bucket and reattached it to the cable. One of them took up position at the winch handles, the other stood on the brink balancing the bucket. He beckoned Dan on to the platform. Dan fixed his hat on his head and walked towards him.

As soon as he left the solid earth, he felt the competing currents of air sweep around him, some rising from the chasm, some soughing across the mountain top, some blowing in off the sea. It made him acutely aware of his balance, where the weight was in his feet, how it shifted as he walked. The boards were springy and there was a disconcerting openness on either side.

The man pushed the bucket over the side and steadied it

with one hand. He hesitated, cast an enquiring look at Dan. *Are you sure?* But Dan did not change his mind, and the operator showed him how to grip the rope with both hands, one level with his ear, the other at his stomach; where to place his foot in the bucket; how to rest his other leg on the rim. He took care over this, pausing to make sure Dan had understood. Then he invited Dan to step into the bucket.

For a few seconds, Dan hung in space with nothing but the strength of the other man's arms to stop the bucket swinging away from him, leaving him at the mercy of his own momentum to plummet to the ground. Then his foot found the bucket and he was in position, the winchman stepped away, and Dan began to move slowly downwards, the winch squealing, the sinews of the rope cracking. His instructor joined his companion at the machine, the rope played out more quickly, and within seconds their faces were gone and there was nothing but air above, beside and below.

After a few minutes, he noticed the smoothness of his progress. The bucket was heavy, but he found that if it started to swing or spin, he could control it by shifting his weight. The rope was taut, and though thinner than he had expected, it felt trustworthy. He felt able to look about him and notice the way the rock face changed colour, from pale orange, to pink, to grey. Below him, men toiled, their mallets rising and falling. The thudding, clinking, shouts, and occasional laughter echoed around the rock face.

He felt a jolt and, to his surprise, realised he had reached the bottom. The rope slackened. He stepped out of the vessel and let go. A moment later, the bucket began its way back to the top and he realised that he much preferred the feel of the ground under him after all.

Evans reached his side a few minutes later. Dan helped him prise his fingers off the rope and supported him as he stumbled on to the dusty ground. While Dan gazed up at the platform, impatient for the captain to appear, the constable pulled out a handkerchief and mopped his beaded brow. He whipped the cloth back in his pocket before Dan turned and saw him. Dan already had seen, but he let the constable preserve his dignity and gave no sign of it.

When Williams was still a few feet above them, he took one hand off the rope and waved his hat. He jumped down before the bucket touched the ground, his face flushed.

"What a descent!" He slapped Evans on the back. "An exhilarating ride, eh, Constable?"

"Extremely," Evans said brightly.

They set off to the section the clerk had indicated. They stopped to check the way with a group of men who had taken a break from their work to pass around a jug of beer. The men were slow to answer, weighing up how much information they should give away to the foreign law officers.

Eventually, a boy, having received the silent approval of his elders, said, "That's them there."

Avoiding pools of scummy water, they picked a path through the dust and rubble to a boulder-strewn cave which ran a short way back into the rock. It was wide enough to accommodate two men easily, and high enough for them to stand upright. A man worked at the back of the cave, hacking out the ore. No timbers had been put up and he could still work by daylight, but against the side wall lay a pile of props and boxes of candles in readiness for working the tunnel when it was excavated. On top of these were the men's satchels with their lunches, and a flask of beer.

Outside the cave, two men broke up stones and loaded them into a half-filled bucket. They stopped work and watched Dan and the others draw near.

"We're looking for Robert Griffith," Evans said in Welsh.

One of them called to the man in the cave, who gave a final mighty swing of his pick and leaned it against the wall. He wiped his hands on his trousers, snatched up his hat from the woodpile, and went outside.

"I'm Robert Griffith."

The Griffith brothers were a burly lot, thick of arm and neck. Thick of head too, Dan judged, with what wits they possessed being concentrated mainly in Robert and petering to almost nothing in the youngest. Like most of the miners, they wore short trousers over heavy ankle-high boots, with old hats and jackets. Robert was in his shirtsleeves. Their clothes were dirty and crumpled, and every now and again the breeze forced their stale, musty smell into Dan's nostrils.

"What makes you think we know anything about Wat Jones?" demanded Robert as Evans translated.

"I'd heard you were friends," Dan answered, "and that you worked together as partners."

"That was a long time ago."

"You must have seen him since then."

"He hasn't been round here for years. Got more sense."

"Did you have a falling-out?"

"You could say that. Bastard bilked us, didn't he? Told us he'd fixed the price of our ore at fifteen shillings a ton, when he was selling it to the owners for a pound."

"He pocketed the difference?"

"Thieving weasel," squeaked one of the brothers.

"Swindling bastard," agreed the other.

Robert twisted his head on his massive neck and told them to shut up. Meekly, they obeyed.

"So you wouldn't be inclined to help him escape from gaol?"

"Be more inclined to see him strung up," the Welshman answered.

"Then do you know who would help him? Or where he might go?"

"As to where he'd go, I'd say the most likely place is hell. As to who would help him, it isn't us."

Dan thanked them and the officers walked away. Behind them, Robert said something to his brothers which set them laughing. Dan gritted his teeth. Was the incident with the handcuffs going to dog every step he took on the island? He glanced at Evans for confirmation he was right about the joke, but the constable was staring glumly at the cliff and had not been listening.

Williams looked up at the platform. "How do we attract their attention?"

Dan kept walking. "We'll go back by the track."

Evans sighed, almost deflating with relief. Dan smiled to himself. Whatever else the constable was, he was no coward. He had proved that by the fight he put up at Cadnant. There was no reason to test his courage unnecessarily.

"Just get a move on," Dan said, without looking back.

# CHAPTER SIXTEEN

When they got back to the inn, Dan would have ordered the horses harnessed at once, but Williams refused to go a moment longer without food and drink. The look on Evans's face made it clear he felt the same. They settled in the parlour, where four of Amlwch's respectable townsfolk, one of them a clergyman, were enjoying their final bottle of claret amidst the remains of a feast. The only other person in the room sat at a table in the window, his nose in a book.

"You got more out of the witnesses than I expected, Foster," said the captain. "Even so, we still have no idea where Watcyn Jones has gone, or who his accomplices are. And though they aren't often caught out in the truth, I don't believe the family know anything either."

"No," said Dan, "and I don't think he's the sort of son or brother who will risk his neck to say a fond farewell to them. We won't catch him that way."

"Can we be sure they were telling the truth?" asked Evans. "Considering that Owen and Elin Jones knew that the threat to arrest them was a bluff."

"You think it was?" asked Dan.

"You would not really have gone to the trouble of locking them up?"

"Never make a threat you don't intend to carry out, Constable."

"Sound advice," Williams said. "But it doesn't alter the fact that we are at a dead stop."

"Not necessarily," Dan said. "It may be that Sir Edward's reward will persuade someone to give us information."

"I think it's unlikely," Williams answered. "Even if loyalty doesn't keep people's mouths shut, fear of their neighbours' wrath will. No one likes a snitch."

"I've known money to be effective in overcoming such scruples."

"You don't know Anglesey. Laws made in England don't mean much to folk here. They'll not help you, not even for money."

"Murder is murder wherever the law's made."

The clergyman's chair scraped back. He rose to his feet and held up his glass. "To Church and King!"

His companions echoed his words and raised their glasses. Captain Williams picked up his wine and joined the toast. Evans followed the captain's example. Dan, his thoughts running on the investigation, stared moodily at the table top.

"And what will you do when the reward fails to entice?" asked Williams.

They were interrupted by a second toast. This time it was the man in the window who proposed it with raised mug. "To Fox and Liberty!"

A scandalised chorus erupted at the clergyman's table. The reverend thumped the boards with his fist, setting the cutlery dancing. Up went his glass again.

"May all Democrats be guillotined!"

"Hear, hear!" applauded his friends.

The clergyman shot a triumphant glance at the man in the window and sat down.

The Democrat gave, "May all fools be guillotined!"

"What is wrong with the fellow?" exclaimed Evans.

Dan looked over at the window and recognised the pedestrian. "He was up at the mine."

"Was he?" said Evans. "Well, he's an ill-mannered lout."

The clergyman, spluttering and purple in the face, bobbed up and demanded, "What did you say, sir?"

"Pardon me, but I was not addressing you, sir. Preferring rational company, I was talking to myself."

"You insolent puppy! You Jacobin dog!"

"Better a Jacobin dog than a blockhead, sir."

The clergyman danced forward and put up two bony fists. Two of his friends grabbed his arms and pulled him back. The third took advantage of the commotion to empty the wine bottle into his glass.

"Things are getting a little out of hand," said Williams.

"Shouldn't we do something?" asked Evans.

"You go ahead," said Dan. "If you get into trouble, let me know."

Williams laughed and stood up. "Come on, Evans…That's enough, gentlemen. The next person to speak will find himself in front of a magistrate tomorrow morning."

"I protest!" the clergyman cried. "Your intervention is a gross impertinence, sir."

Williams held up his hand. "Enough, I say!" He turned to the Jacobin. "As for you, you've finished your drink and you've no reason to be here any longer."

"It is a public place. I have the right to sit here as long as I wish."

"You have the right to end up in gaol for sedition."

"And affray," said Evans.

"And affray. Gather up your things and get out while you still can."

The young man scowled but, seeing that he was outnumbered by his enemies, did as he was told. In the doorway, he stopped and yelled, "Death to all tyrants!"

The clergyman broke free of his restraints. "I'll give the rascal a thrashing he won't forget, so help me!"

The Jacobin laughed and skipped away. Evans blocked the divine's path, allowing his friends to recapture him and press him into his seat. They rang for another bottle to soothe his offended patriotism.

Dan asked the servant who brought the drink to order the coach. The landlord himself came in with the bill; the captain's uniform and Sir Edward Lloyd Pryce's carriage commanded respect.

While Dan paid, Williams said to the landlord, "You should be more careful about who you admit to your establishment. The man who just went out is a republican."

The landlord paled. "Lord bless us! I didn't like the look of him when he came in, travelling on foot as he is, but he spoke like a gentleman. Besides, he showed me he had the money to pay for his accommodation."

"I wouldn't be surprised if he got that money from French paymasters," Williams answered. "They send these fellows slinking around the docks and factories to stir up trouble amongst the ignorant poor with their talk of equality and no King. He was seen up at the mine earlier."

"Heaven preserve us! I'll have the fellow out at once." He hurried after his unwelcome guest.

Dan pocketed the receipt and they left the room. The landlord had caught up with the republican in the passageway.

"But I have paid for the room," the young man said.

"And I've given you your money back. You're not welcome here."

"But where shall I go? Where shall I sleep?"

"That's not my concern. Be off with you."

Dan and his party were outside by now. They had not gone many steps when the inn door burst open and the pedestrian shot into the street, propelled by a shove. The landlord threw a knapsack after him, scattering clothes, books, soap and razor, and slammed the door. The young man protested, but seeing he was only railing at a door, he gave up. Sobbing with rage, he dropped to his knees and stuffed his belongings back into the bag.

# CHAPTER SEVENTEEN

Captain Williams arranged to accompany Dan and Evans to Beaumaris the next morning, where Dan had a couple of leads to follow. First was to consult Commander Bevan about the Irish vessel which had rendezvoused with Watcyn Jones's gang the night he was arrested. Second was to speak to the prison guards in the hope – admittedly a slender one – of picking up some clue as to who had sprung Jones from detention.

While they waited for Williams to arrive, Evans and Sir Edward discussed the local hunting over their breakfast coffee. A pity, thought Dan, the constable did not show as much enthusiasm for chasing criminals as he did hares and foxes. He left them to it and went outside for some fresh air.

Work on the alterations, which had been going on since the builders arrived early that morning, had stopped. The men were on their break, and from the cheers and shouts drifting from the side of the house, it sounded as if they had found something exciting to fill the time. Dan strolled around the house to see what it was. He found them sitting on the ground, the scaffolding or piles of bricks, drinking from stone bottles and munching on slabs of bread and cheese, while they watched a couple of their mates sparring on the lawn.

One of the boxers was the bricklayer who had listened in on Dan's conversation with Sir Edward when he introduced himself and Evans the day they arrived at Henllys. He had taken off his shirt and tied back his curly hair with a length of ribbon, probably a favour from a local girl. His opponent was taller and a few years older, a wiry, sly-looking man. The foreman looked on, watch in hand, enjoying the sport, but mindful of the need to make sure the men were not late back at work.

Dan leaned against the wall and watched the men dance around one another, releasing sharp jabs and punches. Their blows were few and far between, and lightly given, the aim being more to prove they could get over one another's defences than cause any serious harm. The taller man was nimble on his feet. His defence concentrated on springing out of harm's way rather than parrying the other's punches. The bricklayer was no laggard, though. Keen-eyed, too; quick to spot any opening and more often than not bring a single swift blow home. The pattern seemed so well-established that he was caught completely off-guard when, just after he delivered one of these taps, his opponent reversed his movements, darted forward and landed two blows on his ribs. Winded, he doubled over. The audience applauded, and there were many witty remarks thrown out at his expense.

They were not the only ones who thought the match was over. The victor was strutting about enjoying the applause when the bricklayer sprang up and landed a facer on him. Caught off balance, the tall man got his feet in a tangle and toppled backwards. He lay on the ground, working his arms and legs like a beetle on its back while his mates hooted in delight.

Dan chuckled. "Good hit!"

"That's the first time I've seen you laugh."

Dan had been so intent on the fight he had not heard Evans come up behind him. He swung round.

The constable quailed under his fierce look. "That is…I meant…I mean…"

Dan let him flounder for a few seconds, then said, "It's an entertaining match."

The defeated pugilist scrambled up, dashed the blood from his nose, laughed as heartily as the rest and shook hands with the winner. As he did so, he caught sight of the Bow Street men. His laughter died away. The others, their attention drawn to the intruders, sank into a resentful silence. They put away their bottles, snapped their satchels shut, and without waiting for the foreman's instruction, shuffled back to their work places.

The bricklayer said something to his sparring partner, who guffawed. The others, pausing in the act of picking up their tools, smirked at the Londoners. The young man played up to his audience, puffing out his chest, giving a thumbs up, winking and pulling faces.

"What did he say?" asked Dan.

Evans hesitated.

"I brought you with me so you could translate for me. So translate."

"He asked if you could do any better."

"No, I didn't," the bricklayer said in English. "I said, I bet I could kick your arse into the middle of next week."

"Then," said Dan, "let's see you do it."

No one needed to understand the language to know a challenge had been issued. They crowded around the bricklayer, some shouting encouragement, others urging caution, a few doubting he had the nerve to carry it through. The foreman hopped up and down, issuing increasingly desperate orders to return to work, but no one heard him, and they would not have taken any notice if they had.

It seemed that the sceptics were right. The bricklayer was in no hurry to take on the contest. He looked Dan up and down, gauging his chances. Dan guessed how he looked through his eyes: an opponent of similar build and age to the man he had just knocked down, but who would not have the same strength in his arms as someone who laboured in the building trade for a living.

"Let's see what you've got, then," the Welshman said. "Name's Dai Prichard," he added. "I know who you are."

"You can't really mean to fight him," said Evans, when the other had turned away to brag about an easy victory to his friends.

"Why not?" asked Dan. "It's just a friendly bout. Take my pistol." He took off his coat, scarf and shirt and thrust them into the constable's arms.

"Is this wise? He's heavier than you."

Dan did not bother to answer this. He circled his shoulders and tilted his head from side to side. The men were quiet now, eager for the match to begin. The foreman had given up the attempt to get them back to work, and was as keen as the rest to see the sport. He even turned a blind eye to the betting.

"First knock down?" asked Dan.

Dai agreed, and also declared that the bout was going to be short and not so sweet for the Bow Street man. He raised his fists, stooped low, and stamped his right foot forward. Dan's pose looked feeble by comparison. He held his hands higher, level with his mouth, and did not clench his fists so tightly nor brace himself so rigidly.

They eyed one another for a few seconds, then Dai went on the attack. He swung a punch with his right which Dan deflected with a clumsy swing. Dai swung again, and again Dan parried awkwardly. No fighter who had his opponent on the defence before he had so much as thrown a punch could help concluding that he was the better man, and Dai was no exception. Dan could see it in his face and guess how his mind was working: he had only to drive in with a few more rapid blows to break through Dan's inadequate guard and finish the fight. All would be over in less than a minute.

It was. As Dan calculated, Dai went in again and threw a right which would have caught Dan on the ribs if he had not wriggled away. But Dai had already started with a follow-up to the chin with his other fist. His right arm was still extended and his left had moved away from his body when Dan powered forward, swung a rapid one-two-three – stomach, ribs, jaw – and Dai went down.

Used only to fairground or tavern brawls, the onlookers had never seen a man despatched so coolly or so quickly. Never mind that it was their own champion who sprawled on the ground. The Runner had played a good trick on Dai the boastful, and no one could fail to appreciate his skill.

A caustic voice cut across the cheers. "Very impressive."

The startled men turned and saw Captain Williams and Sir Edward. The captain had joined the applause, but the magistrate surveyed the idling men and half-naked combatants with distaste. Dan helped Dai to his feet.

The foreman tugged his forelock. "Sir, they was on their break, sir, just having a friendly knockabout—"

"So I see. And incapacitating themselves for work into the bargain."

"It was my fault, Sir Edward," Dan said. "I challenged Dai. But as you can see, no harm done."

Dai backed this up by shaking Dan's hand, pulling on his shirt, and skipping back to his place at the scaffolding to prove his fitness. The foreman gazed anxiously at Sir Edward, but the magistrate could hardly make more of it after Dan had claimed the responsibility.

"Very well, carry on," he said finally, "but we'll have no more of this horseplay in future."

The men dispersed, and seconds later were sawing and hammering with unusual enthusiasm.

Williams was not cowed by his friend's disapproval. "I had no idea you were such a first-rate pug, Foster! I've never seen such a fast hitter. Who trained you? For you've been trained, and by someone who knows the science, that's evident. Who is he? He must be someone well known. Not Bill Ward?"

"No," said Dan, taking back his shirt from Evans. "It's time to go."

He had just finished dressing when Davies the butler rounded the corner, followed by a tall man in riding boots. He was armed with a cavalry sabre and a pair of pistols.

"It's one of Bevan's riding officers," Williams said. "Perhaps they've found something. Our luck could be on the turn, Foster. What's the message, Llewellyn?"

"It's Commander Bevan, sir," the man answered. "He's dead."

# CHAPTER EIGHTEEN

Dan waded through the gorse towards a rocky hummock at the top of the cliff. Below him lay a white semi-circular beach flanked by dark rocks. Despite the grey water's restless swirling, it was a still and silent place. A lonely place to die, lamented only by the keening birds and the wind sighing over the heath.

Bevan lay on the ground on his left side, his knees bent, blood from his gashed throat pooled beneath his head. His body was already cold and stiff: he had probably been lying there all night. His hat had rolled away from the cliff edge and was wedged in a clump of gorse halfway down the landward slope. Just below it Llewellyn and the other five revenue men huddled together near the horses, talking quietly.

Sir Edward, Williams and Evans accompanied Dan. Williams lived close by, so he knew the area well and had been able to bring them by the quickest route. It had been one of those occasions when speed and the terrain required Dan to travel on horseback. Evans had relished the ride, had looked as if he had been placed in a saddle at around the time he learned to walk. Dan was glad to be back on his own two feet.

They had arrived to find the manager from a nearby limestone works waiting for them with the quarryman who had raised the alarm. The quarryman was more than happy to repeat his story, would, Dan guessed, be repeating it many more times yet. He clutched his hat close to his heavy corduroy jacket with scarred, scabbed hands and, with Evans translating, told them he had been walking to work from his father's farm when he had come across the riderless horse.

"I knew it was Bevan's bay from the star on his face and the snip on his nose. I guessed something was up – he'd been thrown, maybe – so I had a look around, but I couldn't find him so I took the horse to the works and told Mr Beatty."

"How is he so familiar with Commander Bevan's horse?" asked Dan, who would not have been able to tell a star from a snip.

Evans put the question.

"Everyone knows it," the quarryman answered. "Him and his men are always galloping about the island, poking their noses into stables and barns, hiding behind bushes and jumping out on a fellow when he least expects it, making him turn out his pockets and being most insulting when there's nothing in 'em. Mr Beatty also knew the animal at once."

"Indeed, indeed, as Rees here says, Commander Bevan and his officers are familiar figures as they go about their task," the works manager agreed hastily in English. "Work that is, after all, so vital to the well-being of the nation, and of course those of us who have nothing to do with this disgraceful free trade are as eager as these brave officers to see the rascals behind the wicked business brought to justice, and for my part it is my unfailing practice never to purchase so much as an ounce of tobacco unless I am sure that all the legal duties have been paid and—"

"All I need to know," interrupted Dan, "is how you found the body."

"Indeed, indeed, indeed…I gathered half a dozen men and we set off along the coastal path. It's not much used, hardly a path at all, but I thought it most likely that a revenue officer would have been up here, scanning the coves for signs of smuggling vessels. We found Commander Bevan as you see him. I sent one of the men to Beaumaris for Mr Llewellyn, the rest back to work."

The quarryman scratched his nose. "I suppose we'll be making his gravestone now."

Dan thanked the two men and sent them away. He crouched beside the body and patted the pockets. The dead man still had his pocket book, along with a watch, a purse of coins, a tobacco pouch and portable tinderbox. Dan turned the blood-drained face towards him, ran his hands over the skull. Evans watched him handle the body with a look of disgust. Not to your taste, eh, young gentleman? Dan thought, lowering the head back down. There was something in the right hand. He loosened the fingers.

"What's that you have found, Officer Foster?" asked Sir Edward.

Dan held out his hand. A large brass button with shreds of cloth still attached gleamed in his palm.

"Looks like Bevan tore this off someone." He handed it to Evans. The constable shrugged and handed it back. Dan gave it to the magistrate, who examined it and passed it to the captain.

"Means nothing to me, apart from that it's cheap and shows a want of good taste," Williams said.

"But we've all seen it before," said Dan. "On a dirty blue jacket."

"Watcyn Jones's jacket!" cried Williams.

"You think Jones committed this murder?" exclaimed Sir Edward.

"It looks like it," Dan answered.

The magistrate frowned. "Then he's been on the island all this time?"

"Or not far off." Dan looked down to the cove. "He may have got here by boat and climbed up from the beach."

He stood up, pulled out a handkerchief and wiped his hands. He crumpled the bloodied cloth into his pocket, ignoring Evans's fastidious sneer, then walked away from the rock, eastwards in the direction of Penmon, until he came to a patch of muddy ground marked with two sets of footprints. One moved towards the hummock, the other headed away.

"Or these might be his footprints and he came along this path," he said.

He retraced his steps. Back at the body, something caught his eye. He stooped and picked it up. "There's no point following the path the other way. The workmen came from that direction and they've trampled all over it."

"But why would Jones stay on the island when he could have been well away by now?" wondered Sir Edward.

"Perhaps he and his friends wanted to do a little trade before they left," Williams suggested. "And Bevan came upon them. He and Jones fought, and Jones killed him."

"I don't think it happened like that," Dan said.

"What do you think happened?" asked the captain.

"Bevan didn't draw his gun or sabre. There's no bruising on his face or knuckles, nothing to suggest he has been in a fight. The quarrymen say none of them moved the body, so this is how he fell, with his knees bent. He was sitting down when the blow was struck. He couldn't have been attacked from the front because there are no knife wounds on his hands or arms."

Evans, overcoming his repugnance, looked again at the body. For the first time, he appeared to see it as Dan saw it: as a scene to be read, a puzzle to be solved.

"So his killer crept up behind him," he said slowly. "Cold-blooded murder."

"That's right," Dan answered. "Remember what Jones said in the prison?"

It seemed such a long time ago, though it was only two days.

Evans thought for a moment. "That he'd see all the officers dead."

"So this is a revenge attack because Bevan arrested him," said Williams.

"It's possible," said Dan. "But it still doesn't make sense. Why was Bevan sitting on a rock if he came up here to investigate something?"

"Looking out to sea?" Sir Edward suggested.

"And making himself conspicuous. He even lit a pipe." Dan showed them what he had found: the broken stem and bowl of a clay pipe. "He comes up here, makes himself comfortable, and lights a pipe. He's waiting for someone."

"Which means he had an appointment with his killer," said Evans. "So it couldn't have been Jones."

"Jones could have come upon him while he was waiting," Dan said, "or after whoever it was had gone."

"A woman, perhaps?" offered Williams.

"Bleak spot for a lovers' meeting," Dan said. "But whatever the reason, I don't think he was here on excise business. If he was, why come alone?"

"He could have been meeting an informer," offered Evans.

Williams rolled his eyes. "As I've said more than once, Constable, you're unlikely to find one of those on Anglesey."

Evans reddened, his newfound detecting enthusiasm crushed.

"Let's go and ask his men." Dan held his hand out to Williams for the brass button and put it in his pocket with the pipe.

"Did you find anything?" asked Llewellyn as they approached.

"Hard to know yet," Dan said. "Constable Evans has some questions."

It was the first time he had entrusted Evans with a witness. The constable glanced at him in surprise, but Dan had chosen that moment to check the contents of his pockets and wasn't looking at him.

"We…er…I wondered why he was out here on his own. I mean, was it usual for you to work alone? Revenue men, I mean."

Llewellyn shook his head. "No, we usually make sure there are at least two of us. I don't know what he was doing up here."

"Maybe he got a tip-off," one of the others said.

Evans glanced at Williams. "But I thought the smugglers never peached."

"Nor do they very often," Llewellyn answered. "Unless it's to settle a score. It's more likely to have been one of the respectable householders, though why anyone respectable would be out here at night beats me."

"There was something about a French spy a few days ago," said a short, pugnacious-looking man with a Liverpool accent, who had hardly taken his gaze off Sir Edward's eyepatch since he first saw him. "The commander told us he'd had a report from the curate at St Michael's Church."

"Llanfihangel Din Sylwy," Llewellyn said. "It's not far from here," he added for Dan and Evans.

The Liverpool man showed no interest in mastering the local place names and ignored the correction. "He said he'd seen someone signalling out to sea in the daytime."

"The curate is always seeing French spies," Llewellyn said. "And if it was broad daylight, I don't know what he thought the man was signalling with. His handkerchief?"

But the other man did not want to let go of his spy theory. "He also said he'd seen someone suspicious hanging around. A young fellow carrying a satchel. He had a telescope and said he was here on a walking tour."

"The Jacobin we saw at Amlwch," cried Williams. "I thought that young spark was up to no good."

Llewellyn sucked his lip. "But even if the commander took

the curate seriously – which would be the first time – why wait until last night to come here? And why not mention it while we were out looking for Jones the night before?"

"I think we'll have a word with our young republican," Dan said. "First, though, I'm going to search Bevan's lodgings. Perhaps we'll find some answers there. And we need to tell Doctor Hughes that he's got two inquests to organise now." To Llewellyn, he said, "You can move the body."

Llewellyn had arranged for the loan of a cart from the quarry, but they would have to carry the body over rough ground before they met the vehicle at the nearest track.

"Bring him to Henllys," Sir Edward said. "He is family, though we are only distant cousins. I will ride on ahead and prepare Lady Charlotte."

The revenue men went about their business, the spy enthusiast finally tearing his gaze from Sir Edward's face.

When the riding officers were out of earshot, Williams said, "There is one other thing, Ned. Jones's threat was made to officers, squires and justices."

"You think I'm in danger?"

"If, as seems likely, it was Jones who killed Bevan, and if it is a revenge killing, it's possible."

"If I'm in danger, then so are you. So are Llewellyn and his men, and Officers Foster and Evans if it comes to it. Are you suggesting Jones intends to slaughter us all?"

"It was you he went for in the gaol on Wednesday morning. And if he's killed once, he may well kill again."

# CHAPTER NINETEEN

The arrival of two London officers and Captain Williams of the Loyal Anglesea Volunteers on Mrs Pugh's doorstep threw the widow into a flutter from which it seemed she might never recover. They left her in the parlour with her daughter, brandy and smelling salts and went upstairs.

It was a small house on Baron Hill at the edge of the town, as dainty inside as out. The furniture in Bevan's rooms was old and solid, the more up-to-date pieces having been reserved for downstairs display. There was a four-poster bed with thick curtains and a huge, creaking wardrobe that looked as if the house had been built around it. Time-dimmed paintings of landscapes and faces long since forgotten hung on the walls. All was clean, comfortable, and well-suited to a bachelor, especially one who kept his clothes folded away, his spare boots on trees, his shoes in a neat row, and his shaving equipment, tooth- and hairbrushes laid out in a line in front of the spotted mirror on the dressing table.

On the leather-topped desk, Dan found recent copies of *The Chester Courant*, state lottery tickets to the value of £15, paper, ink, sealing wax, letters from friends and family in Shrewsbury, and bills from tailors, bootmakers, gunsmiths and saddlers. The latest ones dated back no more than a couple of weeks and the earlier ones were marked as paid. Bevan had kept his finances as tidy as his belongings.

The drawers yielded a pack of cards, pens, a well-thumbed copy of a book on naval signals, a North Wales almanac, and a miscellany of papers. There was also a pocket-sized notebook. Starting halfway through 1796, it contained lists of place names and dates under headings by year. In many cases, the place name before the date had been crossed out and another written after it.

"What do you think this is?"

Evans replaced a tin of tobacco on the mantelpiece next to a rack of pipes and went over to take a look.

Captain Williams, who was rifling the contents of a sideboard, straightened up and said, "What's that you have there, Officer Foster?"

Dan handed the captain the book. The other two looked on as he flicked through the pages. When he reached the last entry, Dan said, "Notice anything about the date?"

"'Thursday 31 October'," read Evans. "Yesterday's date."

"And Thomas Bevan's last in this life," said Dan.

"It's a rendezvous! You said he was meeting someone. But there's no place or time next to it."

"There might not need to be, if it was a regular meeting. What do you make of it, Williams?"

The captain sucked in his breath. "I…I hardly like to…I must be wrong…it can't be…"

"That's explained it," Dan said.

"Forgive me. What this suggests seems so fantastical. That Bevan, of all men—" He hesitated. "You see these names? Moelfre, Traeth Coch, Amlwch, and all these other bays and coves? They are all places where smugglers are known to land goods. And these dates, or at least the ones I recognise, refer to nights the riding officers were on patrol." He put his finger on one of the entries. "This night, for example. I remember it because I and some of my men went out with them. And this one, and this."

"So these are patrol rotas?"

"Yes. And in each case, the place that hasn't been crossed out is where we went, and in each case, it is miles from the place that has been crossed out. So here, where Traeth Benllech has been crossed out, we were down by Llanddwyn island. They're practically on opposite sides of the island."

"Meaning what?"

"Meaning that for some reason, the patrols were sent as far away as possible from certain places on certain nights."

"So a gang could have landed goods without worrying about being disturbed by the revenue men?"

"That's right." Williams shut the book. "But you could say that of any night. There aren't enough revenue men to watch every mile of coastline. I expect I've misunderstood. We'd have to check the dates against the revenue patrol's log book to be sure. Though – no."

"Though?" prompted Dan.

"It's probably nothing, but Bevan was at Henllys on Tuesday evening. He would have known we were planning to take Jones from the prison the next morning."

"And if he was working with the smugglers, he could have arranged the ambush," Dan said.

"But, Captain, you said it was Bevan who arrested Jones," said Evans. "Why, then, would he rescue him?"

"It wasn't Bevan who made the actual arrest," said Williams. "The commander led the operation at the cove, but it was one of his men who captured Jones, and that was after Bevan had ordered us to fall back. We were on the retreat, and I think the officer was as surprised as the rest of us when he snared one of them. Even more so, when it turned out to be Jones."

"Do you think Bevan was as surprised as the rest of you?"

"Yes, I think so."

"I wonder if that was because he wasn't expecting Jones to be there – or because he wasn't expecting to make any arrests. Didn't you say the rest of the gang got away?"

"Yes, but there's nothing unusual in that. The revenue men are usually outnumbered by smugglers. In truth, making an arrest is something out of the ordinary."

"Which, if he was in league with the smugglers, Bevan would have been relying on to explain his failure to catch the gang. Even the most corrupt officer has to look as if he's doing his job. The encounter with the smugglers could have been put on for show, and Jones's arrest was a mistake – one which Bevan put right at the first opportunity."

"So you think Bevan is a smuggler?" asked Evans.

"I think we can't draw any conclusions until we've checked the log book. We'll finish here first. You can search the bedroom."

"I'll give you a hand," Williams offered. He returned the book to Dan.

Dan studied the notebook. Was Williams right? Had the patrol commander deliberately diverted his men from one part of the island so that goods could be landed at another? Even if the revenue riders' log book confirmed that the entries in Bevan's notebook were patrol routes, how could they prove it? They would not find anyone willing to tell them if the smugglers had come into Traeth Benllech the night Bevan sent the patrol to Llanddwyn. But if Bevan had been working with the contrabandists, perhaps his fatal encounter with Watcyn Jones had not been an accident. Perhaps it was Jones he went to meet. Only why would Jones kill him? Had there been a falling-out amongst thieves? Over what?

"Mr Foster!" Evans called from the next room. "I think you'd better come and look at this."

Dan thrust the book in his pocket. Williams knelt on the bedroom floor by the window, a short length of floorboard propped up on the wall beside him. Evans stood next to him, leaning over with his hands on his knees, peering into the space beneath the floor.

The captain looked up. "The floorboard was loose when I stepped on it."

Dan had wanted proof that Bevan had been working with the smugglers and here it was. The cavity was packed with boxes labelled "*tabac*" and the address of a warehouse in Nantes. There was also a packet that turned out to contain lace, some packets of tea, and two small kegs of brandy.

"My cousin is lying in a shroud upstairs and this is how you honour his memory?" Sir Edward demanded.

"Edward," Lady Charlotte murmured, "pray compose yourself."

He snatched his arm from his wife's grasp, strode to his desk and spun round to face the three men with the dust of their day's riding still on them.

"I don't believe it."

"I'm sorry, Ned, but I don't see what other interpretation you can put on it," Williams said. "We checked the log books with Mr Llewellyn at the watch room. All the places and dates in Bevan's notebook match the patrols."

"That proves nothing. Officer Foster said himself that there is no way of knowing that goods were landed at the locations Bevan listed. For all we know, he was avoiding them because he thought it was unlikely that goods would be brought ashore there."

Dan stood by, his hat under his arm, and left it to the captain to reiterate what he himself had reported to the magistrate. He had known Sir Edward would not like what he had to say, but the facts were the facts. They were no more to his liking than Sir Edward's, though not for the same reason.

"It's unlikely that a man would write down a list of places where he thought nothing was going to happen," the captain said. "And there's the contraband in his room."

"A few packets of tobacco for himself, tea for the landlady, a bit of lace for the landlady's daughter. About as much as you'd find in the average clergyman's house. Peculation, and disappointing enough, Lord knows, but not enough to suggest he was in league with the smugglers."

"But you were there in the gaol when Jones said there was someone in authority running the trade on the island," the captain pointed out. "Who so well placed to be that man than a revenue officer? And as Officer Foster also said, it would explain how he came to be out alone at night in company with Wat Jones. And, of course, it was he who arranged the attack at Cadnant."

"Making him complicit in murder too? No!" Sir Edward slammed his hand on the desk. "I will not have it, Foster. I will not have you and your – your – thief-taking accomplice coming here and making these foul accusations. I will write to Sir William Addington at once and I will let him know in no uncertain terms what I think of your methods. The pair of you will be lucky if you ever work anywhere again, let alone in the police." He swayed and clutched the desk for support.

"Thief taking?" cried Evans, stung by the insult.

"As to that, Sir Edward," Dan said, "you may well find that Sir William has already arrived at it himself without you troubling to involve yourself in the matter. Not only has Jones escaped, leading to the death of one man in the process, he's gone on to kill a man while at large, and if anyone is to take the blame for that, it's me. It has nothing to do with Constable Evans, who was merely obeying my orders."

"Yes, for heaven's sake, Ned, be reasonable," Williams said. "Foster has done his best."

Sir Edward might have told them what he thought of Dan's best, but he was shaking too much. He looked almost as distressed as the night Dan found him wandering outside, or at least not far off it.

In an attempt to calm things down, Dan said, "Nothing is

final yet, sir. Before we draw any conclusions, there are one or two matters that are still not clear."

It was too late. Sir Edward's eye rolled back in its socket, the blood drained from his face, and his seared skin flared into prominence. As his knees buckled Lady Charlotte sprang forward to catch him before he hit the ground. Dan flung his hat aside and rushed to help her. He and Williams manoeuvred the stricken man to the sofa and laid him down. Lady Charlotte sank to her knees beside him, smoothed his hair from his damp forehead and loosened his collar.

"Bring me some brandy from that decanter over there," Williams said.

Evans hurried to obey. Williams dribbled a few drops into Sir Edward's mouth. He coughed and his eyelid fluttered, but he did not revive.

"We must get him upstairs," Lady Charlotte said.

"Foster, you take hold of one arm," Williams said.

Evans hovered anxiously. "Can I help?"

"No, you wait here," Dan answered.

# CHAPTER TWENTY

Dan had hardly closed the library door behind him before Evans jumped up. "You haven't left her alone with him? Sir Edward can be violent when these fits are upon him."

"What makes you say that?"

Evans hesitated. "Feverish people often are."

"Is that a lucky guess, or have you seen the bruises on her wrists?"

"You know about those?"

The answer was obvious and Dan did not bother giving it. He was more interested in how the constable had found them out.

"Captain Williams is helping her put him to bed. When did you see the marks?"

"After dinner on Tuesday night. I saw her showing them to the captain in the hall just before he left. I didn't mean to overhear their conversation, but I confess I was so shocked, I didn't immediately make my presence known. By the time I did, she had already said enough to make it clear how she'd got them. Even then, she spoke more from regret than anger. Her loyalty and patience are—"

Dan interrupted the constable's hymn of praise. "Showing them to the captain?"

"He is an old family friend and a great support to her. He

and Sir Edward are like brothers; there are no secrets between them. Their fathers were close, and the two practically grew up together. Captain Williams used to come here for lessons with Sir Edward's tutor and stay for weeks at a time. The boys were inseparable."

"And how do you know all this?"

"By talking to Mrs Jenkins."

"And what else did Mrs Jenkins tell you?"

"That Sir Edward treats Lady Charlotte abominably, but she never complains. What makes it all the more dreadful is that she need not have married him at all. When he came by his injuries, he would have released her from their engagement, but she wouldn't hear of it, though he's sadly changed, and not only in his appearance. How a man could be so weak as to accept such a sacrifice from such a woman is beyond me. But she is devoted to him, in spite of it all. Mrs Jenkins thinks she's a saint."

"That's what Mrs Jenkins thinks, is it? Seems you've been enjoying a good gossip with the servants."

Evans flushed. "She's a garrulous old biddy who needs very little encouragement, and I was concerned about Lady Charlotte. Though I own I don't know that I can do anything about it, even though her plight is worse than I first realised."

"You don't have to justify yourself to me. You never know what you can learn from tittle-tattle. But what goes on between Sir Edward and his wife has nothing to do with our job. And that's going to be harder without his co-operation."

"Do you think he will write to Sir William?"

"It makes no difference whether he does or doesn't. This Welsh jaunt has been a disaster from start to finish. Unless I can get a result, I may as well not bother going back to Bow Street."

"But haven't we got a result? We've discovered that Bevan was the man Watcyn Jones told us about, the one running the smuggling gang."

"Except that I'm not sure he was. I was just about to say so when Sir Edward had his fit."

"But what about the evidence we found in his rooms?"

"Half a dozen packets of tea? I agree with Sir Edward. It amounts to no more than a few perks. Payment for keeping the patrol out of the way, probably. And for a man heading a lucrative business, Bevan wasn't exactly living the high life."

"That might have been a disguise, to draw attention away from himself. He was able to pay his debts in good time."

"Yes, I noticed that, but I don't think being able to spend within his limits qualifies a man as an arch villain. Still, you're right, and it may be that he has money hidden away somewhere. It could be he's deposited it in a bank. Where is the bank, by the way? I don't remember seeing one in Beaumaris."

"I don't think there is one on the island. The nearest is in Caernarfon."

"Find out where. In the meantime, I want to track down our Jacobin friend."

"You think he has something to do with Bevan's death?"

"I think it's worth following up. For now, it would be best if we moved to the Bull and left Sir Edward and his family in peace. We'd better go and pack."

"Pack?" asked Captain Williams, coming into the room and heading for the brandy decanter. "Are you going somewhere?"

"Since Sir Edward is ill, I think we should take rooms in the town," Dan replied.

The captain stopped in mid-pour. "You must not leave! If you do, it will distress him beyond measure. He didn't know what he was saying and he almost certainly won't remember it. That's how these attacks usually go. If you leave, he'll insist on knowing why, and if he even begins to suspect that he's offended you, he will be inconsolable."

"We aren't offended," Dan said, "but we should leave him in peace while he recovers."

"The quickest way to help him recover is to forget the unfortunate scene and carry on as if nothing has happened. If he wakes up and finds you gone, he will torment himself with all sorts of imaginings. I beg you, Foster, for Ned's sake, stay. He will be back to his old self by morning, and better able to bear the shock and disappointment about his cousin."

"Then we'll stay, but make sure not to trouble him too much."

"That won't do either. He cannot bear to be treated like a querulous valetudinarian. He is impatient to see Jones brought to justice. He'll want to be kept informed of developments as soon as they happen."

"Then tomorrow we will go and find some developments to report," Dan said.

Williams gulped his brandy. "Where are you going?"

"To Amlwch to look for the young man we saw at the mine."

The captain refilled his glass. "I shall stay here with Ned. Will you take the carriage or ride?"

"The carriage," Dan said before Evans could suggest they went on horseback.

# CHAPTER TWENTY-ONE

They reached Amlwch just before mid-day. While the driver was dealing with the stable boys at the Amlwch inn, Dan and Evans went in search of the landlord. They found him in the otherwise empty parlour reducing one of the maids to tears. Sighting potential customers, he dismissed the snivelling girl with her hands full of broken crockery and went from scowling and scolding to affable and eager to serve. His smile wavered for a few seconds when he recognised the law officers.

"Good morning, gentlemen," he said in English.

"We're looking for the pedestrian who was in here a couple of days ago," Dan said.

The landlord's plump face quivered. "He's not been back, and no more should he. We don't welcome his kind here, I can assure you."

"Do you have any idea where he went?"

"He's not here and that's all I know, and wouldn't have him either."

"You haven't seen him about the town?"

"No, and if I did, I wouldn't give him the time of day. I'll have no truck with troublemakers like him."

The man having made his feelings, though nothing else, clear, Dan thanked him and he and Evans left.

"We should check all the inns and taverns," Dan said when they were outside.

Evans frowned. "All of them?"

"And the boarding houses."

"Psst!"

The scolded maid peered around the half-open door, whispered loudly and crooked her finger at Evans.

"We haven't got time for that," Dan said.

"She says she knows where he is."

Evans moved close to the girl and stooped to listen, though he could have heard her just as well without her lips brushing his ear. There was no need for her to smile up at him so appealingly, bat her eyelashes so flutteringly, or blush so becomingly either.

Dan folded his arms. "Ahem."

The girl skipped back to her work.

"He's staying in a lodging house by the docks," Evans reported. "His name is Sampson Kirby, he's from London, and he says he's a student at Oxford."

"He says?"

"Well, he can't be, can he?"

"Because?"

"It's Michaelmas term. He should be in Oxford."

The sort of thing Evans would know. "Then we'd better go and find out what he's doing here."

The lodging house was one of a row of hovels between the Jolly Pilot and the White Lion, with the Miners' Rest and the Eagle vying for custom in the middle. Not that they had to do much vying. Every alehouse was packed with sailors, miners and dock workers, the grime of their labour still upon them: tar and grease, coal dust in rivulets of dried sweat, caked mud, ash and soot. Inside the taprooms, women flitted between the men. Outside, dirty, barefoot children begged and scavenged.

Carts from the mine creaked and rumbled through the half-drunk, drunk and comatose who crowded the street. When the vehicles snarled up, as they often did, the drivers swore at one another. Some climbed down and exchanged punches. Ore thundered down the chutes from the upper quay into the copper bins below. The smelting furnaces roared, hammers pounded, the copper mill rollers ground, unseen machinery thumped, hissed and whined. The smells of sulphur, hops from the brewery, tallow, smoke and dung heaps hung over it all, along with the rotting debris bobbing against the harbour walls.

Escaping death beneath the cartwheels and avoiding sinking ankle high into piles of manure and rubbish, Dan and Evans ducked through the open door of Sampson Kirby's lodging house. They met a discordance of shouting, banging, crashing, howling, screaming, weeping, and grunting. A heavily built man emerged from the first door in the passage and accosted them in a sing-song voice. Evans explained that he was reciting the prices of a room, bed sheets, spirituous liquor, a pipe of opium, a woman or any combination of these, though Dan had already guessed the gist. Anything was purchasable, including the janitor's co-operation.

When the man had his coin, he led them up the filthy bare stairs to a room at the back on the first floor. Dan knocked on the door. There was no reply, and after listening for a moment, he told the caretaker to unlock it. He and Evans went inside and Dan shut the door in the janitor's face.

Kirby had left the room tidy, though shifting all the dirt was more than one man could have managed. A portable shaving kit was set neatly by the cracked bowl on the wash stand, and a small towel that was too clean to have been provided by the house hung from the rail. He had made the bed, such as it was, and Dan left the unpleasant task of lifting up the stained pillows and mattress to Evans.

Kirby's knapsack was propped against the wall. In it Dan found two shirts, two pairs of stockings, a pair of trousers, brushes, a soap box, a small sketchbook and a box of pencils, chalk and charcoal. The book contained drawings of scenes taken at the mine, as well as a rough plan of the buildings labelled "office", "kiln", "store", "sheds" and so on.

Evans was also looking at a book.

"What's that, a diary?"

"*Lyrical Ballads*. There's a fine verse of Wordsworth's about Tintern Abbey—"

"Which isn't a lot of use to me, Constable. What do you think this is?"

Evans put the poetry back on the scarred bedside table and took the sketchbook. "He's fascinated by the mine, isn't he? Many artists are. I heard Mr Turner was there last year."

"I doubt Mr Turner came to draw huts and sheds." Dan put the book back in the knapsack. "Leave everything as you found it. We'll keep watch for Kirby outside."

After adding the janitor's silence about their visit to their purchases, the two took up position outside the Miners' Rest. People hurried in and staggered out of the alehouses. The line of carts heading to the quay dwindled to nothing. A single cart empty of ore trundled into view and drew up in the street. Instead of going into one of the alehouses, the driver tipped his hat over his eyes, folded his arms and leaned back in his seat, apparently dozing.

It was late afternoon by the time Kirby appeared. He carried a loaf of bread, and a bottle of wine poked out of his coat pocket. The man in the cart pushed back his hat and swung to the ground. The two met in the middle of the road and exchanged a few words. Kirby handed over something wrapped in a handkerchief. The carter unknotted it and satisfied himself as to the contents. In return, he delivered a small keg from under his seat.

"Brandy!" said Evans.

"I'm not so sure," Dan said. "The cart's come from the mines."

"But Sir Edward said the Amlwch miners were involved in the trade. They must be hiding contraband up there and bringing it into town to sell."

"Possible, I grant you. But if a keg of brandy was all Kirby wanted, he wouldn't have to look to Parys Mountain for his supply."

The cart moved off and Kirby went into the lodging house. Ten minutes later, he came out again without the food and drink, and with his knapsack. He hoisted the bag on his shoulders and set off along the street.

"I think he's carrying more than a couple of shirts and stockings," Dan said. "Come on."

They followed Kirby to the outskirts of the town, where he paused and adjusted his load before setting off into the dusk. Ahead of them rose the outline of Parys Mountain. The barren landscape on either side of the dusty, rutted track was indistinct, no more than vague shapes in the darkness. No lights shone in the buildings at the top of the mountain, and the open cast was a vast, silent pit of darkness. Sulphurous smoke still belched from the kilns, but no men hammered and no rock tumbled. The wind hissed over the lifeless ground, the ropes on the windlasses creaked, and water gurgled.

They lost sight of Kirby and moved into the obscurity at the side of the mine office while they scanned the site for him. They both spotted him at the same time, walking along the track from the copper women's shed.

"There must be a nightwatchman somewhere," Dan muttered.

"I can see a light moving up there." Evans pointed to a yellow spot bobbing near the pump house.

"He's on his rounds. Convenient for whatever our friend is up to."

"What is he up to?"

"It's time to find out."

Dodging from shadow to shadow, they moved after Kirby. He turned down the side of the warehouse where they had questioned the storekeeper the day before yesterday. Dan reached for his gun and signalled to the constable to do the same.

At the rear of the building, Kirby lowered the knapsack to the ground. It landed with a thud. He crouched, took something out of it and stood up. He faced the window shutter and raised his arms. Metal ground on wood. He was drilling a hole.

"Burglary," whispered Evans. "Should we arrest him now?"

"We'll wait."

The drill broke through. Kirby tossed the circle of wood away and brushed dust from the aperture with his fingers before reaching through. His groping hand found and lifted the bar with a metallic click. He pulled the shutter open, waited, listened, then drove the drill through a pane of glass. The glass shattered and he waited again, his body tense. No alarm followed so he tapped out the shards of glass, grasped the handle inside and swung the lattice open.

He stuffed the drill into a deep pocket inside his coat, took off the coat and bundled it up. He looked round, prompting Dan and Evans to dart out of sight. There were heaps of boulders dotted all over the mine, one only a few feet away. Kirby hid his coat behind it. This done, he shouldered his knapsack, hauled himself up to the window and wriggled inside. He pulled the shutter closed behind him. A few moments later, a square outline of light appeared around it.

Dan and Evans took up position on either side of the window. Kirby shuffled about inside, shifting crates and kegs. A quarter of an hour passed. The light was suddenly extinguished. Kirby's running footsteps approached the window and the shutter flew open. The knapsack sailed out and crumpled on the ground.

Kirby pulled himself over the sill and somersaulted after

it. He landed awkwardly, rolled down the slope and came to a halt by the boulders where he had hidden his coat. He sat up, blinked, and found himself looking down the muzzle of Dan's pistol.

"Good haul, Kirby?" asked Dan.

"I didn't take anything. I'm not a thief! We have to get out of here!" He tried to get up, but Dan shoved him back.

"You look like a thief to me. A burglarious one at that. That means gaol for you, my lad."

Evans picked up the knapsack from under the window. "It's empty."

"Didn't get what you went for?" asked Dan. "What was that?"

"There isn't time for that, you dolt! We have to get away from here before it's too late."

Dan looked back at the building. "You didn't bring anything out, you took something in. Something in a keg. Evans – run!"

Before the constable could move, there was a roar and a funnel of light tore through the storehouse roof. Dan flung his hands over his head and threw himself next to Kirby. Wood, glass and metal rained down. By the time he was able to raise his head, flames were leaping out of the building. Rubble and dust covered the ground. There was no sign of Evans.

Kirby made another attempt to get away. Dan slammed him back. He still had his gun in his hand, which by some miracle had not gone off. He aimed it at Kirby. The saboteur was too busy gibbering at the weapon to see Dan's fist coming. The blow knocked him unconscious. Dan shoved his gun in his pocket, tore Kirby's scarf from his neck, dragged him into a sitting position and tied his hands behind his back. He used his own scarf to tie his prisoner's legs.

The roaring had not stopped, and it took Dan a moment to realise it was in his own ears. Something trickled down his cheek. He pressed his fingers to his face, brought them away covered in blood and dust. He shook crimson drops out of his eyes, staggered to his feet and clambered over the debris, kicking and shoving it aside. The wall in front of him bulged and a searing heat beat against him. Thick black smoke gusted overhead, shedding choking ash. His eyes stung and it was hard to breathe.

"Evans! Constable Evans! Where are you, man?"

There was no answer.

# CHAPTER TWENTY-TWO

Another explosion inside the warehouse brought down more of the roof, and scattered sparks, tiles and shards of burning timber. Dan ducked and covered his head, caught some blows on his shoulders and back. When he looked up, he thought the end wall was swaying, though he could not be sure if it was the play of flame, smoke and shadow that made it look as if it was moving.

He struggled through the debris, his legs sinking through the unstable heaps, calling the constable's name. Sometimes he stopped and scrabbled at a heap of stones or hauled timbers aside. He found nothing beneath. Sweat poured down his face and it was hard to see anything clearly in the flickering light.

A pale spidery shape moved in the rubble. It disappeared, reappeared a few seconds later, waved, disappeared again. It must be a hand. It must be.

"Evans!" Dan shouted, ploughing through a network of charred beams.

He balanced awkwardly on the wreckage and hauled one of the spars aside. Something shifted behind him and he glanced over his shoulder. Bricks tumbled off the top of the wall. He turned back and dragged another beam free. Clouds of dust rose into his eyes and nostrils. He coughed, wiped the dirt away, and seized another beam. The mound stirred and dust trickled into a cavity beneath. A pale face stared at him through the gap he had made.

"Evans! Can you speak? Can you move?"

"Yes," the constable answered.

Another shower of bricks fell from the wall. Dan clawed at the spars and widened the gap enough to expose Evans's head and shoulders. The constable was curled up inside a hollow which had sheltered him from the fire and falling debris. He pushed at the rubble from the inside.

A column of flames roared from the building and bricks rained down from the wall.

"It's going to collapse! Get out of it, Foster!"

Dan gritted his teeth, put his shoulder beneath a beam, anchored his feet and shoved with all his might. Nothing happened. He took a deep breath, shoved again. Slowly the beam began to move, widening the opening in front of Evans, who dragged himself out. Dan dropped the beam as Evans's feet slithered free.

The constable sat up, ash and charred flakes of wood running off him. "That was a surprise."

The wall swung back and forth, building up momentum, bricks cascading. Dan grabbed Evans's arm and they ran. As they reached the edge of the rubble, the wall finally gave way. It crashed to the ground, obliterating Evans's hideaway. Dan leapt clear. He landed on his knees, Evans staggering beside him. A cloud of dust formed above them, hung for a moment, then settled on and around them.

Evans got to his feet and held out his hand. Dan hesitated, then clasped the outstretched fingers and let the constable help him up.

"Foster, you saved—"

"Better see to Kirby," Dan interrupted.

Their prisoner leaned against the rocks, his head slumped on his chest, groaning. Dan untied the scarf around his ankles and pulled him to his feet. They manhandled him down on to the track. Two men in heavy boots and greatcoats, both carrying lanterns, ran towards them, shouting and waving their arms. One of them pointed a pistol.

Evans shouted back. Whatever he said, it did not convince. The watchman's voice grew shriller and he gestured with his gun: *on your knees*. Evans protested.

"Do as he says," Dan said. He had seen how the man's eyes goggled in fright and the pistol shook in his hand. Worse still, his partner had drawn his own gun, which he held at arm's length and wobbled in front of him without anything resembling an aim. There was nothing more dangerous than a frightened man with a gun who did not know how to use it, and here they were confronted by a pair of them.

Dan pushed Kirby to the ground and raised his hands. Released from his grip, Kirby keeled over.

"Get on your knees, Constable!" Dan shouted.

Startled into obedience, Evans sank to the ground. The first man snapped an order. His partner dithered forward two steps, hopped back, tottered forward again, halted and snarled something that was most likely "do it yourself".

Evans had another go at explaining who they were. The watchmen looked at one another, lowered their guns, snapped them up again, bit their lips, consulted in loud, panicked voices. Evans repeated the name Sir Edward Lloyd Pryce several times, along with "Foster" and "Bow Street". It felt as if he had been speechifying for hours before the watchmen finally stopped waving the pistols around.

"I did it, didn't I?" Kirby crowed. "And if those government lackeys hadn't interfered, I'd have managed more."

He jerked his head at Dan. Evans, sitting on a desk at the side of the mining office, was out of his line of vision. Ward, the surgeon employed by the company to look after the men, was examining the constable.

The watchmen stood behind the prisoner's chair and, alert to his slightest movement, pounced on him and pressed him back in his seat. Kirby's clothes were dishevelled and torn and he was still bleeding at the mouth from the treatment they had given him on the way to the office. Apparently, the two had been convinced he would have got away if they had not kicked, thumped and half-strangled him whenever they got the chance. Dan had been hard-pressed to get him down here in one piece. Though his hands were tied behind his back, they were still sure he was capable of mischief. Knocking over one of the lamps and starting a fire six men would not be able to stamp out, perhaps.

"What did you say, you traitorous villain?" roared Brooks, rushing at the prisoner.

Dan held the manager back. "That's enough."

From outside came the sound of voices and the flicker of torches. The explosion had roused the miners who lived in the hovels dotted around the lower flanks of the mountain. From them, the news had quickly spread to the town, causing an influx of excited crowds. Mr Brooks had set off as soon as he heard what had happened, bringing Ward with him, his coachman laying about him left and right with whips and curses to clear the road.

"So you set the explosion in an attempt to disrupt the production of copper for the Navy," Dan said.

"Not an attempt. I succeeded."

Brooks snorted. "You're a fool if you think burning a few stores will halt operations for a moment."

"And you're a fool if you think you can hold back the tide of progress," Kirby retorted. "The old order is in its death throes. It won't be long before the new dawn. The day of liberty, equality and fraternity. The end of tyrants. The—"

A loud crash interrupted him. They all turned in the direction of the sound. Ward scrabbled about on the floor by

Evans's chair. The constable leaned down and scooped up the short metal probe the surgeon had dropped.

"Much 'bliged," said Ward. He spat on the probe and rubbed it on his sleeve. "If ye'll jush turn y'head to th'right." He screwed up his yellowing eyes in concentration and bent over Evans.

They never found out what the surgeon intended to do with the shaky implement. Dan knocked his arm away, sending the tool flying again.

"I'll not have this drunken quack near my constable another minute."

The nightwatchmen smirked, Brooks huffed defensively, and the drunken quack, who had not heard, shuffled about looking for the probe, muttering, "Dearie me, dropped it."

"Evans, any bones broken?" asked Dan.

"No."

"Then you're fine. And now, gentlemen, we're taking the prisoner back to Beaumaris. There is one last thing, though. We saw Kirby buy the gunpowder on Amlwch quay from one of the carters from the mine. I suggest you try and find out who he is. Unless Mr Kirby here wants to save everyone the time and trouble."

"Why should I betray a comrade?"

"You might if it's the difference between the gallows and transportation," Dan said.

Kirby turned pale.

"Mr Brooks," Dan continued, "would you send a message to Sir Edward's coachman to bring up the carriage?"

There was no need. A brisk knock on the door heralded the arrival of the coachman, who had the carriage waiting for them outside. Dan and Evans escorted Kirby out of the office, pushed their way through the gaping crowd and put him inside.

# CHAPTER
# TWENTY-THREE

"And it is your opinion that Commander Bevan died where you recovered his body?"

"It is," Dan answered Coroner Hughes.

Every seat in the upstairs assembly room in Beaumaris Town Hall was taken, and there were people standing at the back. Goronwy Evans, Sir Edward, Stephen Lloyd Pryce, Captain Williams and the prison governor sat in the front row, Llewellyn and his men behind them.

Hughes had examined Evans that morning and pronounced him fit, apart from a few bruises and cuts. In his late fifties, the doctor was neat in his movements and succinct in his speech. It had been reassuring not to see Evans poked and prodded by a man whose hands shook and whose breath was practically flammable. Of the two officers, Dan looked as if he had come off the worse. His hands and face were battered, burned and bruised, and his movements stiff and painful. However, Mrs Jenkins had done an excellent job of cleaning and mending their clothes, and their appearance was otherwise respectable.

It had been a busy day for Stephen Lloyd Pryce, who had prayerfully laid Thomas Bevan in the family vault at St Catherine's church to await the arrival of his family for the funeral. For the inquest, he had adopted a righteous and juridical air suitable to the occasion, and frequently signalled his approval of Hughes's sterner remarks with a nod and hum. It reminded Dan of the Methodists he had seen at Hurst's sermon in Beaufort Buildings on the Strand – a comparison he was cheerfully sure would displease the reverend.

Braillard stared at a point above Dan's head while he listened to his testimony. He had been careful to point out that his responsibility for Jones ended the instant he relinquished custody of him. Having apportioned the blame satisfactorily, he avoided eye contact with the Bow Street men.

The captain, smart in his volunteer's uniform, divided his attention between the proceedings and Sir Edward. Accompanying his cousin's coffin on the short walk to the church had been strain enough for Sir Edward, and he had looked ill before the inquest started. He was pale and tense, his arms folded tightly across his chest. Dan focussed on his answers, not letting the magistrate's nerves distract him.

"And what did you do after you had examined the body and collected the evidence that demonstrates that Watcyn Jones was present?"

"I caused the body to be carried to Henllys and I went to search Bevan's rooms in the hopes of finding out who he had gone to meet. I was accompanied by Constable Evans and Captain Williams. We found a cache of smuggled goods, as told on the list I gave you, and a notebook with entries in his handwriting which suggest that he frequently altered the revenue patrol's planned routes."

A scandalised murmur broke out. Even Doctor Hughes's composure was disturbed. His pen came to an abrupt halt. Dan had given evidence to the accompaniment of many similar outbursts at the Old Bailey and ignored it.

"He had written last Thursday's date, but no other details. It suggests that there was a rendezvous planned, but whether it was with someone else and Jones happened upon him, or whether it was with Jones himself, is unknown."

Hughes let the implications of this sink in. "You are suggesting that Commander Bevan was collaborating with smugglers? That he occasionally looked the other way in return for the modest reward of a few items of contraband?"

"The evidence points that way."

"Yet you have no proof that contraband goods were landed on the nights he diverted the patrols, no proof of a direct connection between Watcyn Jones and Commander Bevan, and, indeed, no proof that Commander Bevan went out that night otherwise than in the normal course of his duties?"

"My investigations into those matters are not yet complete."

"Of course. I would remind the jurymen that the purpose of this hearing is merely to establish cause of death, and of that I think there can be little doubt. Whatever the deceased's purpose in going to the cove, there is clear evidence that Watcyn Jones was there too." Hughes turned back to Dan. "That being so, Officer, is it your opinion that the murder was committed by Watcyn Jones, lately a prisoner in Beaumaris Gaol, on whom you had served a warrant for the murder of Revenue Officer Barker in Kent earlier this year?"

Dan hesitated. He was not sure it was his opinion yet, but it was difficult to suggest anything else.

"The evidence as it stands points that way, yes."

"Thank you, Principal Officer Foster, that will be all."

Dan picked up his hat and returned to his seat. Mr Llewellyn and the other riding officers had given their evidence and now there was nothing to do but wait for Hughes to consult with his clerk before directing the jury. He had already ruled on volunteer Hudson's death: an unsurprising "Wilful Murder by Persons Unknown", with Jones's role as accomplice noted. The outcome of Bevan's inquest was never in any doubt: "Wilful Murder by Watcyn Jones."

"It is a great calamity," Stephen Lloyd Pryce said, "that Jones is still at liberty. No decent man is safe while such a creature remains at large. Of course, no blame for these horrible murders can accrue to you, Principal Officer Foster. We are all of us merely human, all fallible, all frail flesh. You must not allow the fact that you let Jones give you the slip at Cadnant dismay you."

Captain Williams spluttered into his wine. Sir Edward, who sat by the fire in the parlour where they had gathered after the inquest, toyed with his empty glass and did not seem to have heard his brother's remark. Evans sucked in his breath and looked at Dan as if he expected him to tear off his jacket and challenge the reverend to a bout of fisticuffs.

Instead, Dan smiled. It was not a smile that made the constable look any less anxious.

"I thank you for your kind words, Reverend."

"The Methodistical persuasion has much to answer for," Pryce went on, happily bearing the burden of the conversation. "They have undermined true morality and the ordained order of things, and taught the labouring man to envy his betters and desire equality with his superiors. Their hedge preachers and Sunday school teachers have sown seeds of discontent which have led to lawlessness and riot – synonyms, sir, synonyms for reform and revolution. I would not be surprised if Jones and the man you arrested at the mine were connected. You have surely considered the possibility?"

"I have not," Dan said, "but thank you for the hint."

"It is fortunate that Doctor Hughes's remarks have guided you away from the preposterous idea that cousin Bevan had any involvement with Jones and his smuggling gang."

"As you say."

Sir Edward shivered and lifted his gaze from the flames. "What Mr Foster is too polite to remind you is that Jones was not the only one who broke the law."

Stephen Lloyd Pryce raised his eyebrows. "Come now, Edward, you surely do not put cousin Bevan's regrettable lapses on an equality with three murders, especially when set against years of devotion to his dangerous work. He would, I am sure, have realised upon a little reflection that the course he had taken was unworthy of him and made amends."

Sir Edward shook his head. "We must face the facts, Stephen. Tom was in a position of trust. He betrayed that trust. The only thing we do not yet know is how far his betrayal went. Perhaps it was, as you say, a few regrettable lapses, but Jones told us that there was someone in a position of authority behind the smuggling operations. If Tom was that man, it is Mr Foster's duty to ascertain the truth. We must not interfere with him in the carrying out of his duties."

"Interfere? Is it interfering to drop a few gentle hints?"

Williams stood up and moved over to the decanters. "If it should turn out that Bevan was innocent of so deep an involvement, Mr Foster will be the first to tell us, won't you, Foster?"

For Sir Edward's sake, Dan's answer was sincere. "I hope as much as anyone here that such will be case."

"However," Williams removed the stopper from the decanter, "in spite of what Hughes said, the evidence against him does not make it seem very likely. May I help you to another drink, Reverend?"

Stephen held out his glass.

"How do you propose to advance your investigations?" asked Sir Edward.

"Evans and I will visit the bank in Caernarfon tomorrow," Dan said.

Sir Edward nodded and did not pursue the subject. The door opened and Davies, the butler, came in with a letter for him. He broke the seal, glanced at the writing and handed it to Williams.

"You read it, Jack. I have a slight headache."

"It's from Mr Brooks at the mine. They have discovered the man who supplied Kirby with the gunpowder, which was stolen from the warehouse. It was easy enough to identify him as he did not turn up for work this morning. The Amlwch constable searched his lodgings and discovered a number of pamphlets advocating the overthrow of kings, annual Parliaments, and votes for working men."

"Lord have mercy on us!" exclaimed Stephen.

"The man himself has not been found," Williams continued. "The constable is arranging for descriptions to be sent to the local magistrates."

"Well, Foster," said Sir Edward, "whether Kirby's accomplice is found or not, to have apprehended a French spy is no mean achievement. I congratulate you."

"I did not do it on my own," Dan said. "Constable Evans played his part."

"Now that's the mark of a good officer!" Williams cried. "One who gives credit where it is due, is it not, Evans?"

Evans was too surprised to answer. Superiors who do not take all the credit to themselves were a rarity.

"You look as if a bit of fresh air would do you good, Ned," Williams said. "Why don't we go outside?"

"Yes, I think I will. If you will excuse me, gentlemen."

The two men left the room, the magistrate's pace a shuffle beside his friend's vigorous stride. The walk did him little good, though, and that evening he did not come down to dinner. On his way to bed later, Dan stopped to listen outside Sir Edward's door. All was quiet. He hoped that Sir Edward's night would be a peaceful one.

# CHAPTER TWENTY-FOUR

Dan's eyes flickered open. A figure in white hung over him, eyes gleaming from a pale face surrounded by dishevelled hair. A spectral nimbus flickered about the apparition, deepening the darkness in the rest of the room. He thrust out his hand and his fingers closed around damp fabric as cold as a shroud. A cry of pain brought him to his senses. He released his grip and sat up.

"Lady Charlotte?"

"Mr Foster, I need your help."

"Did I hurt your arm?"

"No. It doesn't matter. It's Edward. He's not in the house and the door's open."

"Can you light me a candle? I'll be down in a minute."

When she had gone, her light tread making hardly a sound on the wooden stairs, he dressed hastily. It was a quarter past two by his watch. He could still hear the wind and rain that had accompanied his drift into sleep. The rain was heavier, the lashing of the trees louder. It explained her tangled hair and wet gown: she had been outside looking for her husband.

He pulled on his coat, wincing at his aching muscles. He looked at his pistol on the desk and, after a few seconds' hesitation, decided to take it. He picked up the candle and grabbed the cover off the bed.

Lady Charlotte stood by the front door peering out at a curtain of rain. The air smelled wet and cold, tanged with salt. He put his light on the hall table and threw the blanket over her.

"Did you see which way he went?"

"I didn't see or hear him. Something woke me, the storm I think, about an hour ago. I couldn't get back to sleep until I'd looked in on him. His bed was empty and cold. I came down and went outside a little way, but there was no sign of him."

"So you don't know how long he's been gone?"

"No, but he doesn't usually go very far. Most of the time he just stands looking out to sea." She fought back a sob. "Tonight I couldn't see him."

"Go and wait for me inside."

She nodded, too consumed by worry to thank him. Not that he minded. It was a filthy night and a man in Sir Edward's state of health should not be out in it. Dan pulled up his collar, twitched down his hat and went outside. She pulled the door shut behind him. He heard the latch click as he moved deeper into the night.

The wind gathered handfuls of rain and flung them against him. It took a few moments for his eyes to adjust to the dark. When they did, all he saw was the outline of swaying trees, crouching clumps of undergrowth, and ahead of him, the roiling grey Strait.

He had no idea which way Sir Edward had gone, so he took the route he had taken last time. He skidded on the wet grass, floundered in mud, slithered on leaves and twigs brought down by the wind. The muddy ditch at the foot of the hill had become a churning stream. He reached the shore, felt the sand give beneath his boots, the coldness of water welling over his feet, the slipperiness of stones and seaweed. He looked left and right along the strand. Nothing stirred, save the water.

He threw a look of dislike at the Strait, always there, always making its presence known, always visible. The moon had set, and the sky was full of troubled clouds. A good night for smugglers, he thought, but there were no boats on the water, or at least none he could see.

He decided to try a zig-zag sweep back up the incline. He inched his way, scouring the darkness, pausing every now and again to listen. Nothing except the wind and the rain, gusting, pattering, rustling, gurgling. He shook his head, spraying drops of water from the brim of his hat.

A noise, something like a long sigh. He stopped, one knee bent to steady himself on the sloping ground, straining his eyes and ears. The hair on the back of his neck bristled. Was someone close by? Instinctively he drew out his pistol.

Again he thought he heard a sigh, but it was hard to be sure with the wind gusting around him. He moved forward, halted after three steps, listened, took three more steps, halted, listened, scanned the trees. Gradually a shape began to form between the trunks, a shape that was not the bole of a tree. Not a standing man either, but a huddled form lying on the ground.

Dan ran the last few steps and dropped to his knees by the crumpled figure. It was Sir Edward, sleeping where he had fallen. His bare feet and legs, washed by the rain, gleamed pale in the darkness. He wore nothing but a nightshirt which was plastered to him. Dan put his pistol on the ground and pulled off his coat.

"Sir Edward! Wake up, sir, and put this on."

He grasped the man's shoulder and turned him over. Sir Edward's head lolled against the grass and leaves. His face was white, his left eye socket a deep pit, his right eye staring into the writhing branches overhead. A deep gash ran across his neck and the rainwater ran red.

The house blazed with lights and activity. Lady Charlotte was in the parlour with Mrs Jenkins, still wrapped in the blanket

Dan had given her. In the kitchen, the cook made tea and the maids served brandy to the soaked, silent men whose duty it had been to carry in the body. One of the grooms had ridden to Ty Coed to fetch Captain Williams, and Reverend Lloyd Pryce had already been summoned. The rest of the servants sat around the table in horrified silence, and for once the cook did not shoo them out of her way. The scullery maid, Mary, had been sent to warm water in the copper for washing the master when "they" had finished with him.

"They" – Dan, Evans and Doctor Hughes – had opened one of the rooms at the front of the house and laid the body on a clean sheet on a workman's trestle table, with another sheet folded at Sir Edward's feet. Dan had closed Sir Edward's eye and now he lay like all the dead, no matter how violent their end, as if in sleep, his mouth set in the faint smile caused by the tightening of his skin.

"He's seen his Maker," one of the men had said of that smile as they laid the body down and the servants had backed out of the room, hats in hand, eyes brimming.

Hughes cut away the sodden nightshirt, revealing the full extent of the injuries Sir Edward had received on board the *Ardent* at Camperdown. His left side and arm were scarred by fire.

"Lady Charlotte woke at around one," Dan said, "found his bed empty, went to look for him, and woke me about an hour later. It was three o'clock by the time I found him, so he'd already been lying out there for at least two hours. He was certainly cold to the touch."

Hughes nodded. "Given the weather and the fact that he was only wearing a nightshirt, it would be hard to tell how long he had been there just from how cold the body felt. The jaw is already beginning to stiffen, though. I'd say he's been dead a few hours."

"Long enough for the murderer to be long gone," Dan said.

He most likely did not see his murderer, he thought. The wound had been dealt from behind, just like Bevan's. There were no other injuries and no sign of a struggle, again just like Bevan. He met Evans's eyes above the table.

"Watcyn Jones," the constable said.

"It looks that way," Dan agreed.

Footsteps ran along the corridor and the door opened without the ceremony of a knock. Stephen Lloyd Pryce swept in. He hesitated, his affronted eye taking in the doctor, the Bow Street men, and the naked figure on the table.

"Have you no respect, Hughes? Leaving my brother uncovered, exposed to the common gaze, an object to satisfy the idle curiosity of strangers?"

Dan turned his common gaze on the outraged clergyman. "I think you know full well who we are, Reverend, and that it is our job to find the man who murdered your brother."

"Which surely does not necessitate subjecting him to these indignities," Pryce retorted. "There is no doubt of the murderer's identity and you should be at your work looking for him, not satisfying low tastes for spectacle."

"We need to examine the body to learn what we can about how and when your brother died."

"One glance is sufficient to tell you how he died." The reverend blanched as he gave that glance. "And as for the when, it was during the night, and you should have been on the villain's trail hours ago."

"Come, Reverend Pryce, this is not fair or reasonable," said Doctor Hughes. "Of course these professional matters are difficult for the family, but I assure you, as your brother's physician, that he has been treated with every respect by the officers. It was Mr Foster who found him and he immediately covered him up with his own coat." He looked at Dan. "And I believe the examination is complete."

"I've seen all I need to see," Dan confirmed.

The doctor took up the folded sheet from the end of the table and covered Sir Edward. He stood there for a moment, head bowed.

"Now I must see Lady Charlotte," he said.

"And I shall start making the funeral and testamentary arrangements," Lloyd Pryce said.

The business side of death meant different things to different people. It could be a comfort, or a distasteful or wearisome necessity. It could be all absorbing or something they thought about only when wills, trusts, conveyances and undertakers' bills were thrust under their noses. In some cases, it could be a barely disguised pleasure. Dan had a suspicion that for the Reverend Lloyd Pryce, it fell into the last category.

When the doctor had gone to the parlour, and the rector to sit at his brother's desk in the library, Dan looked out of the tall sash window. The rain had stopped. The air had the fresh glow that rain leaves behind it and shafts of sunlight played on the peaks of Snowdonia.

He said, "Let's go and take a look outside."

Evans blew out the candles, which had faded as the room grew light, and they went out.

Dan had promised Lady Charlotte that he would not tell anyone about Sir Edward's night-time wandering, and he knew that even after her husband's death, she would wish that secret kept. Perhaps especially after death: her husband's heroic reputation was all he had left now.

"It looks," Dan said, "as if Sir Edward heard a noise and came outside to investigate."

"I don't think so," answered Evans.

"What do you mean?"

"Well, he was a laudanum addict, wasn't he?"

"What makes you think he took laudanum?"

"I spotted it the first evening we were here. One minute he was fine, then all of a sudden he was in the grip of a debilitating pain, and an hour or two later he was well again. There's not much can take away a man's suffering that quickly. With those injuries, he'd have needed it. I expect that's why he started taking it, and then he couldn't manage without it. He'd need his drops in the morning, at night, and more during the day when the pain flared up. I doubt he'd have been capable of noticing much at all by the time he went to bed."

It certainly explained a lot about Sir Edward's behaviour. "Then how do you think he got outside?"

"Sir Edward was a somnambulist."

"A what?"

"When he was in one of his trances he walked in his sleep. Why else would he be out here without his shoes or coat? And what man would leave his bed to investigate a suspicious noise without taking a pistol with him?"

"You're sharper than you look, Evans. But you're not to mention this to anyone else. Lady Charlotte asked me to keep her husband's secret, and I gave my word. Sir Edward was a good, brave man and there's no need to smirch his memory."

"I would never say anything that would embarrass Lady Charlotte. But I thought you knew about his weakness."

"I knew he suffered greatly, and about the sleepwalking. I hadn't realised about the laudanum, but it makes sense now you mention it."

They reached the spot where Sir Edward had fallen.

"You can't expect to find anything now," said Evans. "Not after all this rain."

"Maybe not, but we'd only be doing half a job if we didn't look."

They circled the area, scanning the ground, but found no footsteps, no discarded weapon, and because so many twigs had been snapped and scattered by the wind, no trail to follow. The constable turned an "I told you so" face up to Dan, who had come to a halt on higher ground a little above him.

"Sir Edward was taller than Jones," Dan said. "So Jones must have been standing about here when he killed him."

He looked down at the area around the tree roots. A speck of white fluttered against the bark. He crouched and plucked a few white cotton threads from it.

"This must be from Sir Edward's nightgown."

"Perhaps he was sitting against the tree when Jones found him."

"But how did Jones know he was here?"

"He was lying in wait for him."

Dan looked back towards the top of the rise. "You can't see the house from here, so there wouldn't be any point lying in wait at this spot. Jones must have seen Sir Edward come out and followed him. We'll work our way back up, see if we find anything on the way."

"But what are you looking for? We already know Jones was here."

"Juries like evidence they can look at. And if it comes to it, so do I."

Evans strode off, but Dan called him back and set a slow, sweeping pace. After another fruitless search, they came out on to the lawn facing the scaffolding.

"Jones couldn't have known Sir Edward was going to sleepwalk last night," Dan said, "so why was he here?"

"What else could it have been for, but to try and get in?"

"But what was he planning to do if he did get in? Murder Sir Edward in his bed? Start a fire? Rob the place?"

"He was out for revenge one way or another. 'The squires and justices and officers.' That's what he said in the gaol."

"And now we've had an officer and a squire."

Dan looked across the Strait. The smuggler's friend, the murderer's ally. A man could arrive by boat, come ashore, commit a murder, leave by boat, and who could follow his tracks? And when he was ready, he could make his way to Ireland or France any time he liked.

How was he to follow a man when he had no idea which way he had gone? The way he always did in such cases. With the day now fully broken, he would start making enquiries in the surrounding district, knocking on doors, stopping passers-by, calling into taverns. Someone might have seen or heard something during the night. First, though, they should finish here.

"We'll check for signs of an attempted break-in and make sure all is secure," he said.

They made a circuit of the house. None of the windows had been tampered with, and there were no footprints. They were almost back where they had started when they heard a hoarse bellow followed by a woman's scream.

"It came from the house. Come on, Evans!"

# CHAPTER TWENTY-FIVE

Dan and Evans pushed through the servants clustered outside the room where Sir Edward's body lay. A quick glance revealed the chaos inside: a candlestick broken in a corner, a hat trampled upon, a smashed bowl lying in a pool of water. Captain Williams, still in riding boots and coat, stood by the trestle table, tearing at his dark curls and uttering groans that seemed to issue from the root of his soul. Lady Charlotte hung on his arm, weeping and pleading with him to come away.

"Calm yourself, sir, calm yourself," urged Doctor Hughes. "You are doing no good giving way like this, and you are distressing Lady Charlotte."

Williams turned to Dan. "Was it Jones, Foster?"

"It looks that way. I'm sorry."

"I will kill him."

It was not Jones dead Dan wanted, but Jones alive and at the Old Bailey to stand trial. However, he did not argue with the captain's grief. At that moment he was not sure that if it fell to him to stay the captain's hand, he would do it.

"You should go now," he said. "Sir Edward shouldn't be left here like this."

Williams nodded and allowed Lady Charlotte to lead him away.

"Go back to your work," Doctor Hughes snapped at the servants.

Weeping and whispering, they shuffled off. The doctor followed Williams and Lady Charlotte into the parlour. Evans would have gone after them, but Dan said, "We've got work to do. We'll take a couple of horses and start looking for witnesses."

By now, the workmen had arrived and clustered outside in shocked silence. The death was not only a calamity for Sir Edward's family. There would be no work that day, nor for many days to come, and that meant no wages. There was nothing for it but to put on their hats and walk home, thinking of how to break the news to their wives.

Dan and Evans had just passed through the gate on to the lane when they saw Llewellyn and two of his riding officers approaching. They drew rein and waited for them.

"Good day, Officer Foster," Llewellyn said. "Though there's little good about it. I thought you might like some help. I'd have brought more men, but the others are not yet in from patrol up at Traeth Coch."

"Any help is gratefully accepted," Dan said. "News must travel fast on Anglesey."

"Doctor Hughes sent me word. I gather he is already here."

"He's with Lady Charlotte and Captain Williams."

"I thought the captain would come with us."

"He's taken the death hard," Dan said. Llewellyn was too tactful to press for more detail and Dan continued, "There are similarities between Bevan's death and Sir Edward's so we're working on the assumption that the killer was Watcyn Jones."

"Makes sense. Any idea where Jones went?"

"None. I thought I'd ride north towards his home ground where he might find friends. But now we've more men, it might be useful to split into two search parties."

Llewellyn agreed and they arranged to meet back at Henllys later.

Dan and Evans rode at a slow pace along the coastal path

towards Penmon. There were signs of the island's history wherever Dan looked; Williams and Evans had talked about them on the way to Parys Mine. Circular ridges in the ground marked the site of ancient huts, groups of stones were temples, smooth mounds contained burial chambers. They passed a flat plateau some way off on their left, its steep sides encircled by the remains of defensive walls which were now a network of tumbled stones, overgrown with gorse and trees which created countless grottoes and dells. There were a hundred and one places on Anglesey for a man on the run to hide, Dan thought.

Passers-by were few and far between, and they came upon only one or two lonely cottages occupied by farmers, quarry workers or fishermen's families. No one they spoke to had seen or heard anything: no ships lying off shore, no row boats pulling up on a beach, no shadowy figure fleeing through the night.

They reached a tangled area of woodland from the middle of which rose a round-topped hill crowned with the remains of a castle, inaccessible through the dense vegetation choking the slopes. From there, their way took them past a deer park and on to the eastern tip of the island where they found an ancient church and farmhouse surrounded by roofless ruins that were all that remained of a priory. The wife emerged from her dairy to speak to them, but had nothing to tell them, nor had her dairymaid. Two wide-eyed children stood in the kitchen doorway staring at the visitors and scuttled inside when Evans winked at them.

They dismounted and searched the outbuildings and ruins. Dan poked his head inside a dovecot of ancient grey stone, its roof intact. He recoiled from the smell of heaped up bones and bird droppings. Even the most desperate fugitive would think twice about hiding in there.

Outside, he was joined by Evans, who had been looking in the barn. They had been inside every building, but there was a walled area they had not explored.

"What's up there?"

"A hermit's cell. It's why the priory is here."

They skirted a pond overhung by trees, choked by reeds and coated in sickly green weed, and walked in single file up a narrow path. They passed through a rectangular stone doorway into a muddy enclosure around a low cliff face, twenty or thirty feet high. A small, roofed building stood against the cliff, the area around it paved with uneven stones. Dan unlatched the wooden door, which swung back easily on its hinges. A blast of cold air hit him and the flames of half a dozen candles flickered in the draught. He was about to step inside when Evans tapped his arm and pointed at the ground.

Most of the stone-flagged floor of the tiny chamber was taken up by a rectangular aperture above a clear stream of water which ran almost soundlessly over mossy rocks and shining pebbles. Coins glinted in the barely discernible ripples. The water was surrounded by stone benches. Above these, the candles burned in shallow niches; others had long since gone out and wax accumulated over the years streaked the walls. There were small bunches of flowers on the shelves, some faded and dried, others fresh, along with a strange assortment of objects: buttons, brooches, strips of lace, a pewter mug, a wooden doll with jointed limbs, ribbons, an apron, a baby's bonnet and other small tokens.

Footsteps approached along the path. Dan recognised the mistress's brisk voice.

"She says it's St Seiriol's Well," Evans said in answer to Dan's questioning glance. "This was the saint's hermitage. Those are offerings people bring."

Dan looked at the small, sad gifts. How many, he wondered, had been left in gratitude for sickness cured, how many only in hope?

"She's here in case you want to drink the water," Evans added. "You have to pay her."

The woman had more to add. Evans humoured her with non-committal remarks, but she did not take the hint and go away. Dan recognised the name Sir Edward Lloyd Pryce.

"What did she say about Sir Edward?"

"The sort of nonsense these people talk. That if he had come here, his face would have been healed and his sight restored. She says Mrs Jenkins visited and took some of the water away to give him, without his knowledge, but it didn't have any effect. She says that's because you have to come here to drink it. And if he had, I expect she'd say his eye didn't grow back because he drank it on the wrong day, or forgot to walk three times around the well before leaving."

The woman gestured at Dan.

"What's she saying?"

"She says that you should drink some. It will heal your cuts and bruises."

Understanding that Dan knew what she was saying, she addressed him directly, her face full of concern, her voice urgent and pressing.

"Now what?"

Evans translated. "*You should drink the water. It will mend your hurts, even the ones that cannot be seen.*"

She gazed earnestly at Dan and repeated her words. When it was clear that they had no intention of giving her their custom, her disappointment seemed to have a deeper cause than the mere loss of her fee. She shook her head at Dan with a look as tragic as if she were sitting at his death bed, and left.

There was nothing of interest in the chamber. Evans set off along the path and Dan stayed to fasten the door. *It will mend your hurts, even the ones that cannot be seen.* Cuts and bruises soon went, but there were other pains that did not heal so easily. Evans was already out of sight. On an impulse, Dan went back inside. He crouched beside the spring, cupped his hand in the cool stream, and drank.

Back at the house, the woman offered them some milk, which they accepted. Evans handed over a few coins, so their visit was not without profit for her. They remounted and resumed their search. They followed the route around the coast for several miles, then retraced their steps some of the way before turning inland to travel back to Henllys.

Back at the hall, they found Llewellyn and his men in the kitchen, drinking ale and flirting with the maids. They had nothing to report and, having gazed hopefully into their drained mugs for several moments, put them down with a sigh and left. Lady Charlotte had shut herself up in her room and would see no one but Mrs Jenkins. Captain Williams had gone home, and with no family requiring a cooked meal, Mr Davies told them that a cold supper would be served in the dining room for them. Dan looked at the fire and the foods laid out ready on the kitchen table in front of it: bread, cheese, meat, fruit, puddings and other good things. The dining room was grand, but not so inviting – nor perhaps so informative – as the kitchen.

"Why don't we save you the trouble and eat here?" he asked.

Evans raised his eyebrows, but Mrs Parry, the cook, was pleased by the suggestion. It not only showed that the London men were not stand-offish, but presented an opportunity to find out all about the investigation. Not that her curiosity profited by it. Dan refused to say anything about the case apart from, "It's early days yet."

Dan, Evans, Mr Davies the butler, Mrs Parry, and the housemaid gathered at one end of the table and chatted in English. The rest of the servants huddled lower down and talked in Welsh. Mrs Parry and Mr Davies were too preoccupied with their visitors to check the staff's gossip, which Dan saw was of a sensational nature. There was much whispering and tittering, gasping, jaw-dropping, and rounding of the eyes. It was hardly surprising, Dan thought, when their master lay in the upper regions of the house waiting for his coffin.

Mrs Parry's words brought his attention back to the conversation at his end of the table.

"Anyone would think he was already master of Henllys."

"Now, now, Mrs Parry," Mr Davies said, "the reverend has every right. He is master now."

"And intends to make sure of it!" she retorted. "He spent the whole day in the library going through the deed boxes and papers, and his brother not yet in his grave. I shan't stay, I can tell you that for nothing."

"Nor shall I!" echoed the housemaid.

"It's Lady Charlotte who is to be pitied now," Mrs Parry continued. "I don't doubt she'll have to go back to her father's house in Merthyr, poor lady, and it's said he's a mean, ill-tempered old man." She dabbed her eyes with her apron, and the housemaid dabbed her eyes with hers. Mrs Parry sniffed. "I expect it'll please Mrs Jenkins to go back to—" she put on an affected voice "—'what I'm accustomed to', if it pleases no one else."

The housemaid laughed loudly.

"Come, Mrs Parry, Mrs Jenkins is a good servant to her mistress," said Mr Davies.

They were interrupted by one of the maids at the end of the table whose voice had risen to an indiscreet screech. The other girls screamed with scandalous delight, the boot boy guffawed, and the head groom raised his face from his mug and capped her remark with one of his own, delivered with a wink and a leer.

"And that's none of your business, Miss Saucy-face!" Mrs Parry snapped at the noisy maid. She switched to Welsh to deliver a scolding while Mr Davies aimed a few choice words of his own at the groom, and the housemaid looked stern. The servants hung their heads, twisted their fingers in their laps, shuffled their feet, and smirked at one another when they thought no one could see.

"What's all the fuss about?" Dan asked Evans while all this was going on.

"It's just servants' tittle-tattle."

"I thought we'd already settled that tittle-tattle can be useful. What's it about?"

Evans hesitated. "They wondered if Lady Charlotte will remarry."

"And who do they think she might marry?"

"They don't name anyone."

Evans looked away shiftily. Had he kept something back? If a name had been spoken, Dan would have understood it. Had it been hinted at instead, and had the constable chosen not to pass it on?

"I don't know how they're brought up these days," Mrs Parry grumbled. "Forever prattling and prying into things that don't concern them."

"And it's not just the young ones," Mr Davies answered, looking at the groom, who comforted himself by emptying his mug and reaching for the beer jug.

The scullery maid, who had not eaten with the others, flitted around gathering up dirty dishes, her heavy skirts dragging after her and her draggled black curls springing from beneath her cap. Leaning across the table, she brushed against the prattler-in-chief. Having endured her own scolding, the maid was happy to have someone to berate in her turn. She screwed up her face, drew back as if the touch was contagious, and trounced the cowering girl. Her companions threw in a few supporting insults of their own. Their victim snatched up her tray and ran back to the scullery.

Mrs Parry and Mr Davies took no interest in the scene, which made Dan think it was not an unusual one. He wondered what the scullery maid had done to make herself so unpopular.

"What's her story?" he asked.

"Her!" Mrs Parry sneered. "That's Mary, Sionett Thomas's child, and it's a wonder she didn't leave the island before the babe was born. Sionett lives in a cottage overlooking the Strait, a few miles from here. Some say she's a witch because she has a bit of herb-lore, and like the fools they are, they sneak to her door for cures and potions." She looked at the housemaid, who blushed and squirmed. "As if a potion could snare a certain young bricklayer!"

"I never thought it would work!" the housemaid protested.

"She never cared what anyone thought, that one," the cook resumed. "She turned up her nose at all the island boys, did Miss High-and-Mighty, and then she fell for a coal-black sailor who didn't stay around long enough to welcome his daughter into this vale of tears. You can't look at Mary Thomas without being put in mind of it. Brazen, I call it. I can't see the reverend keeping her on with her dusky face flaunting sin and wrongdoing. And good riddance to her, I say. The girl's a mope and clumsy with it. Yes, there'll be a lot of changes when Reverend Lloyd Pryce takes over. You'd think he would at least try to hide how much he's looking forward to being owner of Henllys."

"He was always jealous of his brother, from a child, wasn't he?" said the housemaid.

"He was. I shan't stay, I can tell you that for nothing," Mrs Parry said.

"Nor shall I!" declared the housemaid.

# CHAPTER TWENTY-SIX

"Mr Madoc will see you now," the chief clerk said.

Dan and Evans followed the creaky old man through an impressive door behind the counters. The two under clerks, who had feigned counting notes and weighing coin while listening to Evans make the introductions, stared shamelessly. It was not every day Bow Street Runners turned up in the Caernarfon branch of Williams & Company's bank.

They entered the manager's office under the gaze of two pairs of eyes belonging to the occupants of two chairs set side by side behind a large desk. One was Mr Madoc, a portly man with a round face, pug nose, soft brown eyes, and a short queue wig. The other was a plump short-haired dog with a sharp muzzle and pointed ears. The man rose to greet them, while the dog remained seated.

Madoc waved his hand. "Please, take a seat, Officers. You don't mind Mint, do you? He doesn't bark or bite."

Dan sat down in the chair in front of the desk. Evans, having looked in vain for another, resigned himself to standing. Dan produced the warrants signed by the Home Secretary, Lord Portland. Madoc examined the documents, the dog looking over his elbow, and when both were satisfied handed them back. Dan returned them to his pocket book and gave a brief account of the murders on Anglesey.

"Sir Edward Lloyd Pryce and Commander Bevan both slain by the same hand?" exclaimed Madoc. "That is dreadful to hear. Sir Edward was held in high esteem, and the commander came of an old, though no longer a wealthy, Shrewsbury family."

"It's Bevan we've come about," Dan said. "Did he bank with you?"

"Yes, he did."

"We need to look at his records."

Madoc screwed up his face. "I am not sure I can allow that. A client must have confidence that his affairs are kept confidential if he is to bank with us."

"Your client is beyond having confidence in anything, and I need to know about his affairs. It may be that he was involved in business that has a bearing on his death. If so, the information will help catch his killer."

Madoc thoughtfully tickled Mint's ear. "He was a commander in the revenue service, was he not?"

"He was."

The bank manager drew his conclusions, picked up a handbell and gave it a brisk shake. When the old clerk reappeared, he asked him to bring Bevan's deed box.

"You are sure you will not take any refreshment? A glass of Madeira, perhaps?" asked Madoc while they waited.

"Y—"

Dan interrupted Evans. "No, thank you. I just want to see the documents."

The box arrived within a few minutes, a labelled key inserted in the lock. Madoc put it on the table in front of him and opened it. He and Mint peered inside.

"Let me see…he had close on one thousand pounds in his account." Madoc laid the paper to one side and extracted another. "An annuity of one hundred pounds settled on his mother." He placed this on top of the first. "Five hundred pounds in government stocks." Another sheet added to the pile. "And the controlling share in the *Paycock*."

"The what?"

"The *Paycock*, as our Irish friends have it." He glanced waggishly at Dan over the sheet. "A cutter called the *Peacock*."

"And who are his partners in that venture?"

"Captain Dominic O'Flaherty. Seamus O'Donnell, tea merchant of Dublin. Brennan O'Dooley, gent. Darragh Tyrrell, printer." The manager tittered. "And Sir Lucius O'Trigger too, no doubt." He met Dan's gaze and his smile disappeared. "Just my facetiousness, Officer."

"It's a character in one of Mr Sheridan's plays," Evans said.

Dan flashed an exasperated glance at the constable. "Could I have a copy of this agreement and a note of the other assets?"

"Of course." Madoc rang the bell again and gave the order to the senior clerk.

They waited in silence, Madoc's attempt at small talk having fallen on deaf ears. Mint sighed, lay down on his cushion and went to sleep. The clerk returned, Dan pocketed the papers and thanked the manager.

He and Evans went back to the Uxbridge Arms where they had left the carriage they had hired from the George at Bangor after crossing the Strait from Gallows Point in Beaumaris. It was a new hotel outside the town walls, and on the expensive side. They ordered dinner and, while they ate, looked over the banking documents.

"So this is where he hid the money," Evans said. "And here's the proof he was running the operation." The constable tapped the partnership agreement relating to the *Peacock*. "Captain Williams was right."

"It must have been Captain O'Flaherty and his crew who rescued Jones," Dan said. He gathered up the notes and pulled his watch from his pocket. "Go and tell them to get the horses harnessed and I'll pay the bill."

Evans snatched up his hat and coat and ran out. Dan settled the account and went outside. The chaise was ready, the driver lounging against one of the wheels, smoking a pipe.

"Where's the constable?"

The man nodded in the direction of the entrance to the stable courtyard. Evans stood inside the archway, talking to one of the maids. She had a shawl over her shoulders, as if she had just been out on an errand. Dan was about to call him away from his latest fleeting conquest when the girl handed him a package. Evans slipped it into his pocket and gave her some money. She counted it and gave him a satisfied smile. Evans turned away and Dan hastily found a spot of mud on his boots which needed scraping off.

"There you are," said Dan, looking up with feigned surprise. "It's time to go."


"The *Peacock*, you say?" Llewellyn scratched his chin. "Then we're in luck. The repairs on the *Viper* have been completed and she'll be going out later today. I'll let the crew know they're to board the smuggling vessel and bring her in if they come up with her."

It was Thursday morning and Dan and Evans were in the Beaumaris Customs House, where they had come to consult with Llewellyn. Captain Williams, who had got over the first shock of Sir Edward's death and was now more determined than ever to help bring Jones to justice, had accompanied them.

When they had left Henllys that morning, there were already visitors gathering to pay their respects. Sir Edward's body had been washed and prepared for burial by the women sent by the undertaker, coffined and placed on a bier in one of the upper rooms. The coffin was covered with a black sheet and surrounded with candles, and the room and staircase had been hung with black drapes. The funeral was to take place on

Saturday, when the murdered man would be laid in the family vault at his brother's church.

Llewellyn gazed glumly at the Anglesey map on the wall opposite his desk. "The men will take it hard. We – they – had hoped the commander did no more than keep back a few packets of tobacco. When the King's warehouses are full to bursting with seized contraband, and there's little in the way of reward for the risks we run, who wouldn't forgive a man for rewarding himself every now and again?"

One glance at Dan told Llewellyn that he would not. "Not that that excuses it, of course," he amended, "and now it turns out that Bevan was in for more than a bit of baccy. The commander was running the show all along."

"It's the obvious conclusion," Dan said.

Llewellyn sighed. He placed his hands on the desk and pushed himself to his feet. "I'll go and speak to the cutter commander."

Dan, Evans and Williams followed him out. The *Viper* lay at her quay in front of the Customs House. She was smaller than Dan had expected, with only one mast and a couple of swivel guns. A few crewmen were loading water barrels, food, muskets and ammunition on board, though not with any sense of urgency. They were in no hurry to get underway.

An ungainly figure rolled along the quay, puffing like a grampus. It was the pockmarked turnkey from the gaol.

"Officer Foster, Officer Foster!" he wheezed. "Mr Braillard sent me to find you. We've just received word from Parys Mine."

He paused, partly for breath and partly for effect.

"They've found a body up there, and they think it's Watcyn Jones."

# CHAPTER TWENTY-SEVEN

Elin Jones twisted the ends of her shawl in her work-roughened hands. "Hugh the Store said they'd heard the fairies under the mountain knocking. It was for him." She looked at Dan across the cart in which Watcyn Jones's sheeted figure lay. "It was you English hounded him to death. If you hadn't been chasing him, he'd never have had to hide up here."

"If he hadn't committed murder, I wouldn't have been after him," Dan said. "And if you'd told me when we first met where he was, maybe he wouldn't be like this now."

"What difference would that have made? You were taking him back to the halter. It's you who's killed him, one way or another. And I wouldn't have told you even if I'd known."

"You still claim you didn't know he was hiding on the mountain?" Williams demanded.

She glared at the captain. "It's true."

"What I want to know," Owen Jones said, "is who's going to pay to bury him? Whose fault is it he's dead?"

"It's his own fault or no one's," Mr Ward said, when Evans had translated this. "Stumbling around in the dark where he shouldn't have been, a trip, a fall, and smash." Elin flinched. "Smash," the surgeon repeated. "Accidental death."

Smelling of spirits and with shaking hand, he'd taken less

than a minute to examine the body. The conclusion he had reached seemed too obvious to doubt, though.

"That's enough from you, Jones," Samuel Brooks said. "You can go now. I'll arrange to have the body brought down to you later."

Elin and Owen Jones moved away, the father still brooding over the injustice of having to pay his son's funeral costs, the daughter with stiff steps, set face, and tears held at bay.

Dan took the brass button he had found near Thomas Bevan's body out of his pocket and pulled back the bloodied sheet. Wat's clothes had been torn and dirtied by the fall, but the gap and hanging threads in the row of buttons on his blue jacket were clearly visible.

"It's a match," said Evans.

Dan put the button back in his pocket. He grasped Wat's chin and rolled his head from side to side. He rubbed his thumb over the yellow marks above his jaw.

"Bruising on his chin," he said.

Ward hiccupped. "I shouldn't think there's a part of him that isn't bruised and broken. They come up after an accident like this rattling like a piece of shattered porcelain."

Dan lifted Wat's hands, turned them over and examined the cut and bruised fingers. He pushed the cuffs back, noted the marks around his wrists and the scratches on his arms, and pulled the sleeve down. His eyes flickered up and down the body, from the bloodied head to the soles of the scuffed boots, which were covered in pale dust and traces of sand. In the pockets he found a pinchbeck watch with the flashy seal still attached to the silver chain, a few pennies, a stub of candle, a tinderbox and, in a deep inside pocket, a knife in a leather scabbard. He pulled this out and examined the blade. It had been wiped, but not very thoroughly, and there were streaks of red around the hilt.

Williams shuddered. "The weapon he used to kill Ned and Bevan."

"I'd say it was," Dan agreed. He handed it to Evans for safekeeping. "Who found him?"

Brooks pointed at three miners standing, hats in hands, a little way off. "They did."

"I need to see the place."

"Eh? Is that really necessary?" demanded the mine manager. "The longer you are here, the longer it will take to get the people back to work."

Dan looked at the men, women and children clustered around the entrance to the mine yard, enthusiastically interpreting to one another the words they could not hear and the actions they could not see.

"I need to know what he was doing there."

"But you already know that. He was a fugitive. There are abandoned workings and shafts all over the mountain where a man could safely hide away."

Dan took no notice of this. "The head of the gang that found him can take us."

Brooks sighed. "Be as quick as you can." He beckoned to one of the three miners. "You – Rhys Gwyn."

Gwyn pointed at himself. "*Pwy – fi?*" He glanced at his companions, shrugged and strode over to the cart. He listened impassively while Evans explained what was required, and merely nodded when the constable had finished.

They set off. The crowd shrank back from them as if afraid of the touch of men whose business was death. They left the mine yard behind, passed the copper ladies' shed with its deserted benches, and beyond that the partly cleared remains of the burned storehouse.

The path led them slightly upwards. To the right a little below them lay the rectangular precipitation pools. The pump house tower landmarked a ridge in the distance. They veered to the left and walked until the main working was a long way behind them. Here, where the silence over the desolate landscape was more profound, the sense of desertion intensified.

The track curved round a waste tip. Gwyn stopped and pointed downwards. A narrow path dropped away from the edge of the valley.

Evans translated. "We go down there. There's an abandoned working where they've dug out all the copper near the surface. A few caves have been excavated, and there are a couple of shafts running into the side of the hill, all thought to be worked out. No one had been here for years until Gwyn and his partners decided to put in a low bid and take another look. They were going to start work here today."

The path was steep and the coating of dust and pebbles sliding under their feet made it treacherous. They hugged the side of the cliff, the way winding down until, when they looked back, the surface was a long way above them. A strange pointed formation appeared in the valley bottom below them. Drawing closer, Dan saw it was a high pyramid of rock shaped by miners' picks.

They reached level ground and came to a halt by the pyramid. It stood in the middle of a narrow depression confined on three sides by cliffs and on the fourth by a tumble of rock. Its silence and enclosure made it a sinister place, suitable for dark deeds, and one the nightwatchmen certainly never frequented during their half-hearted patrols.

Gwyn pointed at the rusty splashes near the bottom of the path.

"He must have been on his way to or from his hiding place," said Williams, "and lost his footing in the dark."

"It's likely." Dan crouched down and examined the spot. When he had finished, he stood up and began to circle away from the bloodstains. Occasionally he stooped to turn over a rock or brush away dust.

By now, the constable was used to Dan's fondness for

carrying out minute and futile searches. With a sigh, he joined in. Williams followed his example. Gwyn stood by, watching them as if nothing the English did could surprise him.

"There's nothing," the captain said after a while.

"No," Dan answered. He scanned the cliffs. "But where was he hiding?"

Gwyn, looking from one to the other, guessed what puzzled them. He jerked his head at the wall of rock on the opposite side of the hollow.

"He says there's a cave there," said Evans.

Dan squinted. "I can't see anything."

"Me neither," said Williams.

Gwyn beckoned. *Follow me.*

He led them towards a narrow vertical crack in the rock. It was about six feet long, but nowhere near wide enough for a man to pass through. Nevertheless, he strode on without slowing his pace. Then he vanished.

Williams laughed. "I'll be damned!"

What looked like a fissure turned out to be a fold in the rock. They slipped after Gwyn and found him standing at the entrance to a tunnel. He took a candle and tinderbox out of his pocket. By the flickering light he provided, they saw that the passage sloped downwards and was wide enough for two men to walk side by side. Gwyn held up the candle and they followed its fragile flame, which looked as if it might succumb to the currents of cold air at any minute and leave them lost in the dark. At the bottom, the tunnel opened out into a wide chamber.

The captain whistled, the piercing sound echoing through the shadows. "Looks like this is the place."

In the dim light they made out the outlines of barrels and crates stacked against the wall.

"*Duw!*" Gwyn stared, open-mouthed, at the contraband.

"There's a lantern on the floor with a candle still in it," said Evans.

Gwyn, quickly recovering his composure, lit it.

Evans rotated the beam around the cave. "I'd say there's at least ten casks of brandy. The same of rum."

"Here's genever, eight casks," said Williams. "And a couple of baskets of wine."

Evans rummaged through an open crate. "Tobacco." He handed one of the packets to Dan.

"From Nantes," said Dan. "The same warehouse as the packets in Bevan's room."

"So this is where he stored the run goods," Evans said.

Dan threw the packet back into the crate. He walked around the cavern, directing Evans where to shine the light. There were plenty of footprints in the dust, but they were too muddled to be of any use.

He had just finished his inspection when the lantern sputtered and went out.

"Time to go. Is the tunnel we came down the only way in?"

Gwyn confirmed that it was.

"Ask him when he was last here," Dan said to Evans.

The answer came back: about a week ago. So the contraband had come in within the last few days, while the revenue men had been busy with the hunt for Jones.

"Evans, go and get Brooks to despatch a message to Mr Llewellyn to bring his men at once, then come back here. Make sure no one gets wind of the find; it might be too much of a temptation. We'll stay and keep an eye on things. You can stay too, Gwyn," he added, in case the miner had friends he wanted to share the news with.

They followed Gwyn out of the cave and into the welcome daylight. Evans set off at a run to the mine manager's office. Dan, the captain and Gwyn sat down with their backs to the cave. From here, they had a good view of Evans toiling up the path out of the valley.

Dan, looking about him, met Gwyn's eye. The miner looked

away. He did not like sitting under the gaze of a Bow Street Runner, that much was obvious. What was equally obvious was that he had not expected to find the baccy and spirits. Dan doubted he would have led them to the cave if he had known they were there.

"Well," said Williams, "it isn't the end we were looking for, but Jones got what he deserved. It feels like justice has been done."

"I don't think the Home Secretary or Sir William Addington will find the outcome so satisfying," Dan answered. "I was supposed to take him back to stand trial in London. I'll be lucky if I still have a job when I get home."

"Nonsense, man, don't be so dismal. You've exposed Bevan as the leader of a smuggling gang, found his cache of contraband, and thwarted a revolutionary plot by the way. I call that quite an achievement."

"And four men are dead because I let Jones slip through my fingers."

"For which no one can blame you. Volunteer Hudson was a casualty of the ambush which Bevan arranged. Jones killed Bevan, and why should anyone lose any sleep when rogues turn on one another and do the hangman's job for him? And no one could have predicted he would attack Ned on his own ground: a lonely road on a dark night would have been more in his line, and that we could have guarded against. As for Jones himself, I can hear Ned saying his fate was the working of Providence, and you can't deny that it was taken out of our hands."

"I can't deny that."

"Besides, you're looking at it all wrong. If Lord Portland and Sir William are disposed to make a fuss about it, you only need to remind them that Bevan was one of the government's own revenue officers. They'll soon get the hint that emphasising the positive outcomes will cause them less embarrassment than kicking up a fuss about an insignificant man like Jones."

"Maybe you're right."

"I am, and I daresay I'll get most of the magistrates on Anglesey to agree with me. It's going to look very odd if the local justices are singing your praises and the Home Secretary's threatening to dismiss you." Williams clapped Dan on the shoulder. "You should be congratulating yourself. I for one am glad Jones is dead and gone, with no chance of slipping through the noose because of some devious lawyer or half-baked jury. So should all scoundrels end, swiftly and surely."

Dan caught sight of someone moving down the path into the valley. He scrambled to his feet. "Here's the constable."

# CHAPTER TWENTY-EIGHT

"It's not such a big haul," Llewellyn said. "A few ankers of spirits, a bit of wine and tobacco."

He and his men had arrived to oversee the removal of the contraband. Under close watch of the revenue men, it was being carried away by miners loaned by Mr Brooks.

"Still," Llewellyn continued, "whatever it fetches at auction will put something into the revenue coffers. Not a bad hiding place, though. Hard of access, and unlikely to attract idle passers-by. Our smuggling friends will miss it."

"It would probably never have been found if Jones hadn't died here," Dan said.

"That was a stroke of luck – for us," Llewellyn agreed. "We can deliver his body to Coroner Hughes if you wish."

"Then I'll thank you and go and tell Lady Charlotte that we've found her husband's murderer," said Dan.

Lady Charlotte was in the library with her brother- and sister-in-law. Even in its pallor, Lady Charlotte's face had more vivacity than that of the thin, limp woman in drab clothes on the sofa beside her. Stephen Lloyd Pryce sat at Sir Edward's desk, estate papers spread out before him.

They arrived in time to hear the reverend say, "I would never have thought my brother would be so thoughtless."

Mrs Lloyd Pryce echoed her husband in a barely distinguishable lisp. "So very thoughtless!" She looked at her husband for encouragement and, having received it by a slight inclination of the head, stroked Lady Charlotte's lace-trimmed black silk sleeve for good measure.

"What is the matter?" asked Captain Williams.

"Nothing is the matter," Lady Charlotte replied, "save that Sir Edward has made me the sole beneficiary of his will with, of course, provision for trusts to be set up by Mr Cadwallader to administer the property, funds and investments on my behalf."

"Oh, my dear!" fluttered Mrs Lloyd Pryce, paling as so many unwomanly words fell from Charlotte's lips.

"That any husband who professed fondness for his wife would burden her in such a way!" cried the rector. "I would not do it."

"Indeed, you would not," said Mrs Lloyd Pryce with sudden animation.

"And, of course," he continued, squinting suspiciously at her, "I am perfectly prepared to take over the management of these complex affairs. I will ask Mr Cadwallader to draw up the necessary documents at once."

"And I have said there is no need for you to trouble yourself," said Lady Charlotte. "It was Sir Edward's wish and explicit direction that I should rely on his man of business, and that is what I shall do." She shook off Mrs Lloyd Pryce's comforting pats and stood up, her hands clasped tightly in front of her. "You have news, Mr Foster?"

"Pray, do not distress yourself, dear madam," cried the rector, rising also. "I will deal with this."

"Pray, my dear, do not," said Mrs Lloyd Pryce, pawing feebly at her sister-in-law's skirt.

"I do," Dan answered. "Watcyn Jones was found dead at Parys Mine this morning. It seems that he had been hiding in a remote part of the site, that he fell to his death during the night, and that his death was accidental."

"I tell you that He will avenge them speedily!" Lloyd Pryce exclaimed. "And so the wicked shall perish and transgressors shall be cut off!"

"It has certainly saved the trouble and expense of a trial," said Williams. "And so I suppose, Mr Foster, that your work here is done?"

"There is the matter of Jones's inquest," Dan said, "and we've been unable to identify the man who killed volunteer Hudson. Unless the revenue cutter seizes the *Peacock* and her crew in the next day or two, there's not much chance of it either. I shall ask Mr Llewellyn to send me word in London, but with every day that passes, the likelihood of finding the ship lessens."

"I should think you've scared the *Peacock* well away from the island, at least for a while yet," Williams said. "Thanks to you, the smugglers have lost their leader, contraband, and hiding place. It'll be a while before they recover from the disruption to their operations."

"I hope you and Mr Evans will remain at Henllys until your business is done," said Lady Charlotte. "To tell the truth, even though Jones is gone, it's reassuring to know you are here. The house has not felt as safe as it did since Sir Edward—" She broke off.

"My dear Lady Charlotte, of course you should not be left alone and unprotected," the reverend said. "Mrs Lloyd Pryce and I can move in at a moment's notice."

"I was thinking of employing a nightwatchman," she said. "Perhaps, Captain Williams, you could recommend someone?"

Dan decided to leave them to their discussions. "It's late in the day, but I'd like to have a word with the coroner if I can."

He beckoned Evans and the two set off on the short walk to Beaumaris.

The castle lay below them, the glittering Strait to the left with the flocks of oyster catchers probing the wet shore. Gently rolling meadows ran up to tree-lined slopes on their right. Sheep grazed on the bright grass, birds rustled in the hedgerow, rooks cawed, blackbirds hopped and pecked, a blue tit bobbed past. There was a sharp mewing sound and Dan spotted a buzzard circling above the treeline.

They walked in silence until they reached the high street and passed the castle, courthouse and gaol. Instead of continuing to Doctor Hughes's house on Church Street, Dan turned aside into the Bull. Evans, taken by surprise, bumped into him.

"Are we going in here? I thought we were going to see the coroner."

"That can wait. I need a coffee."

They found a table in a corner, out of earshot of the rest of the company. Dan put his hat on the windowsill and took a sip from his cup.

"So tell me, Evans, what do you make of it?"

The constable smiled. "I think the reverend is no match for Lady Charlotte."

"I agree. But I wasn't thinking of that. Did you notice anything about Jones's body?"

"Apart from the fact that he was badly knocked about? No. Like what?"

"Did you look at his wrists?"

"They were bloodied and battered, like the rest of him."

"But did you see that the cuts went all the way around? They were made by a rope, and some of them were fresh and raw. The bruise on his chin, on the other hand, was several days old. Those wounds weren't caused by the fall. I'd say Jones had been kept a prisoner somewhere, probably for the last several days."

"But that would mean he could not have committed the murders."

"Or that he couldn't have committed both of them. It would depend on when he was taken captive. The last we saw of him, he was headed to the *Peacock* in the company of a gang of smugglers. Did they lock him up for some reason? If so, he might have been out of the way since last Wednesday and couldn't have committed either murder. Or it could be he killed Bevan and was locked up afterwards. Or that he was being held somewhere when Bevan died, but was freed or escaped after that and killed Sir Edward."

"Does that mean you think there could be two killers?"

"It would certainly complicate matters, wouldn't it?"

"But we have evidence that Jones killed Bevan. And who besides Jones would want to kill Sir Edward? We were there when he attacked him in the prison."

"We have evidence that Jones was at the first murder, and very convenient evidence it is. A distinctive brass button torn off his coat by a man who was sitting with his back to him when he put a knife to his throat. That's an awkward manoeuvre for the victim, don't you think?"

"Are you saying that the evidence was planted? Why? Who would do that?" Evans frowned. "You think someone else killed Bevan and framed Jones for it?"

"I think it's possible. And now he's not around to tell his side of the story, which is also very convenient if there is someone else involved."

"But we know Jones killed Sir Edward."

"Do we? There's something else you didn't notice. Jones's boots."

"Why should I look at his boots?"

"What colour is the soil on Parys Mountain?"

"Red. Orange. Purple. Mostly red, I suppose."

"The dust on Jones's boots was pale, and there was also sand in it. However Jones got up the mountain, he didn't walk."

"You're not saying you think Jones was murdered too?"

"I'm saying there are questions yet to be answered. You asked one yourself: who else would want to kill Sir Edward?"

"But where do we start if we don't even know if we're looking for one murderer or two?"

"As a matter of fact, I don't think we are looking for two murderers. Both Sir Edward and Bevan had their throats cut from behind, and both seem to have been killed by Jones. I think one person is behind all this. To find out who that is, I'd start closer to home."

"Closer to home?" Evans stared. "You mean at Henllys?"

"What's the first question to ask when someone's been killed? Come on, Constable, you must have some idea."

"Who saw them last?"

Dan tutted. "Who stands to gain by their death. Or who thinks they will."

"Stephen Lloyd Pryce? He was so certain he was going to inherit the estate, he's practically moved in already. But it couldn't have been him."

"Why not? We know he was jealous of his brother, and we know he thought he was entitled to his share of the wealth. On the night of the dinner party all he could talk about was how much he needed to pay his son's school fees."

"But he's…he's—"

"A soft-headed weakling? He could have paid someone else to do the actual killing."

"But he hasn't gained anything. His brother left it all to Lady Charlotte, so the theory doesn't—" Evans broke off. "Except he didn't know what was in the will." He snatched up his hat and pushed back his chair. "That could mean Lady Charlotte is in danger! We must get back at once."

"It could," said Dan. "Even if she is, I doubt he'd do the deed in broad daylight in front of his wife, Captain Williams, and a house full of servants, knowing moreover that two Bow Street officers will be arriving back any time."

Evans sank back into his chair. "You don't think it is the rector, do you?"

"No."

"I don't understand. First you say there's two killers, then you say there's one, then you suggest it's Sir Edward's brother, and now you say it isn't. So what do you think?"

"I think you've got brains, but you don't use them, Evans. I've already told you where to look."

"Closer to home. But who? One of the servants?"

"Let's go back a bit. Remember what you saw in the hall on our first evening at Henllys?"

"Lady Charlotte had bruises on her wrists."

"You didn't see the bruises. You saw her showing them to Captain Williams."

"All right, I saw her showing them to the captain."

"Or that's what you thought they were doing, whispering together in the hall."

"What else could they have been doing?" Evans gazed at Dan in horror. "You are not suggesting that Captain Williams and Lady Charlotte are lovers?"

"Such things have been known to happen. The servants had their suspicions, didn't they? And on the day of the ambush Lady Charlotte seemed more concerned for the captain's safety than her husband's."

"Of course she was concerned. They're old friends."

"Friendly enough for him to want her husband out of the way?"

"You think the captain murdered Sir Edward? That's impossible. Jones killed him."

"But Williams knew something Jones couldn't have known: that Sir Edward walked in his sleep when he'd taken laudanum."

"That was just a coincidence. No one could have known Sir Edward would choose that night for one of his somnambulations. Jones was there, saw his opportunity and took it. And what about Bevan? What possible reason could Captain Williams have for murdering him?"

"That I don't know. But it was Williams who stumbled on that loose floorboard in Bevan's rooms where we found the tea and baccy, Williams who explained the entries in Bevan's notebook, and Williams who suggested that Bevan must have learned of our plans for moving Jones when he was at the dinner party. But I don't recall our arrangements being discussed that evening; we'd already been over them in the afternoon. The captain was quick to point out that Jones was the murderer too. And now both Bevan the smuggler and Jones the murderer are dead and unable to admit or deny the accusations. I think there's a lot about the captain that warrants taking a closer look."

"You can't think that Captain Williams murdered his best friend. He was beside himself with grief."

"He was, wasn't he? All that shouting and raving. Only there was one thing he didn't do. He didn't pull back the sheet and look at his friend's face."

"Why would he, when it was such an ugly thing?"

"I'll let that remark go for now. But don't people usually like to take a last look at a dear departed friend? Let's just say it's another unanswered question. Like where Jones was held, who imprisoned him, and why. Once we know all that, we may be closer to discovering the truth."

"I thought we already had discovered the truth. All this time we've been going after Jones. If there was any doubt, why didn't you tell me before?"

"You've seen as much as I've seen, and you know as much as I know. You could have worked it out. Besides, it's all guesswork at the moment. You may turn out to be right about Stephen Lloyd Pryce yet."

"What are you going to do now?"

"We," said Dan, "are going to have a look around the captain's house while he's busy comforting the widow."

# CHAPTER TWENTY-NINE

Evans broke the angry silence he had maintained ever since they left the Bull. "You have no grounds for doubting Lady Charlotte's virtue. She was devoted to her husband. If Captain Williams did kill Sir Edward, it was for some other reason."

Dan had been expecting an outburst like it ever since they set off towards Llangoed on the reassuringly placid horses the inn's stables had provided.

"You could be right," he said. "Perhaps the tears she shed the night he was killed were genuine. Or perhaps, in his muddled state, she persuaded him to go outside, knowing his killer was waiting for him."

"No! Her shock and grief were real. It's madness to suspect her."

"Yet you've come round to the idea that Captain Williams, who grew up with Sir Edward, who cared for him with the tenderness of a brother when he was ill, who Sir Edward trusted to spend hours in his wife's company, might be his killer."

"That's different."

"He hasn't got big blue eyes."

"That's not it at all! And this – this sneaking to his house to spy on him – is underhand. Captain Williams does not deserve to be treated like a common criminal."

"What sort of criminal does he deserve to be treated like?"

"You know what I mean."

"I'm trying to find a killer. You think I should be nice while I'm at it?"

"I'd never accuse you of being nice."

Dan laughed. They rode on for a few moments.

"Tell me, Evans, why you became a constable."

"What's that got to do with it?"

Dan shrugged. If the constable didn't want to answer, he wasn't going to press him. Nothing was more calculated to provoke a reaction than a display of indifference, and he did not have to wait long before Evans blurted, "Because, I didn't want to go into law, medicine or the church."

"You had those choices, did you?"

"My father would have been best pleased if I'd followed him into the church. And rather than go back home after Cambridge and be a disappointment to him there, I decided to go to London. I thought I'd find something I'd like better. I'd discovered I couldn't stand insurance offices, banks or architects' practices when the money ran out."

It was an incomplete answer to a question he seemed to have no clear answer for. Why had he become a constable? He thought for a few moments. When he spoke again it was as if he was trying to explain it to himself.

"Came a night I lost my last few guineas to a pair of sharpers at a game of billiards – at the billiards rooms in Bow Street, as it happens – and was walking home wondering whether it would be worse to throw myself on the bosom of the Thames or the bosom of my father when I came across a pair of brutes amusing themselves by beating a constable to a pulp. I managed to see them off, took the constable to my rooms in Bedford Street, and patched him up. He told me I'd displayed qualities handy in a constable and described the compensations, such as being able to put food in your belly and a roof over your head.

"I'd found the adventure diverting, so I thought, why not? The constable knew a householder who'd been summoned to serve by the vestry and wanted to find a substitute for himself, and for a small fee he made the introductions. I only meant to do it for a few months, but two years on, I've grown used to it. Besides, it's as good as anything else."

He looked at Dan as if expecting some comment, but none came. "All right, then," he said, "why did you become a principal officer?"

"Why not, if it's as good as anything else?"

"I see. This is where you give the 'you're wasting your talents' sermon."

"I'm not going to give a sermon. It's up to you if you've decided that being a police officer is a waste of your talents. I'd have said the waste was being a police officer and not putting your talents into it." Dan pointed at a grey stone house surrounded by a large walled garden, stables and outhouses. "Is that Ty Coed, do you think, to the left of that wood?"

"Coed means wood," said Evans. "So yes, I think that's it."

"We could leave the horses in the trees."

"Without food or water? We'd be lucky to find them when we come back."

"Then what do you suggest we do with them?"

"We passed a farmhouse half a mile back. We'll see if we could stable them there. Then we could approach the house through the wood."

"And risk someone from the farm warning Williams that we're close?"

"We'll tell them we've come to look for an ancient British settlement and need to explore the terrain on foot."

"You think they'll believe that?"

"They'll believe anything of an English tourist with money in his pocket."

Two stone piers marked the entrance to Ty Coed, each with a recumbent stag carved on top of it. Ivy had wrapped itself around the piers, age had blunted the stags, rust attacked the gates, and neglect left the driveway rutted and overgrown. It was a solid old house of two storeys with a plain frontage. Chimneys squatted at either wing, and a steep gable crowned the front door, which had a sash window above it, a blank window at attic level, and two symmetrical rows of three sash windows on either side of it.

They left the drive and kept out of sight by following the perimeter wall. At first impression there seemed to be little need for the caution. There was no one about in the untidy stable yard, nor in any of the unkempt gardens and decrepit outhouses. The curtains on most of the upper windows were drawn, several of the roof slates had slipped, the paintwork was flaking, and the step in front of the weather-beaten front door was half-buried under grass. Only the smoke rising from a chimney at the rear gave any hint that the place was inhabited.

They found things a bit livelier at the back of the house, which faced the Irish Sea. The back door stood open on to a path smoothed by use. Water pooled around a pump in a flagged courtyard. The straggling garden sloped down to a high wall marking the limit of the property. A side wall separated it from the kitchen plot, which was the only well-tended part of the grounds, with its beds cleared or netted and paths kept tidy and free from weeds.

Voices came through an open window. They crept up and peered into an oak-beamed kitchen. A plump woman wearing a striped apron over her blue flannel dress, her black hair covered by a white mobcap, worked at a long wooden table in front of a kitchen range. She was beating eggs in a bowl tucked under one of her muscular arms while she berated the cowed middle-aged man in saggy breeches and tattered brown jacket who stood in front of her. He grasped a pair of dead rabbits by the ears. Every now and again he wafted the conies at her in a feeble attempt to make a peace offering.

The dog at his feet gave a muffled bark, jumped up, and growled at the window. The man muttered a threat at it. With a look which seemed to say, "You're making a mistake, but it's up to you", the dog sat down again and bristled at the Bow Street men.

A younger, rounder version of the cook appeared in the passageway at the back of the room carrying a mop and bucket. She stamped into the scullery. They heard her bang the bucket down and throw the mop into a corner. She went back into the kitchen, ignored her mother's greeting, and with the air of a tyrant with the world to rule gave the man an order. He listened meekly, dumped the rabbits on the table in the clutter of vegetables, butter and milk jugs, shuffled into the passage and disappeared behind a cellar door. The cook rolled her eyes at the bloodied carcasses.

Her daughter picked up a knife and started stabbing the peel off a heap of potatoes and dropping them in a bowl of water. The two women grumbled over their tasks. Without the man to quieten him, the dog showed signs of increased suspicion. Dan and Evans retreated, leaving mother and daughter to their discontent.

"Did you hear anything?" asked Dan when they were out of earshot and hiding in a clump of tangled shrubs.

"They're expecting company tonight," Evans answered, "unless the captain plans to drink the six bottles of wine and keg of ale the old man has gone to fetch."

"I'd like to see who that company is. In the meantime, let's find out where that leads." Dan indicated a door in the wall at the end of the garden. It stood slightly open, giving a glimpse of dark woodland.

This part of the garden was damp and shady, overrun with sage, rosemary and mint. The door opened easily and they stepped over a stone sill into the dim wood. The land sloped into a sunken path running between twisted tree roots and brambles, its surface a mix of stone and sand rilled with water. It brought them out on open ground across which a track ran to the edge of a shallow cove.

"A convenient path to a lonely landing place," said Dan.

"Henllys is not far from a cove, yet you never suggested Sir Edward was a smuggler. And I can't see any ships, can you?"

"That doesn't mean they aren't out there. And Henllys is too close to Beaumaris to be the safest place for landing goods. This is ideal. I wonder if Captain Williams has got anything hidden away in that big house of his. Time to take a look, I think."

"Take a look? How?"

"How do you think? We'll try the windows at the front."

"You're going to break in? But someone's bound to hear us."

"Not if we don't make a noise."

Before Evans could make any more objections, Dan started back to the house, ignoring the muttering behind him. He began by testing the windows on the off chance any were open, but none were. Most of the rooms – parlour, library, drawing room – had empty hearths and a dusty, deserted look. A fire had been lit in a wood-panelled dining room, where it was struggling to reach maturity under a stone chimney. Dan took a knife out of his pocket, slid it between the upper and lower sash and knocked the catch open.

Evans raised his eyebrows. "Have you done that before?"

Dan did not answer. He pushed the lower sash up, nodded the constable through, climbed in after him and closed the window. The air in the room was chill and clammy, the floor smearily damp from the cursory sweeps of the maid's mop. The surface of the old oak dining table was dulled with age, but it had been wiped and plates and glasses stacked up on it ready for arranging later. The rug in front of the fire was worn and needed a good clean, and dust balled in the corners of the room, though a cloth had been hastily passed over the furniture, and around the ornaments on the mantelpiece and jugs and bottles on the sideboard. One or two stains on the wall marked places where paintings had once hung. Most of those that remained were of sombrely clad long-dead inhabitants who had blended to uniform shades of umber, black and ivory. A large damp stain spread across the ceiling.

In the corridor they could not hear any sound from the kitchen, and as far as they could tell, there was no one else in the house. The walls were panelled, and a central wooden staircase led from the hall to the upper floors. A huge unlit log filled the fireplace, over which was a coat of arms which repeated the stag motif they had seen at the entrance.

Dan cautiously opened the door leading to the domestic quarters. The women's sharp voices drifted down the flagstoned passageway. They peered into larders, pantries, wash and still rooms until they came to the door to the cellars. There was no sign of the meek man except for a lantern with a smoking candle in it on a shelf at the bottom of the stairs. Dan took a flint box out of his pocket and relit it.

Racks of dusty bottles, barrels of beer, and labelled kegs of wine, sherries and spirits stood under a vaulted ceiling. Mallets, taps, bungs, corks and jugs lay untidily on top of an empty barrel. A crate of empty bottles and a couple of buckets stood next to it. The place was musty and smelled of sour yeasty spills. Near the foot of the steps was a small empty meat larder with a barred unglazed window in a heavy wooden door.

"It's just an ordinary cellar," Evans said.

Dan held the lantern high. The flame flickered in a draught from the back of the vault. He moved deeper into the chamber. Evans rolled his eyes and followed. The rear wall was half-covered by wooden shelves on which stood barrels of butter, straw-lined crates of vegetables and apples, stone jars of oil. The flow of air was almost a gale here.

"Nothing here." The constable turned away.

"I think there's something behind the shelves."

Dan put down the lantern, caught hold of the wooden case and pulled. Nothing happened and Evans was no doubt about to point out that they were just ordinary shelves when the unit shifted.

"Give me a hand."

Between them, they pulled at the shelving. It swung back, exposing a narrow passageway.

Evans gasped. "A secret tunnel! How did you know?"

Dan picked up the lantern and stepped inside. The roof arched over them and the smell of earth was strong, but it was dry. The way was level and they had taken only a few steps when it opened out into another cellar, bigger than the first. The beam slid over barrels, kegs, baskets of wine, and crates of tobacco. Dan lifted the lid of one of these and took out a cloth-wrapped packet.

"Look at this."

"Tobacco from Nantes," Evans said. "The same address that was on the bags we found in Bevan's room and at the mine. How Williams kept his nerve when we went into the cave, I don't know! He has deceived us all."

"Williams kept his nerve because he wanted us to find the contraband at the mine."

"But why—?" Evans broke off. "So we wouldn't come looking for any more. A small sacrifice to divert the revenue men away from the real cache."

"Now you're getting the idea."

Dan put the packet back in the crate and pulled the lid over it.

"Look!" Evans said. "There's a glimmer of light over there."

The slender line of light came through a small gap between

two trap doors set at an angle above them. Stone steps with metal tracks on either side for rolling barrels led down into the cellar. They pulled back the bolts, raised one of the doors a little way and peered through. They looked out from an earthen bank in an overgrown rose garden. The door into the wood was not far away.

"You couldn't ask for better cover for shifting cargo from the beach," said Dan, "if anyone should happen to be around."

They secured the trap door and went back to the first cellar. They swung the shelves back into place and scuffed the floor to erase the marks in the dust before returning to the foot of the stairs.

"Look at your boots," Dan said.

Evans looked down. "What?"

"Pale dust. Where did we last see dust like that?"

"On Watcyn Jones. He could have been kept down here! In that meat larder, perhaps. We should take a look."

Dan let himself be led by the constable's newfound eagerness to prove Williams a villain. The pantry was long and narrow and lined with empty stone shelves. The door could be bolted from the outside, but there was no fastening on the inside. It was too much to hope that Jones had shed any more convenient buttons and there was nothing else to find apart from dust and cobwebs.

"But this could have been the place," Evans said.

"I think it's very likely."

Dan blew out the candle and left the lantern where they had found it. They crept up the stairs, opened the door, and listened. The women in the kitchen were still clacking away. They left the house through the dining room window and hurried back to the cover of the overgrown garden.

"What now?" asked Evans.

"We wait for whoever it is Williams is expecting tonight. I spotted a summerhouse that would give us a good outlook."

They followed the boundary wall on the edge of the woodland to a small domed building built against it in the corner of the grounds. Half a dozen steps led up to the entrance, which was flanked by four columns and had sash windows on either side. Many of the panes were broken and the door was distorted by damp and clogged with old leaves and dirt.

They pushed their way inside. The floor was filthy with bird and animal droppings, and vast cobwebs hung in the corners. Two windows at the rear mirrored the ones at the front, with views through the woods and to glimpses of the sea. The stone bench around the walls gave them somewhere to sit while they watched.

"You take the front."

Evans sat down near the door, rubbed the grimy glass, and stared out at the bedraggled garden. Dan settled himself facing the woods and turned up his coat collar. He pretended to be unaware of the glances Evans threw his way, and of his nervous attempts to speak.

"Mr Foster," he managed at last, "sir, I just wanted to say…I wanted to tell you…you were right and I—"

Dan stared out at the trees and smiled to himself. "Just keep your eyes open, Constable."

# CHAPTER THIRTY

"There's someone moving along the path," said Evans.

Dan went over to the front window. The manservant shambled towards the garden gate carrying a lantern. He passed into the woods, the light flickering in and out of the trees before it vanished into the sunken path.

"I'm going to see what he's up to," Dan said. "You stay here."

Outside, wafts of mint and rosemary floated on the chill air. He picked his way through the woods and along the dark path. The soughing branches, and then the waves breaking on the shore, covered any sound he made.

He stopped at the end of the path. The servant stood at the cliff's edge, the lantern at his feet, the wind blowing his coat about him. He pulled a gun out of his pocket and aimed it into the sky. A blue flare shot towards the stars, fired by a flintlock with powder in the pan, but no shot. From out to sea came an answering flash. The man picked up the lantern and turned to leave. He was not one to rush himself, and Dan easily got back to the summerhouse while he was still dawdling on the path.

Evans greeted him with, "The captain just came back."

Williams's horse stood near the back door. From inside came a distant sound of running feet and banging doors. The cook appeared in the doorway and called out to the servant who was still shuffling towards the house. He grumbled something in return, altered course, caught hold of the horse's bridle and plodded off to the stables.

"Williams's visitors are coming from seaward," Dan said. "I just watched the servant signal a ship."

"They're landing goods tonight!"

"Looks like it. I want you to ride back to Beaumaris and fetch Mr Llewellyn and as many men as he can muster. I'll stay here and keep an eye on things."

"Is that wise? If anyone sees you—"

"I'll keep out of sight. You'd better get going. And Evans."

"Yes?"

"Be careful."

"Sir."

The constable's light footsteps disappeared into the darkness. The cold suddenly felt more intense, the silence menacing. Dan reached into his pocket for his pistol.

Half an hour passed. A horse and rider appeared at the side of the house. The rider dismounted clumsily and banged on the kitchen door. The cook's daughter opened it and curtsied.

"Good evening, Mr Roberts."

Dan had a feeling he had heard the name recently, but it was too dark to see the man's face and he could not place him. It was not an uncommon name, though.

Roberts followed the maid into the house, patting her swinging rear and making appreciative noises. She laughed and coyly slapped his hand away, an unconvincing protest. The manservant grumbled out of doors again to stable the horse. He went back, the door closed behind him, and apart from the cook and her daughter moving about the kitchen, the house settled down.

It was completely dark by the time Dan heard footsteps and voices approaching through the wood. Two men carrying lanterns emerged through the door in the wall. Williams stood on the threshold to welcome them, the light streaming around him. The three men shook hands and the captain ushered them inside.

The put-upon servant dawdled outside and stood waiting at the top of the garden. Many more footsteps approached, though no one spoke. One after another, a score of men passed through the gate. Some stooped beneath the weight of casks slung over their shoulders, others bent under sacks. Some of them walked in pairs carrying crates slung on frames between them.

The servant greeted them with a few gruff words and guided them around the side of the house to the rose garden and the entrance to the cellar. Barrels, sacks and crates thumped to the ground, the men grunting with relief. The servant slouched back inside. Moments later, the trap doors crashed open. Half of the crew reappeared and made their way back to the cove, where their shipmates must be busy unloading more goods. The rest stayed behind and, maintaining their disciplined silence, sent the barrels and crates rumbling into the cellar.

But these were just the labourers. Captain Williams and his three guests were the ones behind the venture. Dan left the summerhouse and dodged from shadow to shadow. He caught a faint whiff of tobacco smoke coming from the side of the house, the smell strong on the night air. Relays of sailors toiled to and fro, working doggedly and without fuss, their boots churning the damp grass.

Dan got round to the front of the house without being spotted. All he could see of the dining room through a gap in the curtains was a figure crossing the room, a pair of boots stretched out in front of the fire. Glasses clinked, someone laughed; Williams, he thought.

He crept to one of the end windows and repeated the operation with his knife to raise the sash. It was stiff from disuse, made more noise than he would have liked, but he managed to make enough of a gap to climb inside. As a precaution, he left the window ajar.

The dimly-lit corridor was empty. The smell of roasting meat floated from the kitchen, reminding him that he had eaten nothing since breakfast. He tiptoed to the dining room door. The wood was thick and he had to strain to catch what was said.

"…to Liverpool. From there it could be sold to traders with London connections."

It was a voice Dan would not forget in a hurry. He had first heard it threatening to kill a young volunteer at Cadnant: the Irish captain who had led the ambush. The ship anchored off the shore must be the *Peacock*, and according to the documents Dan had seen at Williams & Company's bank in Caernarfon, his name was Dominic O'Flaherty.

Brisk footsteps rapped on the stone floor. Dan slipped into the room opposite, pulling the door to just as the maid came into sight. The manservant trudged behind her, carrying a tray of covered dishes. She opened the dining room door and they went inside.

Dan glimpsed Roberts standing by the table, rubbing his hands and smacking his lips at the maid, or the food, or both. They were slobbery lips and hung over a double chin, with goggling eyes above. Now Dan recognised him. He had crossed to Anglesey from the George at Bangor on the same ferry as Dan and Evans. Then he had been Roberts the economical family man who had dined at the Three Tuns at Porthaethwy with his wife and daughter. Now, he was Roberts the gluttonous lecher, loading his plate at his host's expense.

Chairs scraped as Williams and his cronies took their seats. Wine glugged into glasses, plates and knives clattered. Dan waited for the maid and manservant to go back to the kitchen before he returned to the dining room door. Inside, the conversation had resumed.

"London means top prices," said a sharp, precise voice, expanding on the Irishman's remark. "Taking all costs into account, including the purchase price and the crew's wages, I calculate a profit of fifty per cent."

"It will be our best run yet," said Roberts.

"Indeed it will," said Captain Williams. "And our last."

"But what about us?" cried Roberts.

"We have an agreement!" hissed the precise man.

"Damn you, Williams, I'll rip out your heart and liver if you back down now!" shouted O'Flaherty.

"Gentlemen, gentlemen!" Williams cried. He banged the table, setting the cutlery and glasses rattling. The uproar died away.

Williams answered their objections in turn. "You can go to hell for all I care. The agreement is terminated. And the last man who threatened me ended up with his throat cut."

"Bevan overreached himself when he demanded a greater share of the profits," the precise man said. "But we are your partners."

"And, gad," said Roberts, "why stop now when there's plenty more to be made?"

"Because I have all I want. I, gentlemen, am going to settle down to life as a respectable squire. There's a vacancy for a justice of the peace, and a certain JP's widow possessed of a very pretty property who needs a husband."

"A seat on the bench would enable us to increase our business two-, three-, fourfold," said the precise man. "There could be no safer way of dealing with competitors. There would be nothing to stop us establishing a monopoly on the island's trade – or even expanding to cover the entire North Wales coast."

"The business is finished," said Williams. "I set it up and now I'm winding it up."

"Now just a minute," said O'Flaherty. "It's not up to you to say when it's finished. You can fuck off to your merry widow if you like, but I'm not giving up now."

"As far as Anglesey is concerned, you are," said Williams.

"And what could you do to stop us?" O'Flaherty demanded. "If you turn us in, you turn yourself in too. Don't think for one moment that I wouldn't peach."

"I don't think it, but I have no intention of turning you in. In fact, you ought to thank me for finishing things without any loss or danger to any of you. As far as the world is concerned, Thomas Bevan was behind our operation, and Wat Jones killed him and Edward Lloyd Pryce. I've even got a Bow Street Runner believing it."

"That's what you think," Dan muttered.

"All this talk of peaching will get us nowhere," said the precise voice. "The man who condemns his associates also condemns himself. Surely we can come to a mutually satisfactory agreement concerning the dissolution of our arrangement. Perhaps, Williams, a profit-sharing scheme with you as a sleeping partner might enable us to continue this lucrative trade, and you to retain your respectability?"

"Why should we pay him to do nothing in the business?" said O'Flaherty. "If he wants out, let him get out and have done with him."

"We are paying him for the goodwill," answered the precise voice, "which is a trading asset on which we can set a value."

"Yes, yes, indeed," stuttered Roberts, shaken by all this talk of Bow Street Runners and peaching. "There's no money in falling out."

"What would you offer me?" asked Williams.

For the last few minutes, Dan had been aware of the strains of a fiddle, men singing, shouting and laughing, and boots pounding on a stone floor. The crew had finished their work and gathered in the kitchen for their own supper, a liquid one from the sound of it. The door burst open and the jig spilled into the kitchen corridor, casting crazed shadows into the hall. Dan bolted back into the chill parlour as one of the tars seized the maid, lifted her into the air and swung her past the cold fireplace. Laughing, she pushed him away, straightened her dress, and skipped to the dining room. The men inside were silent and there were no more lascivious comments from Roberts while she cleared the dishes.

The sailors were still prancing around in the hall and kitchen corridor. It was no longer safe to stay in the house. Dan hurried back to the open window. He climbed out, pulled down the sash and set off towards the summerhouse, using the cover offered by the straggling trees. He paused in a patch of shadow and scanned the ground ahead of him before he broke into the open.

There was a sharp click by his right ear.

"Stay where you are!"

# CHAPTER THIRTY-ONE

"Put your hands up and turn round. Slow."

Dan found himself facing a stocky man dressed in loose trousers and short jacket. Drink-inflamed eyes glared at him over a pistol.

"Now your weapon. Slow."

Keeping one hand in the air, Dan reached for his pocket. The bloodshot eyes followed the movement and failed to register the swift flick of Dan's raised fist before it cracked his jaw. The man staggered, sending a shot flashing into the night.

Dan turned and ran. Behind him the kitchen door crashed open. The smugglers stumbled out, shouting and waving their weapons, narrowly avoiding shooting, clubbing or stabbing one another.

"Who fired that shot?"

"It came from over there!"

"No, this way!"

Dan sprinted to the summerhouse, sprang up the steps and slammed the door. He did not slow down, but kept going, straight for the rear window. He had been sitting by it long enough to have seen that age and weather had rotted the wood. He flung his hands over his head and threw himself at it sideways on.

He smashed through in a spray of glass and wood, landed

on the sloping ground beneath, lost his footing and skidded down the incline. Above him, flashes of light filled the empty frame and bullets whizzed over his head.

He rolled to a stop. There was no time to check for cuts and bruises. He scrambled to his feet and pelted through the trees.

The sailors swarmed over the sill and thudded to the ground, boots crunching on the broken glass. The trees stretched ahead of him, seemingly for miles, until all at once he found himself in mid-air again. He had fallen into the sunken track. He landed with a shock worse than the first because it was unexpected. He slid downhill in a miniature landfall of sand, stone and ice-cold water, and felt a stinging pain in his left thigh. He staggered to the opposite bank. He pulled himself to the top by the roots and branches and pushed through the snagging undergrowth.

The track slowed his pursuers who, forewarned by his disappearance, negotiated the drop with more care. He was on moorland now. Somewhere in the dark waters on his right lay the *Peacock*; the charcoal outline of a plateau rose ahead of him. He stumbled through gorse, scrabbled up steep paths on slippery outcrops of limestone, skirted tangled bushes. His trail meandered over the rough terrain, but though he did not seem to be getting anywhere, it worked to his advantage. His twists and turns made it harder for his pursuers to track him.

The pain in his leg became more insistent. His left foot dragged, and though he was moving, he was cold. Worse, he was light-headed and began to fancy an ambush lurked behind every dark shape. Wind-deformed trees swooped down to grab him, rocky outcrops squatted ready to leap upon him, brambles clutched at his ankles. They're just trees, rocks and bushes, he told himself, and flinched as another branch took a swipe at him.

The ground rose to a slight ridge. A group of figures huddled in a circle at the top. There was no hope that they had not seen him and he was limping too badly to run. One of the figures broke away and floated towards him in a dark, whispering cloud. There may have been words in the whispers, but if so, he could not understand them. He blinked, struggling to focus, and realised that a woman stood in front of him. Her loose ill-fitting dress and shawl fluttered in the breeze. Dark hair streamed across her face.

"What are you doing here?" he mumbled. She should be in the scullery at Henllys, her arms elbow-deep in dishwater.

Mary Thomas slipped her arm under his as his knees buckled.

"Hush," she said, followed by what must have been "this way". He let her guide him up the ridge and over the grassy lip at the top, towards her companions. He saw why they had not moved or spoken. They were not men, but stones, arranged in one of the ancient circles that Evans had spoken of.

She led him across the circle. An upright standing stone loomed in front of them. Its neighbour had tilted towards it, but between them they still supported a massive cross stone, fixed now in a diagonal line. It looked like a crooked doorway, though all that lay beyond it was the night. Mary took him across the threshold and they plunged into a thicket. It seemed impenetrable, yet she found a way through.

They moved downhill and further down, seemed to pass beneath the earth. They came to a halt by a hollow at the foot of the stones, well hidden by the trees. He would never have found it on his own. *There were a hundred and one places on Anglesey for a man on the run to hide.*

She helped him crawl inside and sit down, his back against the stone.

"Thank you," he gasped.

He moved his hand down his thigh, felt the blood soaking through his breeches. He had gashed it in his tumble down the sunken path. The loss of blood accounted for his dizziness and confusion. He pulled off his neckcloth, winced as he wrapped it around his leg and tied it tight above the wound. Mary crouched at the entrance of the shallow den and listened to the faint sounds of voices drifting across the moor.

She crept to his side. Though neither of them could see the other's face, they were aware of one another's movements and breathing, gradually calming. She said something, gestured towards his leg. A question. He shook his head; he didn't understand. She tried again, but the result was the same. She patted his shoulder, her voice both reassuring and instructing. Rest? Sleep? Be quiet?

This was no time to rest. His pursuers were still out there.

"You should go." He put his hand on her arm, pushed. "It isn't safe. Go."

She shrugged his hand away. Her skirt rustled as she sat down next to him. He had not got the strength to argue, and besides, the smugglers were not far away. She was probably safer here after all. He would wait for the sounds to die down and compel her to leave as soon as the danger had passed.

Down here was nothing like the cave on Parys Mountain, where the air was chill as death. It was warmer, and there was life in it too. He felt the roots in the soil behind his back. The ancient stone, whatever mysteries it hid, had been raised by men, spoke of human presence and purpose. He and the girl were safe half-buried beneath it, as long as he stayed alert. He rested his pistol on the floor beside him, his fingers loosely gripping the smooth wooden handle, and settled down to keep watch.

His eyes fluttered open some time later. It was still dark. There was a warm weight on his shoulder which in his drowsy state he could not at first account for. Then he remembered Mary. She had fallen asleep with her head resting on him, her body pressed close. He had his arm around her, though he did not recall putting it there. He tried to move, but she did not wake or stir. To prolong the effort was more than he could manage. In any case, he was not uncomfortable. He gave up. She sighed and snuggled closer.

Later still, he woke with a start. The movement, slight though it was, rekindled the pain of his leg wound and all his other cuts and bruises. His head swam and his limbs felt heavy. It was still dark and the warmth of the girl's body had gone. He realised this in the same instant he became aware of voices, footsteps and the glimmer of lanterns. Someone laughed, a triumphant sound.

"Here it is!" Captain O'Flaherty's voice.

They had come straight to his hiding place. Mary Thomas had betrayed him.

The smugglers' lanterns lit up the hollow and dazzled him. He made out half a dozen shadowy figures gathering around the entrance to the cave in a silent semi-circle. He would have time to fire one shot before they overpowered him, and he was going to use it.

He grasped his pistol and tried to lift it, but it was so heavy. He gritted his teeth and tried again, almost fainting with the effort. He shook his head, ignored the pain of stiff, torn muscles, raised the pistol, but no one came at him. They were waiting for something.

Or someone.

A single set of footsteps approached. The smugglers held up their lanterns to light the way, the light falling on Dan where he sat exhausted and bleeding in the shallow cave. A tall figure filled the entrance, pistol in hand.

"It is you, Foster! I thought as much when they told me about our intruder."

The gun shook in Dan's hand and sank down beside him. He could not lift it again. It was over and all he could think was, *but I won't see Alex grow up*. Captain Williams grinned, raised his weapon and took aim. A shot rang out.

The captain spun and crashed to the ground, his gun firing wide of its mark as it flew from his fingers. His men scrambled past him, shouting and clawing at one another. The only way out was back to the stone circle and towards the gunfire. They drew their pistols and charged, firing wildly. Answering shots rang out. One of the crewmen fell and his mates stampeded over him. More shots followed, and cries of panic and pain.

Williams struggled to his knees, clutching his right shoulder. He groped for his pistol, circling on all fours. He collided with a pair of boots and squinted up at the man who blocked his path. He had a gun pointed at the captain's head and there were more armed men behind him. Williams slumped back to sit cross-legged with his head in one hand, his other arm hanging uselessly at his side.

"Cuff him," said the man in boots. He leaned into the cave. "Can you walk, sir?"

# CHAPTER THIRTY-TWO

Dan groaned when he put the weight on to his injured leg. Evans drew a small phial of dark red liquid from an inside pocket.

"Take a few drops of this. It will help with the pain."

"Laudanum? So that's how you knew about Sir Edward's habit. Like drawn to like."

The bottles in Evans's bag, the sneaking around at Porthaethwy, the furtive transaction with the maid at the inn in Caernarfon all made sense now. He'd been slipping out for fresh supplies.

"But where did you go the night we were at the Three Tuns? There's nothing there."

Evans grinned. "I went to the local horse doctor – who's also the local apothecary, bone setter and tooth puller. Here, have some."

"I don't need it, and neither do you."

"You don't know what I need," the constable retorted, pocketing the phial.

Dan was past caring. At that moment, Evans could drown himself in opium if he liked. "Give me a hand."

He leaned on Evans's arm and struggled back up to the stone circle where Llewellyn's men were busy collecting weapons, laying out the dead, and seeing to the prisoners.

"Officer Foster, thank God we reached you in time!" Llewellyn cried. "But where are you hurt?"

"Never mind that now." Dan nodded at two figures lying motionless on the ground.

"Not ours," said the revenue officer. "There's a third over there, still alive. We've tended his wound as best we can, but it doesn't look good. The rest got away."

"Where's Williams?"

Llewellyn pointed at the man seated in a defeated huddle on a fallen stone near the edge of the circle. One of the riding officers stood guard over him, his pistol at the ready should the captain make a bid for freedom in spite of his shackled hands. Dan had hardly limped half a dozen steps when Mary Thomas burst out of the shadows and rushed at him, gabbling excitedly. He shoved her off, more forcefully than he had intended. She tumbled to the ground and stared up at him, speechless with shock.

"What are you doing?" cried Evans. "That's Mary from Henllys."

"What's she doing here?"

"She brought us here."

"She what?"

"She brought us here, and it's a good thing she did. We'd never have found you in time without her. Only someone who knows the area well could find that cave."

"I thought—" Dan bit his lip. "Mary, I'm sorry…tell her I'm sorry, Evans. Tell her I mistook her."

Llewellyn, meanwhile, helped her to her feet. She was sobbing by then, but when Evans relayed Dan's apology it was immediately accepted and her tears wiped away. She gazed rapturously at Dan, talking so rapidly it was some time before anyone else could get a word in. Eventually, she was forced to pause for breath.

Dan looked at Evans.

"She says she's glad you're safe," the constable said.

"Say I'm truly grateful, but we still have work to do."

The constable made the necessary translation and Llewellyn signalled to one of the officers to take care of her.

"So," said Dan, "tell me what happened."

"When I got to Beaumaris – nearly breaking my neck in the process – I summoned Mr Llewellyn and he summoned his men, and then we hurried back to Ty Coed. We found the cook, her daughter and manservant bundling all their worldly goods, and quite a few that weren't theirs, such as the odd cask of brandy and pack of tobacco, onto a cart. It didn't take much to get out of them that Williams and his men had found you, but you'd escaped with the captain in pursuit. We were just setting off to look for you when Mary appeared. We thought at first she was something to do with the gang, and she was so incoherent it took a while before we could get any sense out of her. She'd been visiting her mother, who lives not far from here. She was on her way back to Henllys when she saw the smugglers' lights on the moor. She was hiding in the stone circle when she saw you, took you to the cave and came looking for help. And here we are."

"Williams had three visitors, his partners in the trade. What of them?"

"There was no one else there."

"That would have been too much to hope for. One of them at least should be easy to find, a local man called Roberts."

"Not Mr Roberts of Plas Gwyn?" exclaimed Llewellyn. "But his family has connections with Lord Bulkeley."

"That's him," said Dan. "The Irish captain, O'Flaherty, will be well away on the *Peacock* by now. I didn't hear the other man's name, but I've no doubt one or more of the people we've got in custody will be willing to oblige us. But there's no question who was running things. And now it's time to deal with him…Who fired the shot that hit Williams, by the way?"

"I did," said Evans.

"No mean shot, Constable. It saved my life."

Williams watched dully as the three men drew near.

"Has anyone seen to your wound?" Dan asked him.

Williams gave a mocking smile. "Has anyone seen to yours?" He was still smiling when Dan continued, "John Williams, I'm arresting you for the murders of Thomas Bevan, Sir Edward Lloyd Pryce, and Watcyn Jones. I'll work out the other charges later, but that's enough to be going on with."

Llewellyn, who had not yet had time to get used to the idea that Captain Williams was deep in the contraband trade, staggered under these further shocks. Watcyn Jones not a killer, but a victim. One man responsible for all the deaths, and that man Captain Williams. But explanations would have to come later: Dan had explanations of his own to seek.

"I have some questions for you, Williams," he said.

"I won't answer them."

I think you'll answer this one, Dan thought. "Did Lady Charlotte help you murder her husband?"

Evans started and looked as if he wanted to protest, but Williams's response came back before he had the chance.

"You'll leave her out of this, you bastard. She knew nothing about it. I'll see you in hell if you say otherwise. She's innocent, damn you."

"She's hardly that," said Dan. "She betrayed her husband with you. She had as much reason to want him out of the way as you did."

"And why shouldn't she? He was useless: useless to her, to himself, to everyone. A selfish swine, clinging on to her after what he'd become: a hideous, snivelling wreck. She should have been a queen, and instead he turned her into a nursemaid to a drug-addled cripple."

"She didn't have to marry him. He offered to release her after he was injured."

"Is that what you think? Her father forced her to honour the engagement in spite of Ned's noble offer – an insincere one, by the by. The old squanderer wanted money to expand the mining interests on his estate in south Wales, and knew Ned was good for a loan or two. You should have seen them on their wedding day! That monster and her – it was an abomination."

"I thought he was your friend."

"And would have remained so if he had taken his misfortune like a man. He should have let her go. She had every right—" He broke off. "She had no idea what I was going to do."

"Even if that were true, she must have known, or at least suspected, it was you who killed him. She could have spoken out against her husband's murderer. But she wanted to help you get away with it, didn't she? And that's enough to make her guilty."

"She knew nothing, I tell you."

"Knew nothing of your smuggling activities either, I suppose? Or that it was you who killed Bevan and then made it look as if he was the head of your smuggling gang, the one Jones threatened to expose? Or that you got Jones out of prison so you could kill him before he could tell the truth about you?"

"That was business and nothing to do with her. And Jones didn't know anything about me. If you thought he did, you're as big a fool as he was."

"But Jones was one of your men."

"Jones and his gang were small-time operators. I only tolerated them on the island because they deflected attention from me. That was what Bevan was for, to keep the revenue looking another way."

"And then Bevan threatened to reveal that you were running the real trade on Anglesey unless he got a bigger share of the takings. I imagine he went to your last meeting expecting to make a deal. Instead, you sneaked up on him and cut his throat."

Williams yawned exaggeratedly. "Watching your pudding of a brain struggle to grasp the situation bores me. I'm not going to answer any more of your dim-witted questions."

"That's all right," said Dan. "I've already heard enough tonight to piece it together. You sent O'Flaherty to get Jones out of gaol, kept him prisoner while you made sure he'd be blamed for the murders, and then you killed him, or had him killed. It doesn't matter which. You're still to blame for his murder."

"You think him such a great loss?"

"Maybe not, but it was not your place to end his life."

"Spare me your pious homilies. What are you but a thief-taker who makes his living meddling with what is none of your business?"

"I'm not the one in handcuffs."

# CHAPTER THIRTY-THREE

After they had delivered the prisoners to Beaumaris Gaol, Evans took Dan to the doctor's house. Hughes cleaned and dressed his wound and reassured him that as long as there was no inflammation, it would heal well. He gave Dan some tincture of bark to prevent fever and emphasised the importance of rest, but for the Bow Street men, that must come later. The doctor, used to patients ignoring his advice, uttered a long-suffering sigh and insisted they at least take some refreshment before they left. They ate some breakfast and felt better for it.

It was still early when they reached Henllys and sent for Lady Charlotte. She was already dressed and came down to the parlour looking frail and interesting in her widow's black.

Without any preamble, Dan said, "We have arrested Captain Williams for your husband's murder, and the murders of Thomas Bevan and Watcyn Jones."

It was brutally done and he was not surprised when the lady fainted. He was not moved either. He had seen a similar trick played in the boxing ring many a time when a man on the losing side exaggerated a hurt in order to gain time.

Evans was not so heartless. He ran for Mrs Jenkins, who wafted smelling salts under her mistress's nose, chafed her hands, and dripped brandy into her mouth. As soon as Lady

Charlotte's eyelids fluttered, Dan sent the housekeeper away. It was not her servant's fond face she saw when her eyes opened. It was his, and what she saw there made her shiver.

"I can see that the news Captain Williams has been caught has come as a shock," he said.

"I can hardly comprehend it. The captain was Sir Edward's closest friend. It cannot be true. No one can be capable of such wickedness." She pressed a hand to her temple.

Evans made an impulsive movement towards her which Dan stayed with a curt gesture. The exchange was not lost on her. She recognised the constable as a potential ally, and bombarded him with pathetic and appealing glances.

"I doubt there's anything shocking in that," Dan said. "You and the captain betrayed your husband, and then you killed him."

"That is a vile thing to say. That I…that we…no, it is too horrible."

"It is that," Dan agreed. "But you might as well drop the play-acting. Captain Williams has already told us how the two of you planned it together."

He met her terrified gaze without flinching.

"But—" said Evans.

He bit back his words, but it was too late. She read the truth in his troubled face. Dan was bluffing.

"No," she said. "He didn't say that."

Dan could have brained the constable, but that would have to wait. He stifled his anger and shifted tactics.

"Then why don't you tell me yourself how it happened?"

"Because I have no idea. You know that. You were there."

"And very convenient for you that I was. I think that when you woke me and asked me to help you find Sir Edward, you already knew where he was. You already knew he was dead, because while he was in a drugged stupor, it was you who led him outside to meet his killer. Your lover."

"Captain Williams is not my lover. I don't know why you are saying these terrible things to me. My husband is dead and I—" She sobbed.

"You are all alone in the world? It's true now, Lady Charlotte. The captain is going to hang. Perhaps it will be some comfort to him to think of the woman he's lied to protect enjoying the wealth he should have shared with her. I wonder how much more bitter his death will be when he realises you are as faithless to him as you were to your husband. I wonder if he will remain silent then."

"I was never faithless to my husband. If Captain Williams says so, he is lying, or deluded."

"You're very good, but I don't believe you, and neither, I suspect, will anyone else. No matter how careful you and the captain think you have been, your servants aren't blind or deaf. What has been the subject of gossip in the servants' hall is likely to spread further afield following his arrest. And scandal, once it's whispered, soon becomes a shout. People will start to wonder, and ask questions, and put two and two together." He picked up his hat and got to his feet. "I don't think you'll have the enjoyment of your wealth for long."

He signalled to the constable to follow and limped out of the room.

"You had no right—" Evans cried as soon as the door closed behind them.

"Be quiet." Dan listened at the door. There was no sound from inside: no shriek of fear or despair; no outburst of hysterical sobbing.

The carriage they had hired at the Bull was waiting for them. Dan struggled inside, leaned back in his seat and shut his eyes. Evans climbed in after him.

"You lied to her," he said. "Captain Williams didn't say the things you said."

Dan opened his eyes and turned his weary gaze to the constable. "And?"

"He told us she had nothing to do with the murder."

"He was lying."

"He confessed to Sir Edward's murder. Isn't that enough? What need is there to take things further?"

The carriage moved away from the house and along the drive. Dan looked back at Henllys, standing on its rise above the Strait, its front webbed with empty scaffolding.

"That was where we first saw Sir Edward, talking to the architect, looking at plans, imagining a future he will never see now. She was a party to that."

"It was Williams who killed Sir Edward."

"She may not have struck the blow, but she's as guilty as he is."

"But if you have your way, she'll hang."

"Why shouldn't she hang? Other women hang. Poor women. Old women. Ugly women. Why shouldn't she?"

"What good will it do? Captain Williams has offered to do one fine thing with what's left of his miserable life – protect her. You saw what her existence was, how Sir Edward treated her."

"Sometimes treated her, and only because of his illness."

"If he was a victim of his illness, then so was she. And he loved her, anyone could see that. Do you think he would want to see her die on the scaffold? Is that what you want?"

"No, it's not what I want. But I tell you this, Evans. If I had the proof, I'd arrest her."

"And how are you going to get the proof?"

"Unless Williams tells the truth or she confesses, I doubt I can, and I don't think either very likely. The lady's neck is safe, from me at least."

They were on the lane down to Beaumaris, travelling between trees, passing through alternate light and shadow. Who was right and who wrong, him or the constable?

He shifted his leg, trying to ease the pain.

"Perhaps you're right. She has suffered. And though you might not think it, I'm glad I won't have her death on my mind."

The carriage passed beneath the arch and pulled up in the coach yard at the Bull.

"'Then does that mean—"

"And now I'm going to get some sleep," Dan said, cutting off further discussion.

# CHAPTER THIRTY-FOUR

Dan folded the sheet over the dead smuggler's face. It was the face of a young man, and if Dan had not known he had died of a gunshot wound while resisting the revenue men, he would have said it was an innocent one.

He shifted his weight, favouring his aching leg. Although he had slept last night, he had woken feeling as if he could sleep for several hours more. Fatigue made the pain worse. He looked down at the corpse and weariness of the never-ending cycle of crime and death overwhelmed him. He thought of being at home with Alex on his knee and Caroline at his side, smiling at him the way she used to, all the strife and trouble that had so far gone into their marriage behind them. But there was too much still to do.

"He's not going to tell us anything," he said. "And we'll get nothing out of Williams."

"Surely we've got all we need from the people at Ty Coed," Evans said.

It was true that the cook, her daughter and the manservant, anxious to avoid the noose, had fallen over themselves in their eagerness to tell everything they knew of their master's smuggling activities. But it added little to what Dan had already discovered, and the three were not likely to be of much interest to the Home Secretary in their own right, or to the Anglesey magistracy either. Their part in the business had been negligible, and they were ignorant of what Dan really wanted to know.

"There are two men yet to be found," he said.

"But we can't track O'Flaherty and the *Peacock*; it's up to the revenue cruiser to do that. As for the other, all the servants know of him is that he's called Shotton."

"Then we'll have to see what we can get out of Roberts."

Williams's partner had been arrested at Holyhead last night, trying to board the Dublin packet. He had just arrived at Beaumaris Gaol and waited for them in the governor's office, uncuffed and watched by Mr Braillard and the turnkey. He slumped in his chair, squeezing tears from his eyes, his lower lip wobbling in fright.

Dan pulled up a chair and sat down beside him. Roberts flinched and, before Dan had said a word, gabbled, "I knew nothing about the murders and I had nothing to do with Williams trying to kill you. It was all his doing, not mine."

"You can save your defence for the judge," Dan said. "I want to know about your accomplices. What can you tell me about Captain O'Flaherty?"

"Nothing!" Roberts squeaked. "I had nothing to do with him. Williams and Shotton dealt with all that side of things. All I did was invest in the business. I had nothing to do with the smuggling. I had no idea what they were doing."

"You didn't wonder when the crew of the *Peacock* landed all those barrels on an out-of-the-way cove in the dark and hid them in the captain's cellar?"

"They told me it was just imported stock. How was I to know they hadn't paid the duties on it? It's Williams, Shotton and O'Flaherty who should be in prison, not me."

Dan laughed. "You must be the most innocent man on Anglesey, Roberts. Tell me about Shotton."

"Oliver Shotton. He has an insurance business in Liverpool.

I don't know where. I know nothing more about him. Williams brought him in."

"Do you know where he went after the meeting at Ty Coed?"

"He went back to the ship with O'Flaherty. I don't know where they were going."

"Anything else you can tell me?"

"What else would there be? I knew nothing about what they were doing. I thought it was an honest business investment."

"Your idea of honest and mine must be very different," Dan said, standing. "That's all for now, Mr Braillard."

The governor nodded at the turnkey. "Take him to his cell."

"What now?" asked Evans, when they were outside the prison.

"We're going to Liverpool."

"You think that's where O'Flaherty took Shotton?"

"I don't know, and if he did, I doubt he's still there. Still, it may be we'll find out something useful. We should be seeing Mr Llewellyn this afternoon so we can ask him for advice on the best way to get there. We'll go back to the Bull and pack a few things."

At the hotel, they found a letter waiting for them. It was Sir William Addington's response to Dan's letter sent from Henllys over a week ago informing him of Watcyn Jones's escape.

"What does he say?" asked Evans.

Dan skimmed through the contents. "I'm advised that there's a place in the foot patrol waiting for me when I get back. That's if I bring Jones with me. If I don't, I'll be lucky to be kept on as a messenger. In fact, if I don't recapture Jones, and speedily, I shouldn't show my face in Bow Street at all. Better still, I shouldn't come within a mile of the police office. Indeed, Sir William will be best pleased if I never return to London."

"I see."

"And yes, he does mention you. If you are sure you want to, you can read it for yourself."

Evans was sure. Dan watched his expression change as he read Sir William's opinion of a constable who had been such a blockhead, numskull, and dunce as to follow a superior officer's orders. Perhaps, the chief magistrate suggested, Evans might consider a job in the night watch more suitable to his talents.

Evans whistled. "It's a wonder the old fellow doesn't give himself an apoplexy."

"That old fellow is the chief magistrate of Bow Street," Dan said. It was not that he had much respect for Sir William's rants, which were more to do with the chief magistrate's concern for his own position than anything else, but the constable's careless attitude irked him. What would be a major blow for Dan meant nothing to Evans, who cared little for his job.

"Of course, sir," Evans said. "But after all, it's old news now."

"I'm not sure the new news is going to improve matters. There have been three murders since Jones got away."

"But we have arrested the murderer, and if we haven't got Jones, we've got two of the leaders of the smuggling gang. That ought to count for something."

"Let's hope so. And now we have our prisoners, we need to know what Sir William wants us to do with them. Are they to be tried in Wales, or at the Old Bailey? I'll write to London for instructions before we go. First, though, we have Sir Edward's funeral to attend."

# CHAPTER THIRTY-FIVE

"Elephants," muttered Evans, gazing up at the building. "Why elephants?"

It was late on Thursday morning, and Dan and Evans were standing in Dale Street at the junction in front of the Liverpool Exchange. They had left Beaumaris after Sir Edward's funeral on Saturday. Lady Charlotte had been convincing in the role of grieving widow, but in spite of her performance, Dan had noticed one or two whispering groups clustered around the church after Stephen Lloyd Pryce had read the burial service.

The best way to get to Liverpool had turned out to be going up to Amlwch and waiting for one of the pilot boats to take them to the next ship bound for the city. They had arrived on Monday and taken a room at the Crown Inn in Redcross Street. Their days since then had been spent making enquiries in insurance offices, banks, counting houses, warehouses, and merchants' coffee houses, but no one had heard of Oliver Shotton or his insurance business.

They had lost count of how many times their wanderings had led them back to this spot. It did not improve with familiarity. The Exchange had recently been rebuilt after a fire, but no one had thought to clear away the crowded alleys and hovels that huddled around its north and west sides.

"The Africa trade," Dan said, though Evans's question

had not required an answer. "That's where their money comes from."

In many ways, Dan thought, Liverpool was like London. The hard-faced merchants; the busy streets with their hawkers, beggars and sailors; the snatches of unknown languages; the ships crowding the docks; the noise and dirt and thieving and money-making and filthy courts crammed between proud buildings: all were familiar. Shops selling jewellery, books, musical instruments, fine wines and imported foods fronted fish markets and shambles. Grand houses had factories and foundries for neighbours. Dirty streets piled with rubbish ran past elegant baths and concert rooms. Salt works, whale oil refineries, and shipyards embellished everything with soot, smoke and fumes.

It was not London, in spite of its pretensions, its domed St Paul's, Covent Garden and Islington. From their room at the Crown, Dan had watched coaches set off for London and envied the passengers their forty hours of jolting in close confinement, each jolt taking them further away from Liverpool. But though it felt as if they had covered every inch of the town, they were no closer to finding Shotton.

"Coffee," he said.

They went to the coffee room in nearby Exchange Alley. They had already visited it once to make enquiries, with the usual result. It was good to be out of the cold, noise and dirt of the street and discuss the case in comfort. The conversation was an agreeable hum, the coffee fragrant, and the waiter who took their order reassuringly efficient. He was a middle-aged man with a worried expression which lifted when he had delivered their drinks and been rewarded by Dan's appreciative sigh.

"Pardon me, sir," he said, "did I hear you mention Mr Shotton?"

"Do you know him?" Dan asked.

The waiter reached into an inside pocket and pulled out

a letter. "He was in here a fortnight ago and gave me this estimate for a life insurance policy. It's an exceptional offer, but he told me it expires two days from now and I wanted to tell him I accept the terms. I expected him here yesterday, but I daresay other business delayed him. I can't get to his office in business hours, and as I don't want to miss this opportunity, I was going to send a messenger to deliver my signed acceptance. But perhaps, if you are a business associate of his, you could take it for me?"

"It's an opportunity you will have to miss," Dan said, "and lucky for you if you do. We are Bow Street officers and we're after him in connection with a number of crimes he's committed."

"Bow Street?" gasped the waiter, who had started to look very like the fish Dan had seen on the slabs at the market. "Crimes? Shotton? Bow Street?"

"Yes," said Dan. "Do you have an address for him?"

"His office is near the Old Dock. But Shotton? Bow Street? Crimes?"

"Come on, Evans," Dan said and, before Evans had raised his cup halfway to his lips, was out of the door, leaving his own drink untouched and the waiter standing by the table, muttering his dazed incantation.

"Office" was a grand name for the two dingy rooms at the top of a slippery wooden staircase on the side of a ramshackle building crowded between warehouses at the Old Dock. It was not far, Dan noted, from the much-cheated Customs House. He opened the door without knocking. A dough-faced clerk in a rusty food-spattered jacket, dusty breeches and faded black stockings rose from behind a mound of papers. Before he could ask them what their business was, Dan wrenched open the door into the inner sanctum.

"You can't go in there!" the clerk cried. "Mr Shotton isn't in!"

The room looked as if it had been ransacked, drawers left open, papers scattered on the floor, an empty cash box left upturned on the desk.

The clerk wrung his hands. "Mercy me, mercy me, we've been robbed! But how did they get in? I've been here the whole time. What will Mr Shotton say?"

"Evans, have a look through those papers," Dan said. He turned to the clerk. "Where is Shotton?"

"He's gone out."

"He's been here today?"

"Yes. But who are you? Why are you asking these questions? Those are Mr Shotton's things! You have no right—"

"I'm Dan Foster, Principal Officer of Bow Street, and this is Constable Evans. When did Shotton leave?"

"Of Bow Street? About the burglary? So quickly? Is it a London gang? Did they come in through the window? But how? We're two storeys up. Did they use ropes, do you think?"

"There is no burglary," Dan said. "How long is it since Shotton left?"

"About an hour. I brought him his post. There it is on the desk. Oh dear, he hasn't opened any of it."

"Look at these, sir," Evans said, handing over a bundle of papers. "Unpaid insurance claims. And there's this letter."

The letter was dated some months previously and sent from a bank in Chancery Lane to "Mr Shepherd" at this address. It gave details of an investment the bank had recently made on the account holder's behalf. It brought the account balance up to £6,000.

"A useful sum for a man making a fresh start," Dan said. "Looks like Shotton had his escape plan worked out. Which London coach is he most likely to catch?"

"Mr Shotton isn't going to London," the clerk said.

"He is," said Dan. "That's where his money is. And he won't be back."

The clerk's puffy face seemed to collapse in on itself. "He won't be back?" He sank down onto a chair and, with trembling fingers, pulled out a battered tin snuffbox. "Mercy me! What will become of me? Who will pay my wages?"

"How much does he owe you?"

"Two months."

"It won't be Shotton. He's an embezzler, smuggler and trickster, and it looks like you're one of his victims."

The clerk fumbled with the lid of the box. "He said the bank was being slow to draw on his funds in London. I should have looked for another job at once, but the longer I delayed, the more he owed me. I was loath to leave without it, and then jobs are not so easy to come by."

Dan knew that for a man at the clerk's time of life, it was all too true. Employers favoured bright young sparks with a bit of enterprise and years of hard work left in them.

He held out his hand. "Give it to me."

The startled clerk, thinking his snuffbox must be part of the police investigation, hastily handed it over. Dan twisted the lid open and returned it. The clerk thanked him absent-ly-mindedly, pinched a generous measure between his thumb and finger and inhaled. Calmed by the tobacco, he sat gazing at the floor in stupefied silence.

"What's your name?" asked Dan.

"Mullings."

"Well, Mr Mullings, I need to know where Shotton will go to catch a coach to London. With all that money at his disposal, it could be the mail. Where does that go from?"

"The Talbot Inn on Water Street. It doesn't go until half past nine this evening, though. There is another fast coach at three."

Dan knew Water Street; they had passed along it many times. He pulled out his watch.

"It's two now. Tell me, what does he look like? How was he dressed?"

Mullings snapped the lid of his case shut, stood up, and straightened his shabby waistcoat.

"I'll do better than that. I'll show you."

For a man of his bulk, he moved surprisingly quickly, although he was out of breath by the time they reached the Talbot Inn, from where coaches left for the Swan With Two Necks in Lad Lane, London. He mopped his face with a snuff-stained handkerchief and led them inside. The parlour was noisy and crowded, its customers a mix of men discussing business and travellers cluttering the space around their tables with luggage. Dan peered through the smoke, singling out tables with only one occupant.

"There he is," cried Mr Mullings, pointing across the room.

Shotton, or Shepherd – Dan doubted either was his real name – sat at a small round table with the wall at his back, a newspaper open in front of him, and a waitress standing beside him. He was in good spirits, smiling and winking at the girl as she delivered his glass of brandy. And why should he not be? As far as he knew, there was nothing to hinder his escape. He had not drawn attention to himself by ordering a post chaise, he had money waiting for him when he got to the capital, and it would not take him long to set up a new business in some place where he was unknown.

Mr Mullings's excited outburst carried across the room. Shotton leapt to his feet, grabbed hold of the waitress's arm and pulled a gun out of his pocket. The girl screamed and dropped her tray. Heads turned towards the commotion. Surprise changed to panic as people spotted the gun. They tried to scramble away, tipping chairs, breaking glasses, scattering hats, walking sticks, and bags. The landlord rushed out from behind the bar and, with more courage than good sense, rushed at Shotton.

"Stay where you are, all of you!" Shotton yelled. "Or I'll kill her."

The room froze into silence, broken only by the ticking of a ponderous wall clock, the steady drip of spilled beer, and a bottle rolling across the floor. Shotton manoeuvred from behind his table, pushing the whimpering waitress in front of him.

"Shotton, don't be a fool," Dan said. "Let the girl go."

Shotton scowled. "It would be you, wouldn't it? You're going to let me leave here and you're not going to follow, not unless you want me to blow her brains out."

Evans reached for his pistol. Shotton tightened his grip on the girl's arm. She squealed in pain.

"Put your guns on the table where I can see them. Slowly."

"Do it," said Dan to the constable.

Evans swore, but did as he was told.

"Mullings, bring them over to me."

The trembling clerk looked at Dan.

"You'll be fine," Dan said. "Just do as he says."

Mullings gingerly reached for the guns.

"They can't go off," Dan reassured him. "They're not cocked."

The clerk swallowed and, holding the weapons at arm's length, sidled across the room and dropped them on Shotton's table.

"Move away," Shotton commanded him.

The clerk shuffled off.

"So much as twitch and I'll shoot you," Shotton said to the girl. She took him at his word and stood rigid with terror while he snatched up the guns and pocketed them. "Now walk towards the door. The rest of you, stand back."

Anxious to put as much distance as possible between Shotton and themselves, the company squashed against the counter.

"Move out of my way," Shotton ordered Dan and Evans.

"Shotton, this is stupid," Dan said. "Let the girl go."

"She's coming with me."

"If you want a hostage, take me."

Evans gasped. "But sir—"

Shotton grinned. "I'd be safer with a tiger. The girl will suit me. Open the door, Constable, then step away."

"You're the one with the guns," Dan said. "You don't need the girl. Leave her be."

"I'm taking her with me. You'd better not try to follow either, because if I so much as think I've caught sight of you, I'll shoot her."

"Where do you think this will get you? Even if you get out of the city, you'll have every law officer in the country on your trail."

"I'll be long gone before—"

Shotton never finished. A bulky figure detached itself from the huddle around the counter and reared up behind him. There was a sickening crack and Shotton crashed to the floor.

Mullings stood over the fallen man, clutching a walking stick and gazing in horror at his pale and motionless handiwork. Dan kicked the gun away from Shotton's side and retrieved the pistols. He handed one to the constable, who cocked it and pointed it at Shotton.

The waitress screamed and fainted. A dozen men pressed forward to help her, but the landlord reached her first. He knelt at her side, grasped her hand and crooned, "Maggie, my dear, Maggie, come back to me!" Someone handed him brandy and he pressed the glass to her lips.

Dan patted Shotton's pockets, removed watch, papers, and a pocket book stuffed with bank notes. He looked up at Mullings.

"You can put that down now."

Mullings glanced at the silver-headed stick in his white-knuckled hand. He flung it aside.

"Have I…have I killed him?"

"No." Dan rolled Shotton over and pulled his arms behind his back. Evans handed him a pair of cuffs. When he had shackled him, Dan hauled the groaning prisoner onto his feet and dumped him onto a chair. He opened the pocket book, extracted a Bank of England note for £50 and handed it to Mullings.

"The wages he owes you."

The clerk's eyes widened. "But it was nowhere near as much as that."

"He says it was."

Shotton croaked a curse and rolled eyes heavy with hatred at Dan.

"I…I don't know what to say."

"The money is yours. Put it up safe before every pickpocket in the city sees it."

The waitress woke up and willing hands lifted her onto a chair. Half a dozen men took it in turns to fan her face, offer to unlace her bodice (she refused), and admire her courage. The landlord sat at her side, clutching her hand, jealously fending off the others.

A well-dressed gentleman picked up the walking stick and brandished it proudly. "He used my stick to overcome the villain! Look, there's the blood still on it!"

# CHAPTER THIRTY-SIX

Sir William Addington's second letter arrived three days after Dan and Evans brought Shotton back to Beaumaris Gaol from Liverpool. The chief magistrate instructed them to escort the smugglers to London without delay, and bring saboteur Kirby with them. Sir Richard Ford, the Bow Street magistrate who spearheaded the government's war on spies and radicals, was interested in him.

This time, the party was better protected by a dozen Loyal Anglesea Volunteers along with Llewellyn and his men. The soldiers and most of the revenue men left them at the Porthaethwy ferry, but Llewellyn and two riding officers travelled on with them to London. At the George in Bangor Dan hired two postilion-driven post chaises as the inn had no coach large enough to take the whole party. He employed a groom to ride on ahead to have toll gates opened and refreshments and horses waiting at inns, and they travelled more or less non-stop through two tense days and nights.

The tension was worsened by the three smugglers' bickering and young Kirby's white-faced misery. If they put Roberts with Williams, the captain snarled and sneered at his quivering accomplice. If they put Williams and Shotton together, they sniped incessantly at one another. Shotton traded insults with Roberts, and whoever sat with Kirby complained about the young man's ceaseless sighs and lamentations.

What with the rattling of the coaches, the shortness of the stops and the lack of sleep, it was a frayed company which landed in London late in the afternoon of the third day. The excise men's work was done and they had only to wait for the clerks to organise accommodation for them. For Dan and Evans, rest was still hours off. There was the business of booking in the prisoners and meeting with Sir William to make their preliminary report, and they were due back at Bow Street the next day for more of the same.

The formalities were made more bearable when a message arrived from the Home Secretary saying he was well satisfied with the arrests, and informing them that they could look forward to a reward, the amount to be at Lord Portland's discretion. Not, Dan noticed, the thousand guineas mentioned in the case file he had looked at in the Brown Bear before leaving for Anglesey. That had always seemed too good to be true.

At last, the smugglers were carted off to Newgate and Kirby to the Brown Bear, the tavern opposite the Bow Street office which the police officers used as a lock-up. Portland feared that there were too many Jacobins in Newgate, many of whom went in as ordinary prisoners and were won over to radical views while there. Putting the young man in with them, he felt, would only encourage him.

Dan took Kirby over the road himself, with Evans to assist him. Not that much assistance was needed. Kirby was too depressed to cause any trouble. He sat down and let the warder chain him to the bedstead without protest.

Evans followed the warder towards the door. He was keen to get away, but Dan had not done with the prisoner. Realising he had not yet been dismissed, the constable suppressed a yawn and turned back.

"This is only temporary," Dan told Kirby. "You'll be moved tomorrow, probably to Coldbath Fields and solitary confinement. Newgate is hell, but don't expect that to be any better."

"I don't expect anything."

"What you should be expecting is the rope."

"So you've told me."

"And you don't listen. Someone put you up to this, and they're prepared to let you suffer while they get off scot-free."

"No one put me up to it. Do you think I can't think for myself?"

"You might be able to think, but I doubt you'd know how to lay charges and set an explosion on your own. Did whoever talked you into this explain the risks?"

"I knew what the risks were. Sacrifices have to be made for the cause."

"What cause is that? The cause that says a young man has to throw his life away on a useless gesture? Did you really think you could make a difference? Is that what they told you?"

"I made a difference! I stood up to Old Corruption."

"If it was going to make such a difference, why was there no one else standing up to Old Corruption with you?"

"How would you, a Bow Street myrmidon, understand?"

"What I understand, Kirby, is that unless you give the magistrates something useful, you are going to hang. I only hope you come to understand it too." Kirby made no answer to this, and Dan, who had not expected one, said, "I'll ask the landlord to send you some food."

"I don't want it."

"I'll ask anyway."

"Why are you going to so much trouble with the man?" asked Evans when they left the room. "If he won't talk, it's his lookout."

"That's why," Dan said. "I've seen too many young and foolish men persuaded into rash actions and betrayed by someone older, more cunning and more ruthless than themselves. I was dealing with a case like it before we left London. Two bungling footpads betrayed by the receiver who put them up to it. They will hang, as Kirby will hang unless he turns King's evidence, while whoever led them to the gallows will find others to take their place and continue to prosper." As many of the companions Dan had run with as a street child had ended up, ushered to their deaths by a man called Weaver. He had scooped them off the streets, turned them into pickpockets and burglars, and got rid of them without a qualm when they ceased to be useful to him. Dan might have ended up the same way if it had not been for Noah Foster.

It had started to rain while they were in the Brown Bear. Carriages splashed through puddles. People hurried by, eager to get somewhere warm and dry. If they had somewhere warm and dry to go. Which I do, thought Dan, and I can't wait to get there and kiss my wife and child. Evans fidgeted impatiently: he too must have somewhere he'd rather be. Well, after tomorrow, he could go back to checking beer licences and paving stones and whatever it was he did when he was off duty.

"Don't be late in the morning, and don't turn up looking as if you've spent the night in a brothel," Dan said. He pulled down the brim of his hat and set off towards York Street.

"Officer Foster!"

Dan swung round, his eyebrows arched in surprise. "Still here, Constable?"

"I wanted to ask you something."

"Make it quick, then. I'm getting soaked."

"When we were on Anglesey, you asked me why I had become a constable."

"And I remember it was because it was as good as anything else. What of it?"

"How easy is it to become a principal officer of Bow Street?"

"Easy?"

"I didn't mean it like that. I mean, how would I go about it?"

"You'd join a patrol. It would be a lot like what you're doing now to start with, while you're learning how things are done. Only you'd have to put some effort into it. You'd have to work hard, think for yourself, show you have some skill in detecting."

"Is that how you did it?"

"It is, with some help from the patrol captain, a man called Ned Turner. He was as skilled as any principal officer, perhaps more than some. He taught me almost everything I know. The rest comes from experience."

"So do you think I should apply for a place in the patrol?"

"I think we should get out of this rain."

"But do you think I'd stand a chance?"

Dan hesitated. "Yes, I think you'd stand a chance, if you put your mind to it. And you might want to reconsider your opium habit. But for pity's sake, Evans, I have a home to go to. If you're serious, we'll talk about it tomorrow. And now, goodnight."

A few moments later, Dan dropped his bag in the hall. A line of light showed under the parlour door. As he took off his wet things, he anticipated the scene: Caroline sitting by the fire, her work on her lap, startled by his unexpected arrival, running to meet him, laughing and crying and tousling his hair, scolding him for the dirty boots, the unshaven chin, the grime of the journey…

A startled woman did look up, and she did rise to greet him, but it was not Caroline. It was her sister, Eleanor. He hesitated in the doorway, his tired mind struggling to replace the imagined with the real and confusing the two, so that the woman standing in front of him was his wife, and it was their child who lay in the crib upstairs, and her loving embrace which would enfold him.

But she did not run towards him. "Dan?"

There was something more than surprise in Eleanor's voice. Pity? As if she had guessed his thoughts. His exhaustion had betrayed him, had exposed a pain he thought he had overcome.

Eleanor was not his wife. She was his sister-in-law, married to Patrol Officer Sam Ellis, and Dan still loved her.

"I…I just got back," he said, a remark so obvious it steadied him, made space for the panic to rush in. "What's happened? Where's Caroline? Alex?"

"She's getting ready for bed. Alex is asleep—" Eleanor's cry drifted after him. "Dan…wait!"

He was already halfway up the stairs. In their bedroom, Caroline sat in front of the dressing table brushing her hair, a glass of wine in front of her. Her face was pale with spots of red on her cheeks, thinner surely than when he had left home.

She looked at him in the mirror. Her hand paused, hovered over her head. "See the conquering hero comes."

Her words stopped him dead. She put down her brush, selected a ribbon from the box on the table and tied up her hair close to her head, still watching him in the glass. She gathered the bunch over her shoulder, twisted it, and wound another ribbon around the coil.

She picked up her glass. "What's the matter? Nothing to say after bursting in here as if you thought you were on a police raid?"

"What's that you're drinking?" It was not what he had meant to say, though he did not know what that was.

"You're starting that already? It's a sleeping draught in a little wine. Eleanor mixed it for me. But if you begrudge me a drink—" She twisted round and flung the glass at him. It hit him in the chest, spattered its contents over his waistcoat, and smashed at his feet. She grabbed the hairbrush and flung it the way of the glass. "Begrudge me that too, do you? And that? And that?"

He flung up his hands, too late to bat a jar of powder away. It cascaded down his front. A box of toothpicks struck him on the shoulder and scattered at his feet.

"For God's sake, Caroline!" He saw the combative gleam

his shout sparked in her eye and lowered his voice. "What's all this about?"

For answer she tossed the box of ribbons into the air. The lengths of silk writhed in colourful swirls and drifted down to settle on the rug.

"For God's sake, will you stop it?"

A flicker of lamplight appeared in the glass, Eleanor's white face above it. "Go downstairs, Dan. Tell Aggie to come up." She placed the lamp on the dressing table and put her arm around her sister. "Caroline, dear, you'll make yourself ill. Why don't you come to bed? Things will be better when you've had a sleep."

Dan backed away, but he did not go downstairs. He went into his son's room. Alex was still asleep, his lashes long against his round cheek, his chubby fingers clutching at the blankets. Dan placed a hand on his head, felt the silky curls beneath his fingers as strong as the links of an unbreakable chain. Did the child stir and smile in his sleep? Dan told himself so. He hoped so.

He shut the door quietly and continued downstairs. He called the maid from the top of the kitchen stairs. She appeared so quickly he knew she had heard the racket and had been waiting for the summons.

In the parlour he caught sight of himself in the mirror over the fireplace. He took out a handkerchief, wiped the powder off his face, tried to wipe the stains from his jacket and waistcoat, but succeeded only in mixing them into a sticky mess. He threw the handkerchief onto the fire, sank down into an armchair, and lowered his head into his hands.

# CHAPTER THIRTY-SEVEN

He did not know Eleanor was in the room until she touched him lightly on the shoulder. He clasped her fingers in his. They stayed like that for ever. They stayed like that for seconds. Gently she pulled her hand away and sat down.

"I'm so sorry, Dan."

"She's drinking again?"

"She was for the first few days. Not now. The physician has given her the drops to help her sleep."

"Laudanum." He knew how to recognise it now.

"I give them to her each night in a glass of wine. That's the only drink she has, we make sure of that."

"We?"

"Sam and I. We've been staying here since a few days after you left." She looked away from him. "That is, I have. Sam isn't…can't always be here. He has the night patrol. That's where he is now."

It was not hard to guess the cause of her embarrassment. Who could blame a husband for resenting the time his wife gave to running another household when she should be running his? It was bad enough when Eleanor had been at the old house in Russell Street every day to help Caroline nurse their mother.

"What happened? When I left everything seemed fine. What brought it on?"

Eleanor hesitated. "You did."

That made no sense. He cast his mind back to his departure, to the three of them – no, four, Nick had been there too – in the hall. Caroline had been holding Alex. The child had been crying because his toy horse was broken and she could not persuade him to kiss his dad goodbye. She had been irritated by the accident and barely able to hide it, but she was often irritated and the mood did not usually last long. It had been an unsatisfactory leave-taking, but leave-takings often were, and there had been nothing to suggest it would lead to this.

It was then that he noticed Nick's absence. "Where's Nick?"

"At your father's. We sent him there because Caroline couldn't bear to have him in the house."

Caroline had never liked the boy, always resented the fact that she had had to take him into their home. She couldn't look at him without seeing the filthy street child and pickpocket. It did not matter how many times Dan reminded her that that was exactly what he himself had been before Noah Foster plucked him from the streets.

"You could never have been like that," she would say, sometimes with a fondness that reminded them both of the days before they married. He had been her "Wild Boy" and she'd found his past exciting and romantic. She had been a dazzling, vibrant beauty and her dramatic moods had been part of her attraction. It was only after their marriage that he had discovered what lay behind them: drink.

No, that wasn't it. There was something more behind the drink, a mournfulness in her that made her susceptible. He had fed that mournfulness by disappointing her. He had not given her the life she had dreamed of: married to a famous pugilist, rich, feted, courted by the aristocracy, their names in the papers, heads turning to stare at them in all the fashionable places. He had told her over and over again that he would never make his fortune that way, but she had married him trusting in her influence to change his mind. Even since they had had Alex to reunite them, the fracture in their marriage had never been truly mended. Their reconciliation had only ever been a fragile, easily broken thing. And he still did not know what had broken it.

"Two days after you left," Eleanor said, "Aggie came to Long Acre to tell me that Caroline was ill. She brought Alex with her. They were both upset and frightened. Aggie's barely more than a child herself and she'd been struggling to cope. She told me Caroline had taken to her room, wouldn't dress, wouldn't eat, wouldn't stop crying. Sometimes she'd pace up and down half the night, ranting and raving. And, yes, she was drinking. 'I tried to stop her,' Aggie said, 'but she carried on so bad when I ventured to say that she'd be better off not having any more, I thought she'd bring the house down.'

"We – Sam and I – sent for a physician and he managed to calm her and put her to bed. She was very ill for the next few days, so it was a while before I could discover what had set her off."

Eleanor took a folded piece of paper from the pocket in her skirt and handed it to him.

He read: *"I, Ezekiah Hurst, of Bell Yard, Carey Street, known to the public as a preacher of the Methodist persuasion, having been discovered on the evening of the twenty-fifth day of October 1799 at Mistress Dolly's brothel in Wild Court, do hereby confess..."*

"You circulated that confession and, not surprisingly, Hurst disappeared. But his congregation was left behind, the congregation that had believed in him. Caroline had believed in him. She'd found peace and comfort in his sermons and talk. You took that away from her."

Dan set the paper aside. "I exposed a fraud."

"But he wasn't a fraud to her. And even if he was, it didn't matter. Sometimes people are desperate to have faith in something or someone. They refuse to believe ill of them, or they make excuses for them, and when denial and excuses are no longer possible, when the truth can't be ignored any longer, they decide it's not important. It doesn't matter if they are a cheat or a liar if they are offering something people think is worth having. Caroline had faith, and you destroyed it."

"I did what any man should do, protected my family. He'd have bled her dry if I'd done nothing."

"But you didn't have to be so brutal about it, did you?"

"Brutal? I could have had Hurst transported, or hanged. Do you think I was going to stand by while he robbed my wife, made himself at home in my house, guzzled my food and drink, bullied my son?"

"No, Dan, I don't. I'm trying to tell you how it looked to her. Why couldn't you have talked to her before you took action, explained the situation, helped soften the blow?"

"Because I didn't have time." He sprang to his feet, almost welcoming the pain in his leg. That was something he could understand. He leaned on the mantlepiece and stared bitterly into the pulsing coals. "Is that what she meant by me begrudging her everything? When I've begrudged her nothing. Ever."

"I know, but you must try and understand. She isn't well in her mind. If she was, she wouldn't have fallen for Hurst's lies, and she wouldn't have taken his fall so badly."

"You're telling me she's mad? Is that what the physician says?"

"He says she has a melancholic disorder and that a period of calm and rest will restore her."

"And how much has he charged for that opinion?" He turned to face her. "No, I'm not having this, Eleanor. She will have to face the fact. Hurst is a swindler."

She shook her head. "I know what a terrible homecoming this is for you. It's no wonder you're angry and disappointed. But it's not that simple, and you know it in your heart."

His heart! What, he wondered, was the point of talking about what was in his heart?

"Very well, I can see it must have been a shock for her when she saw one of the handbills. But she ought to be over that by now."

"The handbill she saw fell out of your pocket when you were leaving. Nick picked it up and gave it to her. That's why she couldn't bear the sight of him, because it upset her so much."

"The boy can hardly be blamed for that. His reading isn't that good yet. He can't have known what it was."

She took up her sewing and busied herself folding a sleeveless shirt.

"What is it?"

"He'd had plenty of time to read it. He didn't give it to her until the following day." She put the fabric in her workbox, fiddled with a skein of thread. "Caroline thought he gave it to her meaning to upset her. Nothing would persuade her otherwise. That's why we sent him away."

"Why would he have done that? That's Caroline, wilfully misunderstanding. Whatever he does, she sees bad in it. I hope you didn't let Nick think it was his fault."

She hesitated. "Sam agreed with her. He thinks the boy is sly and spiteful."

"He saved my life. In return, I promised him a home, and I will keep my promise. I'll fetch him back tomorrow."

"It might be best if he stayed at Mr Noah's, at least until she is better."

"And when will that be? When she doesn't pelt me with wine glasses?"

"The physician said it might be wise to send her away for a while. He has a house in Clapham."

"An asylum? No. I won't send her to one of those places. I won't send her away, not now, not ever."

"Oh, Dan, I hoped you would say that. But she will need looking after for a while."

"I can see that. I can't thank you enough for all you've done, Eleanor, but you can't be expected to carry the burden for ever. Nor can Aggie be expected to cope with the house, a child and an invalid. Someone will have to be found, a nurse or attendant or whatever you call it. I know it's asking more of you, but could you help me? You will know better than me what is required."

"Of course I will. In fact, Sam and I have already discussed it. We didn't want to do anything until we'd spoken to you. I do have someone in mind. Mrs Valentine is a widow with a son who is a medical student at Guy's Hospital. He lives in rooms with some fellow students so she could move in here for as long as she's needed. She's a capable, motherly woman and I am sure she will be a soothing influence on Caroline."

"When can you speak to her?"

"I will call on her tomorrow. There is the question of her salary."

"I'll take care of that."

He watched her close the lid of her workbox. "Is Sam coming tonight?"

"He's on patrol and he usually goes straight home to Long Acre afterwards."

"Do you want me to walk you back?"

"I'll stay here tonight, but I will need to go home tomorrow." She hesitated. "I usually sleep with Caroline. I think it would be best if—"

"Of course. I'll sleep in Nick's room."

She took one of the candles from the mantlepiece and paused at the door. "Will you lock up? I've checked the shutters and windows...Goodnight, Dan."

"Goodnight."

He listened to her footsteps on the stairs, the opening and closing of the bedroom door, the floorboards creaking slightly as she moved about the bedroom. The fire was all but out. He kicked the ashes, finally extinguishing it, and blew out the candles, saving one for himself. He went into the hall and locked and bolted the front door. Then he pulled off his boots and went upstairs. He did not go to Nick's room on the second floor, but back to his son's.

Alex lay sprawled under his blankets, one hand thrown across his pillow. Dan put the candle on the chest of drawers and folded the child's arm under the covers. There was an old armchair near the crib where he or Caroline would sit to tell Alex stories before he fell asleep, or comfort him if he woke in the night. Dan sat down and loosened his cravat and waistcoat.

His foot knocked against Alex's toy horse, broken the day he left for Anglesey. He picked it up. One of the wheels hung at an angle: it had not been repaired. Nick had forgotten to see to it after all. He would take it with him when he went to Cecil Street to see the boy tomorrow, ask his dad to mend it. He could have asked Sam Ellis, whose daytime trade was carpentry, but preferred not to demand any more of his brother-in-law's patience.

He put the toy down, blew out the candle, and rested his hand on Alex's huddled form. Alex's body moved gently up and down with the rhythm of his breathing. Dan shut his eyes.

The shadows shifted around the room. Grey light began to creep across the sky, illuminating a jumble of chimneys and spires wreathed in shreds of mist off the river, mingled with coal-tanged smoke. Traders clattered into the Covent Garden marketplace, backing carts and horses, banging crates and boxes, laughing, bantering, arguing, chaffering. In the dens and clubs, drinkers took one more glass and gamblers made one more throw in the futile hope that this time the result would be different. Blear-eyed drunks staggered out of the all-night taverns and coffee houses; bright-eyed porters, gardeners and drovers took their places. The grey light stole into the room, illuminating the sleeping forms, the child in his crib and the man clinging on to him, muttering in his dreams.

## THE END

# NOTES

**Alamode beef**

A savoury stew of beef, bacon, herbs, onions and wine, usually accompanied by bread roll, beetroot or salad.

**Anker**

A measure of wine or spirits, varying from seven to ten gallons; the cask or keg used to transport spirits. Smugglers often used half ankers to make goods easier to carry.

**Bilk**

To cheat.

**Bully**

A man hired to protect brothels; a ruffian.

**Caudle**

A warm drink of wine, ale or milk mixed with gruel, eggs, sugar, etc and given to invalids, the elderly, or pregnant women.

### Cobbers

Women and children employed to break ore into small pieces with a hammer. At the Parys Mine the women were known locally as *copar ledis* (copper ladies).

### Cully

Someone who is cheated; someone who is easily fooled; a dupe, simpleton.

### Downy cove

Downy – someone who is wise to tricks, alert, aware. Cove – a man, fellow, rogue.

### Hedge preachers

A hedge preacher or hedge priest is an illiterate or vagabond preacher.

### Jack Ketch

The hangman. (Jack Ketch was a seventeenth-century executioner.)

### Link boy

A boy hired to carry a torch (link) to guide pedestrians at night.

### Nabber

A police officer. To nab is to arrest or imprison someone.

**Queue wig**

A queue is a long plait of hair.

**Sharp 'un**

A quick-witted one.

**Trap**

Policeman, constable, thief-taker.

# ACKNOWLEDGEMENTS

I would like to thank everyone who helped in writing this book. Special thanks go to editor Alison Jack. Also to Helen Hollick and Debbie Young who have been much more than beta readers, and generous with their support and help at every step. As ever thanks to my husband Gerard who must have made enough cups of tea to float a man o'war, and to my sisters Susan and Glynis for their advice and encouragement.

**Stay in Touch**

For news of books, events, and special offers sign up for my newsletter at www.lucienneboyce.com/newsletter/

**Spread the Word**

If you have enjoyed *The Contraband Killings* please consider leaving a review on line. Reviews are a great way for helping a book to reach more readers